AG.

HARRY DANCER—wanted by both sides in a savage undercover war, he was the target of twin tentacles of seduction

SALLY—the blond specialist in sex whose assignment was to enslave Harry Dancer's senses with every trick of her erotic expertise

EVELYN—the female operative assigned to use every wile that females have employed since Eve to capture Harry's heart and control his loyalty

But as both sides learned, seduction can be a double-edged sword when the man in the middle is determined to come out on top . . .

The Loves of Harry Dancer

Berkley books by Lawrence Sanders

THE ANDERSON TAPES
THE CASE OF LUCY BENDING
THE FIRST DEADLY SIN
THE FOURTH DEADLY SIN
THE LOVES OF HARRY DANCER
THE MARLOW CHRONICLES
THE PASSION OF MOLLY T.
THE PLEASURES OF HELEN
THE SECOND DEADLY SIN
THE SEDUCTION OF PETER S.
THE SIXTH COMMANDMENT
THE TANGENT FACTOR
THE TENTH COMMANDMENT
THE THIRD DEADLY SIN
THE TOMORROW FILE

Lawrence Sanders

The Loves of Harry Dancer

BERKLEY BOOKS, NEW YORK

THE LOVES OF HARRY DANCER

A Berkley Book/published by arrangement with
the author

PRINTING HISTORY
Berkley edition/January 1986

ISBN: 0-425-08473-6

A BERKLEY BOOK ® TM 757,375
Berkley Books are published by The Berkley Publishing Group,
200 Madison Avenue, New York, New York 10016.
The name ''BERKLEY'' and the stylized ''B'' with design
are trademarks belonging to Berkley Publishing Corporation.

PRINTED IN THE UNITED STATES OF AMERICA

A new building, ten stories high, on Federal Highway south of Commercial Blvd., in Fort Lauderdale. Sheathed in glass tinted so dark a green that denizens look out on a watery world, imagine themselves fish gaping from an aquarium.

Top two floors leased to Narak Exporting Co., specializing in hellish gimcracks, including miniature Statues of Liberty with bulbs in the torch, Venus de Milos with electric clocks stuck in their bellies, small chromium sailboats afloat on blue mirrors.

Outer offices presided over by a lanky Florida blonde with sun-streaked tresses down to her buns, and a small, chubby Lebanese with skin like felt on a billiard table. They actually export the geegaws on display—and make a nice penny out of it, too.

At the rear of Narak's offices, a locked door of pickled pine—veneer over an inch of bulletproof steel alloy. A peephole at eye level. A small TV camera focuses on visitors. Monitor within on the desk of an armed guard.

Granted entry through that vaultlike door (electric lock: *buzzzz*), you come into a wide working area of desks, whirring computer tapes, ringing phone banks, stuttering Teletypers, flickering TV screens. On the interior wall, an enormous map bearing the legend SOUTHEAST REGION, showing states of Florida, Georgia, South and North Carolina, Tennessee, Mississippi, Alabama.

Color-coded pushpins in the map indicate activities of the Department: white for state headquarters, blue for large city branches, green for smaller satellite offices in the boondocks. Red pins show sites of current actions.

Temperature in this enormous room, unbroken by walls or room dividers, is a constant 72° F. Air smells always of wild cherry disinfectant. Desks and machines are staffed by men and women in their twenties and thirties. Supervisors are older. Three shifts of workers keep the operation humming twenty-four hours a day, seven days a week.

Wide, carpeted staircase in the rear leads to the upper executive level. There, offices are private, with walls to the ceiling, and closed doors. Voices are never raised; the only sounds are clicking of typewriters, lulling drone of the rooftop air conditioner.

The Regional Director's office is a suite of three chambers: secretary's office, large enough for leather couch, several chairs, computer console, L-shaped desk; a door leads from this open room to the Director's private office; next to that, via double doors, is a conference room with a table long enough to seat twenty.

On the afternoon of April 17, 1985, a Wednesday, Norma Gravesend, the Regional Director's secretary, sits before her IBM Selectric, working rapidly on a stack of personal correspondence. Her typing is precise, accurate. The only mistake she makes—habitually—is to put the "i" before "e" in "weird."

Gravesend is a woman of forty-four, of a thinness almost anorexic. She is all bone, muscle, tendon. Parchment skin of her face stretches tightly. Scanty gray hair, hard and wiry, is gathered back in a small knob, secured with hairpins.

Still . . . not totally without charm. Eyes are a warm brown, gaze direct and understanding. Her laugh can be mischievous. There is gossip about her and the Director—rumors that circulate in executive suites of every large corporation—but nothing has ever been proved, and never will be.

She is interrupted at her work by a young woman in a tailored suit of ashy linen. Carrying an attaché case of maroon calfskin. Gravesend looks up from her typing.

"Yes? May I help you?"

"I'm Sally Abaddon from the Atlanta office." Tentative smile. "I have an appointment with the Director at three o'clock. I'm a few minutes early."

"Of course, Miss Abaddon. Please have a seat. I'll see if he's ready for you."

Secretary knocks once on the inner door, then enters. She is back in a moment.

"The Director will see you now." Then moves closer to the visitor, sniffing. "You're not wearing perfume, are you, dear?"

"Just the approved. And very little of that."

"Good. The Director is allergic to other scents. This way, please."

A big man, thick through neck and shoulders. Snowy hair elaborately coiffed. Rubicund complexion. Teeth like tiny tombstones. He is wearing a black three-piece suit of raw silk. Woven into his tie is the Department's logo: a blood-red rowel.

Standing, knuckles down on his desk, leaning forward. Abaddon comes close in case he wishes to shake hands. He does not. They smile, exchange greetings. He motions her to the armchair alongside his desk.

"That Miller case—" he says abruptly. "Was the violence necessary?"

"Yes, Director, it was."

"We have an unwritten agreement with the other side. We don't eliminate them; they don't eliminate us."

"Except in certain cases," Abaddon reminds him. "We were well within the guidelines. Miller's life was threatened. They would have had him before we had a chance. Their agent was quite ruthless. We did what we had to do."

"You did it?"

"No. My case officer, Briscoe."

"Very well, I'll accept that. In any event, Miller defected. So all's well that ends well. You've never been in Florida before?"

"No, sir."

"Good. We need a stranger to handle a local case. Florida agents might be recognized. The subject is a recent widower. Harry Dancer. Not Henry or Harold. Just Harry. Our informant is a friend and neighbor. From what he tells us, I believe we have a good chance of turning Harry Dancer. Your case officer will be Shelby Yama. Do you know him?"

"No, sir, I don't."

"I'll introduce you in a few moments. He'll

brief you. Meanwhile, I think we should become better acquainted.''

"Yes, Director."

He picks up the phone.

"Miss Gravesend," he says, "please hold my calls."

That night Norma Gravesend leaves her Pompano Beach apartment. Carries a small white shopping bag. Within, two books.

In the library on Atlantic Boulevard she looks about casually. Spots her contact. A man she knows only as Leonard. They move back into the shelves.

"Have you read this?" she asks. Takes a book from her bag. Charles Dickens' *Hard Times*.

"Interesting?" Leonard says.

"Very," she replies.

An hour later Leonard is home with *Hard Times*. Uses a simple book code. Transcribes Gravesend's message. Converts it into a series of five-digit numbers.

Switches on his radio transmitter. Begins sending. He is careful with the name "Dancer." A slight mistake will transform it to "danger."

Headquarters of the Corporation are in a non-descript building on Northwest H Street, Washington, D.C. Tarnished brass plaque reads: SOCIETY FOR UNIVERSAL COMITY.

Radio room on top floor logs in Leonard's transmission at 1:24 A.M., April 18, 1985. Tape recording is hand-delivered to night code-clerk at 1:43. Transcription is brought to Chief of Operations when he arrives at his desk at 8:00 A.M.

Small, shrunken man. Face crisscrossed with worry lines. Wispy hair combed sideways on balding skull. Fussy, afflicted with dyspepsia. Wears tweed suit too heavy for fragile frame.

Reads the decoded message from Leonard in Florida. Chief doesn't like Department's Director of Southeast Region. Man has won too often. Assignment of Sally Abaddon to case of Harry Dancer is a challenge.

Moves to his computer complex. Connects to personnel files of active agents. Punches in physical, intellectual, emotional requirements. Printer starts chattering. Three names. By two o'clock that afternoon, Evelyn Heimdall is in the office of the Chief of Operations.

He is brusque. Wastes no time.

"Have you ever operated in Florida?"

"No, Chief, I have not."

"Good. The subject is there. A recent widower named Harry Dancer. Your case officer will be Anthony Glitner. He'll brief you. Get down to Florida as soon as possible."

"Chief," Evelyn says, "I have vacation time coming in August."

"No problem. Harry Dancer will be won or lost before that."

Harry Dancer. Grief gnaws at his gut like a rat. Joy is gone. Sleep escapes him. Injustice! A *thing* so small it can only be seen through a microscope. Yet powerful enough to bring that splendid woman down.

Worse, his anguish is fading. Shredding around the edges. Pain remains, but dissolving into memory. How long can a man bleed? He remembers her beauty but must look at old photos. Good times. Laughs. But recollection dilutes sorrow. He tries to hang on to his woe. Hug it. But he cannot.

"Life goes on," Jeremy Blaine tells him solemnly.

A slap. The world should have come to an end. But it did not.

He functions. Eighteen hours after the funeral he is at his desk. Dancer Investment Management, Inc. Listens to condolences. Nods. Then, whey-faced, picks up the phone. Goes on. Lives.

Friends try. Invitations. Dinners. Cocktail parties. Barbecues. Introductions to other women. Rejects all. Rattles around a beach home south of Boca Raton that wasn't big enough for two, and is too large for one.

Alcohol doesn't work. Nor pills. Nor pot. The ocean helps. Shimmering there. Swim down the moonpath to forever. Let go and sink. Mouth open. Bubbles lazing up. But always he returns to shore. Leans against the undertow. Plods through sand to his empty house. Empty world.

Taut man. Muscled. Dark eyes and coppery skin. Stern features. Weathered by tragedy. Moves with tennis grace. Determination dulled now. But there, waiting. Everything his for the grasping.

"I want it all!" he had told his wife.

But it has spilled away. No need. No want. Now he moves sluggishly through a life without savor. Pollution is in him. He decays.

"Hey, old buddy," Jeremy Blaine says, "we've got to snap you out of this. Let's you and me go out for a night on the town."

"No," Harry Dancer says.

"Stop feeling sorry for yourself."

"You think that's what I'm doing?"

"Of course. It's all self-pity."

"All right," Dancer says, "let's go."

They drink. Drive up to West Palm Beach for grilled pompano. Drink. Drive back home. Stopping at old places and new places to drink more. Shout. Sing. And Dancer hates himself. Betrayal.

After midnight. Somewhere around Lighthouse Point. Jeremy Blaine, a mouthy guy, says:

"Whoop-de-do! Hey, old buddy, there's a new topless and bottomless joint in the county. What say we check it out?"

"What the hell for?" Dancer says. "I've seen skin before."

"Come on! Don't tell me you don't get a surge out of a young chick sticking her bare ass in your face. We'll have a drink or two, stay like maybe a half-hour, hour at the most, have a few laughs."

"Hour at the most," Dancer says. "I've got a seminar in Miami in the morning."

Called Tipple Inn. Barn of a place with tables no larger than bandannas. Stand-up bar. Three raised stages. Two girls at a time on each stage. Dancing for fifteen minutes to a four-piece rock combo. Replaced by another shift of dancers.

Primly dressed waitresses. For contrast. They order.

"Oh man!" Blaine says. Touching a knuckle to rusty mustache. "Look at Miss Boobs over there on the left. It's a wonder she doesn't fall on her face."

Set ends. Dancers leave the stages as a new crew comes on. Patrons beckon. Girls leaving the stages come over to climb onto tables, perform private gyrations. Wearing a single garter to hold their tips.

"They're good for three or four hundred a night," Blaine says. "Tax-free. How does that grab you?"

Dancer doesn't answer.

Smells. Cheap perfume. Sweat. Stale beer. Urine. Eye-watering disinfectant.

"Hey, old buddy, let's have one. Our very own naked lady. How about that blonde on the center stage? I like the shaved pussy."

"Whatever turns you on," Dancer says.

Music stops. Blaine stands. Waves at the blonde.

She threads her way through the tables. Breathing hard. Glistening.

"How do, gents," she says. Smiling. "Private performance? Twenty minimum."

"You bet," Blaine says. Takes out his wallet.

Tucks a twenty into her garter. "You're a big one."

"The bigger they are," she says, "the harder they fall."

They help her onto the table. Waitress brings another round without being asked. Music starts again. Their nude dancer begins to snap her fingers. Writhes. Pumps her pelvis. Shakes her breasts.

They sit drinking. Looking up at her with silly smiles. She looms over them. An amazon. Spreads her legs. Pushes shaved pubes close to Harry Dancer's face. Strange, stirring scent. Almost like ash. Dead fire. Burnt odor.

Dances frenetically. Flings her body into fierce contortions. Abandoned. Blaine reaches.

"Look but don't touch," she says. Gasping.

Music ends.

"Another set, gents?" she asks. Hands on hips. Legs apart. Staring at Harry Dancer.

"Sure," he says. Reaches for his wallet. "What's your name?"

"Sally," she says.

Agents from the Corporation arrive in Fort Lauderdale on April 20. Led by case officer Anthony Glitner. He organizes things. Apartment and ID for Evelyn Heimdall. Motel suite for cutout and communications man. No need for a safe house. Yet.

Glitner flies back to Washington. Reports to

Chief of Operations. They go over Harry Dancer's biog. Their game plan. Looks good. To them. But the Chief is uneasy. Swigs Maalox.

"Tony, it's a killing job," he says. Skittish man.

"Got to be done," Glitner says. He returns to Lauderdale.

On April 25, Evelyn Heimdall calls Dancer Investment Management, Inc. Asks to speak to Mr. Harry Dancer.

"May I ask who's calling, please?" receptionist says.

"My name is Mrs. Evelyn Heimdall. Mr. Dancer doesn't know me, but you might tell him that the Reverend Perry Stone suggested I call."

(Reverend Stone has been alerted that he may be contacted by Dancer. Case officer Glitner knows the drill.)

"Just a moment, please."

Click.

"Harry Dancer. May I help you?"

"Mr. Dancer, my name is Mrs. Evelyn Heimdall. The Reverend Perry Stone suggested I call you."

"Oh, yes. How is the Reverend?"

Laugh. "Still smoking those vile cigars. He said to give you his best. Mr. Dancer, my husband passed away six months ago, and I have just moved to Fort Lauderdale from New Jersey. I'm in the process of shifting my assets down here, plus what my husband left me. I'm trying to understand all the financial things, but I must admit I find myself confused. What on earth is a Ginnie Mae, for example? I was wondering if we might meet and discuss the possibility of your advising me."

"Of course, Mrs. Heimholtz. You could—"

"Heimdall."

"Heimdall. I beg your pardon. You could come to our office, Mrs. Heimdall, but I'd prefer an informal meeting at first—if that's all right with you. Just to get acquainted. Could we have lunch, do you think?"

"I'd like that. But I'm a stranger in town, Mr. Dancer. Can you suggest some nice place?"

"Do you have a car?"

"Oh yes."

"Well, there's an interesting beachfront restaurant on A1A in Pompano Beach. It's called the Sea Watch. Could you meet me there at twelve-thirty tomorrow?"

"Sea Watch. A1A. Pompano Beach. At twelve-thirty tomorrow. I'll be there. Thank you, Mr. Dancer."

"Thank *you*, Mrs. Heimdall."

Intelligence Section has done its usual efficient job. Using the dossiers provided, Glitner briefs Heimdall for hours. Concentrates on Dancer's deceased wife, Sylvia.

"Dark lady," he says. Reading from the document stamped TOP SECRET. "Marvelous tan. Brown hair cut short. Brown eyes. A tennis buff."

"Like me," Heimdall says.

"Why do you think you were selected? Here's the only photo we could locate. Taken when she won Women's Singles at her club. Published in the *Sun-Sentinel*."

"Good legs," Heimdall says. Studying the blow-up.

"So do you. I've noticed. You're about the same height and weight. You've got a little more up front than she had, but that's all to the good. Your hair is longer than hers. Can you have it shortened?''

"Of course. And I'll have it styled like hers. A gamine cut."

"Fine. She liked vodka gimlets. Had a thing for Caesar salads and romance novels. Wore little makeup. Always bare legs. Smoked long Benson and Hedges menthols. Are you getting all this?''

"I'm getting it. What did she wear?''

"Mostly designer things. Other people's names on practically everything she owned.''

"Ugh. Well, I suppose I can do it. Right-handed or left?''

"Right. You mean you can do either?''

"Tony, I have talents you haven't even guessed.''

"I believe it. You may have an opportunity to exhibit them. This Sylvia Dancer was reputed to be a tiger in the bed department.''

"Now how on earth did Intelligence get onto that?''

"Easy. Harry Dancer's personal physician is one of ours. He reports that Harry had some worries about keeping up with his wife. He was taking B-12 shots.''

"*Was* taking? Recently?''

"No. The worries date back a few years. Oh, one other thing—Sylvia Dancer liked the horses. Apparently she wasn't a degenerate gambler; just two-dollar bets. But she loved to see them run at Calder, Hialeah, Gulf Stream—wherever. She owned a pony when she was a kid; maybe that started it.''

"Anything else?''

"Background stuff. Parents, education, and so forth. But at the moment I want you to concentrate on your first meeting with Harry Dancer. Let's go over it again."

Evelyn Heimdall dresses carefully for the Sea Watch luncheon. Pale linen Halston sheath. Hair shortened. Lightened slightly. Bare legs. Minimal makeup. Benson and Hedges in her Mark Cross handbag. She has managed two hours in the sun that morning. Skin a bronzy tan.

It all works. When the hostess brings her over to Dancer's table, she sees the shock in his face as he stumbles to his feet.

Small table. Small talk. Both face the ocean at an angle.

"What's across?" she asks. Gesturing at the shimmer. "If you sail directly east, what do you hit?"

"Portugal," he says. "I think."

She thinks it's West Africa, but doesn't say so. Takes the long menthol cigarettes from her handbag. He snaps a lighter. Holds it in a hand that trembles.

Waitress hovers. "Cocktails?"

"Vodka gimlet," Heimdall says. "With a piece of lime, please."

He orders a gin martini straight up. When it comes, he drains half in a gulp. She sympathizes. Silently.

"What would you like?" he asks. Studying the menu. Not looking at her. "Their seafood is good. And a really big hamburger."

"I wonder if I could get a Caesar salad?"

"Of course," he says. Strained voice. Then orders another martini.

She doesn't want to hit him too hard too quickly. Turns the talk to her finances. Says she has approximately eight hundred thousand. How should she handle it?

"Play it cool," he advises. "At least forty or fifty percent in fixed-income investments. I'll have to know something about your tax situation, dependents, living expenses, and so forth. I'm conservatively oriented. I wouldn't put you into high-risk things."

She smiles.

They discuss his fees, problems of transferring assets, tax-exempts versus zero-coupon bonds, insurance. He is very knowledgeable. So is she. But doesn't let him know it.

Pleasant luncheon. Iced black coffee and Baileys Irish Cream later. Lazy talk about South Florida. Her reactions. Places to go. Things to see.

"I've got to get out to the tracks," she says. "I love racing. I'm not a heavy bettor. I just enjoy the scene."

He hangs his head. "You're so like my wife," he says. So low she can hardly hear him.

"Oh? I'd like to meet her."

"She passed away." Raises his head to stare at her. "About a month ago."

"Oh my God," she says. Stricken. Reaches to cover one of his hands with hers. "I'm so sorry. I didn't know. I went through it six months ago. It's hard, isn't it?"

"Yes. Hard."

"The worst thing," she says, "the absolute worst, is that gradually the pain goes. You're convinced you're going to suffer for the rest of your life. But slowly the sorrow dulls. Even your memories fade. And that seems so shameful that you can hardly live with it.''

"Yes," he says. Looking at her wonderingly. "That's the way it is."

He signs the check. Pays with plastic. While they're waiting for the receipt, she decides to give him a final jolt.

"By the way," she says. Lightly. "I'm a tennis nut. Can you suggest a court? Some place nearby?"

Before they part, they've made a date to play at his club in Boca the next day. Saturday. Heimdall gives him her address and phone number.

"I'll reserve as soon as I get back to the office," he promises. "I'll call you. I imagine everything is booked for the morning. If we play in the late afternoon, perhaps we could have dinner later."

"Love it," she says. "How shall I dress?"

"For dinner," he says. Happy. "Bring your tennis things in a bag. You can change there. I'll pick you up."

"Sounds like fun," she says.

He presses her hand.

Back in the motel suite, Anthony Glitner debriefs her. Takes her over the entire meeting. What did he say? What did you say then? What cocktail did you order? What did he have? What did you eat? What did he? How did he look? What's your take on him?

"I like him," Evelyn Heimdall says. Slowly. "Very much. Right now he's vulnerable. It can go either way."

The Department has two moles in Corporation headquarters in Washington, D.C. One is the night code-clerk. The Department turned him by getting him hooked on cocaine. Now on a daily ration. Enough to keep him wired, but not so much that he can't function.

When the transmission comes in from Leonard concerning Harry Dancer, the night code-clerk makes a duplicate of the transcription. Passes it along to his coke contact. He, in turn, hands it over to the Department's Resident in Washington. That agent forwards it via microfilm to the Department's headquarters in Cleveland.

There the information is printed, evaluated, added to the computerized file. An alert is immediately sent to the Director of the Southeast Region in Fort Lauderdale.

This process takes almost a week. By the time the Regional Director receives the intelligence, he knows the Corporation's team of agents is already in place, zeroing in on Harry Dancer.

That fact doesn't disturb him half as much as the question of how the Corporation learned of the Department's interest in Dancer. The only answer to that is a leak, a serious leak, within Regional headquarters. The Director calls in his Chief of Internal Security. Ted Charon.

They huddle in the Director's office, make a list of all personnel with knowledge of the Dancer operation: The Director himself. Secretary Norma Gravesend. Agent Sally Abaddon. Case officer Shelby Yama. And a dozen others: computer operators, file clerks, aides who set up Sally's employment at the Tipple Inn.

"And Jeremy Blaine," the Director adds. "Don't forget him. He tipped us to Dancer, but maybe he's playing a double game. Check him out."

"Yes, sir," Charon says. "I have a feeling the leak is at a low level, but we'll cover everyone. Do you have any idea how large a team the Corporation has sent down?"

"I've asked Cleveland to query our moles in Corporation headquarters. Nothing yet, but we'll be getting names and numbers shortly. The Washington Resident knows his job. But while we're waiting for intelligence, I'm bringing Briscoe down from Atlanta."

"Briscoe? Isn't he the one who terminated the Corporation's agent in the Miller case?"

"That's the man."

"I don't know, Director," the Chief of Internal Security says. Frowning. "The guy's supposed to be a hothead. A real pistol."

"We may need a pistol before this is over," the Regional Director says. He shows his tombstone teeth. "When you're in this business, anything goes."

Sunday nights are the worst. When Sylvia was alive, they were the best. Just idling. Soft laughter and light rump slaps. Cold dinner. Shrimp or Florida lobster or crabmeat salad. A bottle of something chilled. Teasing each other.

They'd eat on the patio. Sometimes they'd take

the remainder of the wine, two plastic cups, and
wander down to the beach. Sit on sand still warm
from the sun. Watch the moon come up. Listen to
susurrus of waves. Smell salt tang. Content.

Then, later, arms about each other's waist, back
to the house. Slow climb to the bedroom. Slow
lovemaking. Everything drowsy and right. Pillow
talk. Finally, sweet sleep.

All gone.

Harry Dancer tries. On that Sunday night he
makes himself a chef's salad. With slices of
garlicky salami. Opens a jug of California chablis.
Planning the routine. Then puts the salad in the
refrigerator. Trades his wine for a double gin on
the rocks. Takes his plastic cup to sit on the beach.
Looks up at a cloud-clotted sky. Then hangs his
head.

Thinks of the previous day. Mrs. Evelyn Heim-
dall. Lovely woman. Perceptive. And so like
Sylvia he can't stop staring. Good tennis player.
Great legs. Great body.

Her husband has died; she has been through it.
At dinner they talk about grief and what it does to
you.

"You learn," she says, "that all the old plati-
tudes are true. 'Life goes on.' 'Time heals all
wounds.' And so forth. But even knowing all that,
you're left with an emptiness. A big void in your
life. Not knowing how to fill it. But you try."

"What do you do?" he asks. Hopefully.

"Religion helps. Faith. Are you a religious
man?"

"Not especially."

"Well, what works for me may not work for
you. But it's something to think about. If you're

looking for an explanation. Not a reason, but an explanation. Think about it."

"I will."

"Promise?"

"Of course. Would you like a brandy?"

Now, on the dark beach with his iced gin, he tries to think about it. But cannot. He cannot conceive of any explanation or any reason. Only chance. Accident. Senselessness.

If life is without meaning or purpose . . . Well then? Well then? Intelligent men gather ye rosebuds while ye may. Is there any other choice?

Gin finished, he struggles to his feet. Plods back to his empty home. Phone begins to ring the moment he steps inside.

"Hey there, old buddy," Jeremy Blaine says. "Blanche is having one of her famous headaches. How about you and me wandering out to the Tipple Inn and inspecting the beavers?"

"All right," Harry Dancer says.

They sit at the same tiny table. Order beers. Dancer looks around at the gyrating girls on the three stages.

"Looking for someone?" Blaine asks. Grinning.

"Just checking the action."

"Uh-huh. How about that brunette on the right? She's got a tattoo on her tush. Can you *believe* it?"

Drink bottled beer for almost an hour. Shifts of nude women come and go. Girls, really. All young. Firm-bodied. With bikini tans. Something piquant there, Dancer decides. Light and dark. Like marble cake.

Finally Sally comes on. Golden girl. No bikini marks. Overall glow. And long wheaten hair that could be a wig but looks natural. Her total shaved nakedness provokes. She has a soft sheen. Frenzied oscillations. But graceful for such a big women. Choreographed.

"Let's have her over again," he says.

"Sure," Blaine says, "go ahead. I've got to trot out to the trough for a minute." He leaves.

Set ends. Dancer stands. Waves. Sally sees him. Smiles. Comes over.

"Another private performance?" she asks.

He tucks two twenties into her garter. Helps her up onto the table. Her flesh is whipped cream.

"Can we meet?" he asks. Suddenly.

"Sure," she says. "You got wheels?"

"Not tonight. We came in my friend's car."

"I don't do doubles," she says. "Want me to get another girl for your friend?"

"No."

"Then call tomorrow. Ask for Sol. He'll give you my number."

"I'll do that. Thank you, Sally."

"You're welcome," she says. And starts dancing.

Seated, he looks up at her foreshortened body. Thighs and breasts seem immense. She caresses her belly and buttocks. With secret delight.

"You like?" she asks.

"Yes. Very much."

He catches the burnt scent again. Exciting.

"You'll call?" she says. Staring at him.

"Oh yes."

"I'll be good for you."

He thinks so, too. And wants to tell her. But then Jeremy Blaine comes back to the table.

"Hey, hey!" he says.

Norma Gravesend sends another message to Corporation headquarters via Leonard. The Chief of Operations studies the transcription. Summons Anthony Glitner back to Washington. They talk in a soundproofed room, wired to prevent electronic surveillance.

"Tony, we've got problems," the Chief says. Slips a Tums into his mouth. "In addition to Sally Abaddon, the field agent, and Shelby Yama, the case officer, the Others are bringing in Briscoe from Atlanta. He's the man who terminated our agent on the Miller case."

"Damn!" Glitner says.

"Watch your language," the Chief says. Sharply. "It's an indication of the importance they attach to this Dancer action. I think we better counter with some muscle of our own."

"Chief, we've got no one like Briscoe," the case officer says.

"I know that. I suggest you hire a local. A mercenary."

"You think that's wise?"

"I think it's necessary. He'll be an Other, of course, but it'll be divine justice to defeat them with one of their own. Tell the muscle as little as possible about the assignment. Make it sound like a drug deal or a divorce case or *something*. I'm sure you'll be able to con him.''

"I'll get on it as soon as I get back."

"Good. Now our second problem is this: The Department is aware that we learned of the Dancer thing through a leak in their Regional organization. Our mole there reports they have begun an Internal Security search.''

"That doesn't sound good. Are you going to pull the mole?''

"No. She's too valuable; we need her there. She knew the danger when she turned. But that isn't what worries me so much as this: If the Department knows of our interest in Dancer, there must be a leak *here*, in this building. I have alerted Counterintelligence, and they have started an investigation. Tony, be very, very careful. The Others are probably aware by now of your presence, and your team's, in Fort Lauderdale. They'll stop at nothing; the Miller case proved that. So watch your back. And warn your people. And keep your communications to a minimum.''

"I'll do that, Chief. Now I understand why you feel we should hire a muscle.''

They sit in silence for a moment. Brooding. The Chief puts a knuckle to his lips to stifle a small belch.

"Tony, do you think Evelyn Heimdall is going to work out? She seems to be moving slowly.''

"Following the game plan,'' Glitner says. "She's right on schedule. She's made contact. Spent a day with Dancer. Started her pitch. Today she's at his office, going over her investment planning. I expect her to meet him again for lunch or dinner or whatever. Chief, she is a very talented, sincere, and persuasive woman. She believes in what she's doing. I have faith in her.''

''I hope you're right. What kind of a man is this Harry Dancer?''

''Big. Handsome in a craggy kind of way. Athletic. He's still shook from his wife's passing. Hurt. Confused. Uncertain. He's become moody —which is understandable. He was married for nine years, and now he's alone. Evelyn is providing sympathy and companionship. She's a very *solid* woman, and there's no doubt he's attracted to her. He's drowning, and she's offering a life preserver. I'm very confident of the outcome.''

But on the plane back to Fort Lauderdale, Anthony Glitner admits to himself that he isn't all that certain.

He is a tall, attenuated man with the big hands of a basketball player. Charmingly ugly. Scimitar of a nose. Wide mouth. Enormous, floppy ears. But it all comes together when he smiles. Joyous smile.

He knows that people devoured by sorrow sometimes act in eccentric and unpredictable ways. Abruptly change their lifestyle. Discard habits. Take on a new persona. The meek become bullies. Bullies weep. And all seek excess as a blanket on their anguish.

Glitner fears Dancer may be falling into that trap: forgetfulness through intemperance. If that is happening, the case officer isn't sure that Heimdall's life preserver will be grasped—or even welcomed.

He meets with her in Lauderdale that evening. She reports on her meeting with Harry Dancer.

Nothing significant. Dancer is cordial, speaks vaguely about another tennis game, another dinner, a possible visit to the track. But makes no commitment.

Glitner tells Evelyn about the Chief's warnings. Cautions about her personal safety. Then he tells her of his anxieties concerning Dancer's emotional stability.

"He may go off the deep end," he says. "A common enough reaction to grief. I think you better press a little harder. The Department is fielding a tough, experienced team. We've got our work cut out for us. Can you get together with Dancer in, uh, an intimate setting?"

"If I press too hard," Heimdall says, "I may turn him off. I'm sure widows and divorcées are after him. Either directly or through friends. Well, all right, Tony, suppose I invite him over for dinner at my place. He can't very well refuse; I'm a new client of his. I'll lighten up a little, and we'll see what happens."

"It couldn't hurt," Glitner says.

Case officer Shelby Yama had been a theatrical producer when the Department recruited him. But "recruited" is inaccurate. Yama volunteered.

He is an "—ish" man: shortish, plumpish, youngish. And hyper. Confreres think he is on something, but he is not. Just his own adrenaline. He cannot sit still. Cannot contemplate his navel.

No mantra for him. He must be *doing*.

The Harry Dancer campaign is his first important assignment. He doesn't mean to fail. He knows the penalty for failure. The Department never forgives. Punishment is eternal.

Because of his background and training, he sees the quest for Harry Dancer as theater. There must be scripts, sets, costumes, props. And, of course, heavy analyses of the actors' motivations. Shelby Yama already knows the plot. With luck, the denouement will be his.

He requisitions a motel suite in Pompano Beach leased by the Department. He redecorates it as a three-room boudoir. Mirrors on the ceiling over the waterbed. Swagged silken drapes. Plump pillows everywhere. On the walls, portrait nudes in oil and pastel. Pornographic cassettes for the VCR.

"This is where you'll bring him," he tells Sally Abaddon. Showing her around. Demonstrating the devices in the bathroom.

"He'll laugh," she says.

"Sure he will," Yama agrees. "He's an intelligent man. He'll laugh to show his superiority to all this sexy kitsch. But it'll get to him, doll. Believe me, it will. He'll say to himself, Well, why the hell not? He'll surrender to it. And to you. It'll make him forget. That's what he wants at the moment: oblivion."

"He seems nice," Sally says. Sadly.

"So? Does that change anything?"

"I guess not."

"Just do your job, and we'll win this one. There are enough mikes in here to wire Radio City Music Hall. The TV cameras start when he comes in and you flip the wall switch to turn on the overhead light. Got that?"

"Yes."

"There's grass and coke in the top drawer of the bedside table if he's so inclined. I don't think he will be. He'll go for the booze; I'll bet on it. There's plenty in the sideboard, and wine in the refrigerator."

"You've thought of everything."

"I hope so," Shelby Yama says. "If I haven't, this show is closing after one performance. I'll be in the parking lot with Briscoe. Black Mercedes. If anything goes wrong, you know where to find us."

"What could go wrong?"

"Nothing. I hope. Just don't be too eager. I mean, play it cool. Don't lean on him. He can stay as long as he likes. Set his own pace. You go along with anything he wants to do."

"Are you trying to tell me my business?" Sally Abaddon demands.

"No, doll. I know your credits. I just want it to go right."

"It will," she promises.

Harry Dancer shows up promptly at nine o'clock. Carrying a bottle of champagne.

"Greeks bearing gifts," he says. Grinning foolishly.

"Are you a Greek?" she asks. Switching on the overhead light.

"No. It's just an expression. May I come in?"

She is wearing a long, black velvet hostess robe. Covering her from neck to ankles. Wide zipper down the front. Long sleeves. Shelby Yama insists on it.

"Look, doll," he says, "the guy has seen you naked. Now you're covered up. It kills him. He imagines. Sexual tension grows. The longer you keep the robe on, the more frantic he gets."

"Teasing?" Sally says.

"Right. Teasing. You'll have steam coming out his ears. All he'll be able to think about is how to pull down that zipper. Play him. Like a fish."

"Wow!" Harry Dancer says. Looking around at the apartment. Laughing. "Talk about your love nests!"

"You like it?"

"Well . . . it's different. Who posed for the paintings? Not you."

"Friends. And friends of friends. How about a drink?"

"Splendid idea."

"The champagne?"

"No, that's warm. Do you have any gin? Or vodka?"

"Both. Which?"

"A gin on the rocks would be nice. Are you having anything?"

"Of course."

She goes into the kitchenette. He looks around again. Feels muffled. Suffocated. Air conditioning is on, but the apartment seems warm, steamy. All that silk. Ruffles. Nudes on the walls. Soft drapes. Everything overstuffed. Chotchkas without end.

What am I doing here? he asks himself. What *am* I doing?

He is swallowed by an armchair. So plump and deep he seems to be supine. She brings his drink. Coils onto the floor at his feet. Gracefully. She has a glass of white wine. Raises the glass. Puts a warm hand on his knee.

"Here's to nothing," she says.

"I'll drink to that," he says. Smiling bravely.

He sips. Reaches to touch her long, flaxen hair.

"Yours?" he asks.

"Every bit. Want to tug and see?"

"No. I believe you."

"And natural. My collar and cuffs match."

"But you're shaved. Doesn't it itch when it grows back in?"

"Sure it itches," she says. Laughing. "Want to scratch?"

This intimate talk inflames him.

"How long do I have?" he asks her.

"As long as you want. I don't have a meter."

"How much?"

"As much as you want to give."

"That's not fair," he protests. "Not fair to you, not fair to me."

"We'll decide later," she says. Hand moving higher on his thigh. "I trust you."

He looked up at her when she danced on his table at the Tipple Inn. Now he is looking down at her. Sees pellucid complexion. Clear features. Wide, denim-blue eyes. Innocence. Youth.

"How old are you?" he asks.

"Two hundred and forty-six," she says.

"No, seriously, how old are you?"

"Getting close to the big three-oh."

"I don't believe it," he says. "You look nineteen."

"Thank you, sir," she says. "That's because my heart is pure."

"I'll buy that," he says. Leaving her to decipher

his meaning. "Sally, I'm uncomfortable. Would you mind if I moved to a harder chair?"

"The waterbed is hard enough," she says. "Gel. And take off your jacket, kick off your shoes. Make yourself at home. How about some music?"

"Whatever you like."

She puts on a cassette. Ella Fitzgerald singing Cole Porter. Dancer looks at her in astonishment.

"How did you know? That's my favorite."

"Mine too."

"You're too young for Fitzgerald and Porter."

She smiles.

Out in the parking lot, in the black Mercedes, Shelby Yama and Briscoe listen to the conversation on their receiver.

"I think it's going well," Yama says. "Don't you?"

"So far," Briscoe says.

"I have some wild TV cassettes," Sally Abaddon tells Dancer. "Would you like to watch? Put you in the mood."

"No," he says. "Thanks. I don't need them. I'm in the mood."

"I thought you were," she says. Unbuttoning his shirt.

"Hey," he says, "let me do the work."

"Whatever turns you on," she says. Rubbing knuckles lightly on his cheek.

He unzips her. Slowly.

"Oh!" he says. "My!"

"You like the merchandise?"

"I *love* the merchandise!"

Puts his drink aside. Bows his head. Touches his lips to her breasts.

"Manna," he says.

"Don't be afraid to hurt me," she says. "I won't break."

"Why would I want to hurt you?"

He stands shakily. Undresses. She wriggles out of her opened robe. Falls back on the gently heaving bed. Splays her long hair over two pillows. Inspects him.

"Look what's happening to you," she says.

"Sorry about that."

She smiles lazily. "Never apologize for *that*. You're sure you want to do the work?"

"I'm sure."

"Do I get my turn later?"

"If you like. We'll see."

He finds what he seeks in her body. Grief is banished. Memories fade. Her flesh narcotizes him. One erect nipple becomes a universe. He wants to dwell in her.

"What perfume are you using?" he asks.

"Something special. Do you like it?"

"It's different. Exciting."

"Smell here," she says. Moving his head down with her palms. "There. I doused myself. Good?"

"Oh yes," he says. Not sure. A troubling scent.

He is a tender lover. Wanting to give her joy. She moves gently with content.

"Sweet," she says. "So sweet. I love you."

"Is that in the script?" Briscoe demands in the parking lot.

"Well . . . no," case officer Yama admits. "Not exactly. But she has permission to improvise. She's an old hand at this. She knows what she's doing."

Briscoe doesn't reply.

"Roll over," Harry Dancer says. "Let me kiss your beautiful back."

He straddles her. Softly massages neck, shoulders.

"Magic hands," she murmurs. Eyes closed.

He bends down to drift lips along her spine, ribs.

"You're too much," she says.

He has learned from Sylvia. Sylvia—his dead wife. He knows the places. The touches. He kisses. Kisses. And caresses.

"Oh . . ." she breathes. "Where have you been all my life?"

"Your two hundred and forty-six years?" he asks. Thinking her reactions are faked. Whore's talk.

"That's right. I've been waiting for you."

"I don't like this," Briscoe says. Listening in the black Mercedes. "She's deviating too far from the scenario."

"Give her time," Shelby Yama says. "She's just going along with him."

"I don't like it," Briscoe repeats. "I believe she's losing control."

"I think now would be a good time," Harry Dancer says. "Don't you?"

"Oh yes," she says. Rolling over to face him. "Please."

Her arms are strong about his back. Muscled thighs clasp him. Close, they stare into each other's eyes.

Technique deserts him. He is free and soaring. Outside his rational self. Finding the oblivion he needs.

She holds his face in her palms. Making no ef-

fort to kiss his lips. Her body becomes inflamed.
Scent stronger. She moves in anguished thrusts.
Eyes closed.

He is dimly conscious of her heat. Searing fire.
Looking down, he sees her flesh harden. Become
rigid. She changes before his eyes. Quintessential
passion. Lips drawn back from gleaming teeth.
Breasts flinty. Vaginal muscles pulling at him.

He is suddenly fearful. Death is here. He surrenders with a sob. She rises to meet him. Their
sharp yelps . . .

"Got him," Shelby Yama says. With satisfaction. Glances at his watch. "A little over a half-
hour. He'll never be the same. Right, Briscoe?"

"We'll see," the other man says. "This is just
the start."

Dancer doesn't move away. He lies atop her.
Strokes her hair. Face. Nuzzles her neck.

"Sally," he says. "Sally."

She opens her eyes. Flesh of face and body
softening. Death's-head gone. Looks at him with
wonderment.

"Are you really *you?*" she asks.

He laughs. "No, I'm Jack the Ripper. Of
course I am me. What kind of a question is that to
ask?"

She doesn't answer.

"Are you all right?" he says. Anxiously.

"If I felt any better I'd be unconscious."

"May I take a shower now?"

"No," she says. "Let me give you a tongue
bath."

The two men in the parking lot listen to the talk
and sounds for another hour. Then, when Dancer
leaves, Shelby Yama switches off the receiver.

"Good, good, good," he says. Rubbing his palms. "He's hooked. He'll be back again."

"I don't know . . ." Briscoe says. "The tone was off. Something wrong there."

"Wrong? What could be wrong? She followed orders, didn't she?"

"Oh yes. She did her job. But some of her responses bother me. What did she mean by, 'Are you really *you*'?"

"I don't know," Yama says. Puzzled. "That bothered me, too. I'll ask her about it."

"You do that," Briscoe says. "I'd hate to lose that lady."

Case officer Anthony Glitner finds his heavy by the simple expedient of looking up "Detective Agencies" in the Pompano Beach Yellow Pages. The first three he visits are unsatisfactory: their organizations are too large, too legitimate. They are more interested in providing security services than personal investigations. And they're not hungry enough.

On the fourth try, he finds the man he wants. Herman K. Tischman. Retired New Jersey cop. But young enough that Glitner figures he has been nudged into retirement. For whatever reason. Squat, thick man with caterpillar eyebrows. Lips browned from the cigars he chews. And hungry.

He runs a one-man office on Federal Highway. "Domestic investigations our specialty." His fee is a hundred a day, plus expenses.

"You have a permit to carry a handgun?" Glitner asks him.

"Uh-huh. But why ask? You say this is a cheating husband thing. Why would I need a piece?"

"You never know," the case officer says. "The man's name is Harry Dancer. I'll leave you his home address, business address, and a photo. See what he's up to. We'll meet again in a few days and decide what to do next."

"Uh-huh," Tischman says. Chomping his cold cigar. "Three bills in advance would be nice."

They meet four days later.

"Yeah," the investigator says. Flipping pages of a pocket notebook. "The guy's playing around. At a motel. The bimbo is named Sally Abaddon. A nude go-goer at the Tipple Inn. Skin for hire."

"That's fine," Tony Glitner says. "That's what we wanted to know."

"You want me to keep on it?"

"Oh yes. We don't want to stop now."

"Uh-huh," Herman K. Tischman says. Examining the wet butt of his chewed cigar. "You told me this is a possible divorce action. Mrs. Dancer figures her husband is cheating. You're her lawyer."

"That's right."

"Funny," Tischman says. "The wife has been dead for almost two months now. If you're a lawyer, you're not licensed to practice in the State of Florida. Also, while I was planted in that motel parking lot, I saw two other guys on a stakeout. Black Mercedes. What's going on here?"

"You really want to know?" Glitner asks.

"Sure, if it means my ass. Is it drugs?"

"No. Not drugs. This Dancer is the trustee of a

family fund. I represent the children of the decedent. They're trying to prove that Dancer is not morally fit to administer the trust. Preparatory to bringing suit."

"Who were the guys in the Mercedes?"

"I have no idea. They could have been waiting for a friend."

The detective stares at him a long time.

"Two hundred a day," he says. "Plus expenses."

"All right," Glitner says.

The case officer meets with Evelyn Heimdall. Repeats what Tischman told him.

"The Others have the first round," he says. Bitterly. "Ev, we've got to *move* on this."

"Not to worry," she says. "Dancer is coming over tonight for dinner."

"Good. It's heating up. I've asked Headquarters for information on this Sally Abaddon. The detective is going to try to get a photograph."

Heimdall leans forward to pat his cheek.

"Relax, Tony," she says. "It's just the beginning."

"She's a nude dancer," he says. Mournfully.

The agent laughs. "We have our weapons, too. Don't we?"

Harry Dancer shows up at Evelyn Heimdall's apartment carrying a bottle of Frangelico.

"Greeks bearing gifts," he says.

"Why should I beware of you?" she says. Smiling. "You don't scare me."

"I don't? Good. What a *great* apartment!"

It is. Fifty yards from the beach. Fronting the ocean. Living room, bedroom, bath, kitchen. And a fine east terrace, wide enough for chairs, lounges, a cocktail table. Sixth floor.

"Beautiful view," he enthuses. Standing at the railing. "Looks like you could dive into the water."

"No, thanks," she says. "But notice that no one else can look onto my terrace. I can suntan out here in the altogether."

"Watch out for helicopter pilots," he warns.

He thinks her apartment charming. Clear. Airy. Lots of Victorian wicker. Ceiling fan. Everything open and clean. Thin billowing drapes. Basket of fresh fruit. Flowers everywhere. Floors tiled in a black-and-white checkerboard. With a few worn oriental rugs.

She serves gin martinis and tiny, chilled crab claws. On the terrace.

"I may just move in," he says.

"Please do," she says. "I better warn you: you're going to be a guinea pig tonight. I've made a—a what? Kind of a stew, I guess. I invented it. Chunks of chicken breast, spicy sausage, little shrimp. All sautéed with garlic, scallion greens, sweet red pepper, and little bits of this and that. With enough white wine so we can spoon it onto rice."

"I've already gained five pounds," he says. "Just listening. Do you want to talk investments tonight?"

"Not really. Do you?"

"No way! I get enough of that at the office. Were you born in New Jersey?"

"Maine. My father was a minister. And please don't ask me how long ago that was; I don't like to think about it."

"May I guess your age?"

"If you like."

"Thirty-eight."

She smiles. "Close, but no cigar. Thank you for your kindness."

"Older?"

"A bit."

"You look marvelous, Mrs. Heimdall."

"Can't we make it Ev and Harry?"

"Splendid idea. Where did you learn to mix martinis like this?"

"Not dry enough?"

"You kidding? Just right. Did you do a lot of entertaining when your husband was . . ."

"Quite a bit, yes. I love to cook. How are you getting along with meals since your wife . . ."

"I manage. Simple things. Steak and a baked potato. Salad. Stuff like that."

"Lonely, Harry?" she asks. Looking at him curiously.

"Oh yes. You?"

She nods. "It comes with the territory."

"I guess. Planning or hoping to remarry?"

"Not right away. Not until I get my life to-gether."

"You're joking. Ev, you're the most together woman I've met in a long, long time. May I have another martini?"

"Of course. Let's finish the pitcher. Want more ice?"

"I'll get it—if I may. Let me wait on you."

"A pleasure," she says.

He brings the pitcher back from the kitchen. "I lifted the skillet cover and smelled. Dee-licious!"

"There's a bottle of chablis in the fridge, and a green salad."

"I saw it, and stole a leaf of endive."

He swirls the pitcher. Fills her glass. His. They finish the crab claws.

"Lovely night," she says. Staring up. "How many stars are there?"

"Six hundred million, four hundred and thirty-one thousand, eight hundred and fourteen. I counted."

"I think it's eight hundred and fifteen," she says.

"Then another one's been added."

"Your wife," she says.

He picks up her hand. Kisses the fingertips. "Thank you," he says. "That was a sweet thing to say."

Candlelight dinner. White tapers flickering in hurricane lamps. They sit close. Eating. Talking. Laughing. Easy with each other. Comfortable.

"Will you marry again?" she asks. "You asked me. Tit for tat."

"Watch your language," he says. "Maybe. Someday. Not for a while."

"That's wise. Don't rush into anything. While you're lonely and vulnerable. I mean, don't try to duplicate what you had. Wait awhile."

"Good advice. And good food. I'm making a pig of myself."

"Please, let's finish everything. No dessert, but we can have coffee and your Frangelico on the terrace."

"Perfect," he says. "Perfect evening. And you're perfect."

"No one's perfect, Harry."

"You come as close as anyone I know."

Outside, they sit in armchairs of white plastic

webbing. Sip their coffee. Hazlenut liqueur.

"You loved her very much?" she asks.

"Very. Remember Carole Lombard? A fey spirit. Sylvia was like that. Always up. She was so good for me. I'm inclined to be a grouch. She used to call me 'Grumps.' It's true; I get moody at times. She could always get me out of it. She was the light of my life. Sounds like a pop song, doesn't it? But it's true. I never heard her whine or complain. Even when she was dying and knew it. A very courageous woman. I'm not sure I could be that brave. I must be boring you to tears."

"Of course you're not, Harry."

"Let's go to the track," he says. "How about Saturday? Make a day of it. Dinner in Miami. It won't be as good as what we just had, but we'll manage."

"I'd love to go. Just tell me the time."

"Give you a call."

Then they sit in silence. Content. He takes her hand. Holds it. They look at the spangled sky with wonder. Kissing breeze. Perfumed air. Hissing of the sea. Darkness whirls. Drone of airliner, light flashing.

"Thank you, Ev," he says.

"For what?"

"Everything."

It is time for him to leave. They stand reluctantly. Move slowly through the ghostly apartment to the door. Turn to face. He stares.

"Am I so like her?" she asks. "You said I was."

"Were. I don't see her in you anymore. I see *you*."

"I like that better."

"So do I."

He kisses her. Once. On the lips. Warm pressing. Their bodies tight. He touches her cheek.

"Sweet," he says. "So sweet."

"I'll see you Saturday?"

"Of course."

"Don't go away from me, Harry," she begs. "Don't drop me."

"I won't," he vows. "Can't."

She looks into his eyes. "Promise?"

He raises a palm. "I swear by God Almighty."

"That's good enough for me," she says.

He goes home to his empty house. Stares at himself in the foyer mirror. No change. Strange; he had expected to be completely changed. He isn't, but his skin is sallowish. Tan fading.

"Got to get some sun," he says aloud.

That's another thing: he's talking to himself. It bothers him; he tries to control it. He could, he supposes, get a dog or a cat for daily companionship. But what if he starts talking to the pet?

"Hey, Rover, let's have hamburger tonight."

"How do you like my new shirt, Tabby?"

That's what happens to lonely people: they start talking to themselves, animals, goldfish, birds, plants. Otherwise the voice gets rusty. And the brain.

He pours himself a small cognac. Takes it out onto the patio. Lies on an upholstered lounge. Waits for despondency to overwhelm him. But it doesn't. He is shocked by his contentment. Can't believe it.

He reviews the evening. What he said. What Ev said. Wonders if he can go to bed with her. Does he want to? Does she want to? Oddly, it doesn't seem important. Just being with her is important. Holding hands. Kissing or not kissing. Being with her . . .

Because of Sally, he guesses. She can handle all his sexual needs—and more. He gave her a hundred, and she seemed genuinely appreciative. So he is paying for a service—is he not? Except . . . Except . . .

What is it? Her physical beauty, of course. Incredible. Unearthly. And her uninhibited sensuality. A fever in his blood. He did things with her he had never done before. Not even with Sylvia. And Sally has promised more treats. Hinting at arcane tricks that will dissolve him.

He finds himself preening. Cock of the walk. Two beautiful women. Sultan of an exclusive harem.

Then he realizes it is more than just fucking. Reality or promise. He has made contact. Two women he can talk to. Laugh with. Tease and be chivied in return. Intimacy. Yes, that's what it is. What he has missed since Sylvia's death.

What would his life be without it? That tension. Push-pull electricity. Conflict that gives savor to living.

He cannot get it straight. Physical or emotional intimacy? Or both? He cannot define his own needs. Both women seem put-together. Certain and definite. While he churns. Seeking to know himself.

He groans. Comic despair. Tells himself he has everything. And tells himself he doesn't know what he wants. Can't decide. His mind as cluttered as Sally's motel room. Cuckooland.

But despite his inchoateness, there is satisfaction. Life is more than T-bills, commodity futures, and project notes. It is an intricate circuit of human relations. And he feels he is plugged in again. For better or for worse.

A meeting is held in the Regional Director's conference room. Present are the Director, case officer Shelby Yama, Briscoe, agent Sally Abaddon, Chief of Internal Security Ted Charon. And secretary Norma Gravesend taking shorthand notes of the proceedings.

"Ted?" the Director asks.

"Nothing definite yet, sir. We've checked all employees of the Department with knowledge of the Dancer operation. They appear to be clean. We're digging deeper, of course, but at the moment Jeremy Blaine, the informant, seems to be our best bet. He knows about the action. He knows Sally Abaddon is assigned. And he's a very unstable character. It's quite possible he's been turned. I'd like permission to put a twenty-four-hour tail on him."

"Instead of that," Briscoe says, "why don't you set a trap and see if he walks into it? Feed him disinformation. If the Corporation reacts, we'll know Blaine is theirs."

"Excellent idea," the Regional Director says. "But what kind of disinformation? Any suggestions? From anyone?"

Silence.

"How about this," Shelby Yama says. "We tell Blaine that Sally has herpes or AIDS. If he's a double, he'll get word to the Corporation, and they're sure to warn Dancer."

"Thanks a lot," Sally Abaddon says.

"That's garbage, Yama," Briscoe says. Roughly. "Your nonsense may prove Blaine is a double, but it also takes Sally out of the campaign. And that we don't need."

"Oh . . . yes," Yama says. Confused. "I didn't think of that."

"How about this," Ted Charon says. "We know the Corporation is aware of Sally. They know where she's living. We tell Jeremy Blaine she's got heavy drugs on the premises. If the cops show up to search, we'll know Blaine either tipped the cops himself or reported to the Corporation, who informed the cops."

"One thing wrong with that," Sally says. "There *are* drugs on the premises."

"No problem," Briscoe says. "We'll take them out before we tell Blaine. I like it. Simple. Neat. If the cops show up, Sally, let them tear the place apart. They won't find any drugs, but we'll know Blaine has been turned."

"What about those freaky TV cassettes?" Sally asks. "And the other kinky stuff?"

"We'll take it all out," Briscoe says. "Temporarily. If the cops don't show up, it goes back in. And if they do show up, search, and find nothing, then it goes back in after they leave. We can't lose."

"Fine," the Director says. "Let's go ahead with it. Sally, can we have a progress report?"

"I think Dancer is hooked," she says. "I'm seeing him tomorrow afternoon. On his lunch hour! I'm beginning to complain to him about working at the Tipple Inn. I want him to come up with the funds. To keep me. I'm moving cautiously; I don't want to spook him. If he goes for it, and agrees to pay the bills, he'll want to see me a lot more often—to get his money's worth. Then I think we'll reel him in. That's the scenario."

"It'll work," Shelby Yama says. "It's been done before. *The Blue Angel*. Emil Jannings crowing like a rooster and painting Marlene Dietrich's toenails."

They sit in silence. Awaiting the Director's reaction. He stares straight ahead. Not seeing them. Snowy hair in artful waves. Black suit with razor creases. Milky eyes revealing nothing.

"All right," he says. "Proceed along those lines. But remember, this is not a simpleton we're dealing with. Dancer is an intelligent, complex man. While his wife was alive, he believed in the verities. Now he feels his life has no foundation; he's skating on Jello-O. He's confused, temporarily without faith. We've got to give him a faith— or nonfaith. Now I want to tell you what we're up against. The Corporation has fielded an extremely strong team. Case officer Anthony Glitner, an experienced man. Agent Evelyn Heimdall—very capable. A cut-out and a communications man. And recently Glitner has taken on a hired gun: a

private detective named Herman K. Tischman. I
don't like that. I want him turned or eliminated.
Briscoe, you should be able to handle it. He's an
ex-cop running a two-bit operation in Pompano.''

"Doesn't sound like a serious problem, Director. I'll get on it right away."

"Good. Anything else? No? Then let's get to
work. Norma, dear, will you type up a report to be
coded and sent to Cleveland? By tonight, if possible. They're very interested in this action. Briscoe, could you wait a moment, please."

Others file out. The Director closes the double
doors behind them. Comes back to the long conference table. Takes the chair next to Briscoe.
Stares at him.

"What's your personal take on Shelby Yama?"
he asks.

"A lightweight," Briscoe says. "He's treating
this whole thing like a TV sitcom or a paperback
novel. He doesn't realize the importance."

"It's the first big campaign he's handled."

"I think he's going to blow it."

The Regional Director considers that.

"You might be right," he says. "I don't want to
lose this one. He'll remain in nominal command,
but I authorize you to overrule him whenever you
feel it's necessary. He'll retain the title of case
officer, but the final responsibility will be yours.
If we succeed, you'll be suitably rewarded. You
understand?"

"Yes, Director. But it may become necessary
to, ah, remove Yama. For the good of the Department."

The Director nods. "Check with me first," he
says.

The Chief of Operations in Corporation headquarters in Washington is given wide latitude by his superiors. They are interested only in results. Bottom-line mentalities. They get weekly computer printouts: successes and failures. They are not concerned with methods or excuses. Only numbers.

So the Chief, on his own, makes life-and-death decisions every day. Swigs Maalox, pops Tums, prays and asks forgiveness for hubris and errors. He is acutely aware of the importance of his duties. Indigestion, he acknowledges, is a small price to pay.

A case in point is the latest communication from Norma Gravesend. Because of the leak in Corporation headquarters, the Chief has tightened security precautions. Leonard flies up to Washington. Hand-delivers Gravesend's message to the Chief in clear. Bypassing radio—and the Corporation's code clerks.

The Chief reads the report three times. Several disquieting things there. One, that the Department is aware of the personnel of the Corporation's Dancer team. Two, they have already learned of the hiring of Herman K. Tischman. And are moving to neutralize him.

But the most urgent intelligence, the Chief feels, is the Department's search for the leak in their organization. Suspicion has fallen upon Jeremy Blaine, the informant. A trap has been laid. If Blaine comes up clean, the search will continue. In time, Norma Gravesend may be compromised. The Chief cannot let that happen.

He considers what he must do. Moral judg-

ment. Sacrifice one of theirs to save one of ours.
Does he have the right? It is an ethical choice. All
his choices are.

It doesn't take long to decide. He knows the
Corporation cannot abide inaction. Succeed or
fail. But *do* something.

He sends a coded message to Anthony Glitner:
Sally Abaddon has heavy drugs in her residence.
Inform local police anonymously.

Briscoe. No one knows his first name. If he has
one. Sullen man. Hunched and brutish. Glowering
eyes. Hair trimmed like a Marine recruit. Absolute
loyalty to the Department. Loyalty up, and loyalty
down. He has never failed. He is compensated.
But that is not important. His job is his life.

He tells Shelby Yama how to handle Jeremy
Blaine. Yama has lunch with Blaine. Hands over a
small bonus for Blaine's "remarkable work" in
bringing Harry Dancer and Sally Abaddon together. Mentions casually that Sally has plenty of
drugs in her motel suite. Hopes to hook Dancer.
Jeremy nods brightly.

Meanwhile, Briscoe cleans all the junk out of
Sally's place. Two days later the cops show up.
They're polite but insistent. No warrant, but Sally
lets them in. A half-hour later they're gone.
Apologizing.

"All right," Briscoe says. "It's got to be Blaine.
He's corrupted. You phone him, Yama, and tell
him to expect a call from me. A new assignment.

More money. I'll take it from there.''

Jeremy Blaine is eager. A new assignment? More money? Sounds good. Briscoe calls, then picks him up at his home. At midnight. Heads north on I-95. Driving a three-year-old Honda.

"Best place to talk," Briscoe says. "In a car. No chance of a tap if the car's been swept."

"Yama said something about a new assignment."

"That's right. A big job. We think you can handle it."

"Hey," Blaine says, "you better believe it. I delivered Harry Dancer, didn't I? The whole thing was my idea."

"That's right," Briscoe says. "The Department values your work highly."

He gets the Honda up to seventy. Watching for his chance. He sees it coming. A big tractor-trailer heading south, in the left-hand lane, making speed. Briscoe wrenches the wheel. Plunges across the medium. Jeremy Blaine has time to shout, "Hey!"

Briscoe crashes the truck head-on. The Honda is crumpled. Then bursts into flame. Blaine is killed instantly. In the confusion, Briscoe walks away into the darkness. Unhurt.

The Department takes care of its own.

"You remember him," Harry Dancer says to Sally Abaddon. "The guy I was with when I met you at the Tipple Inn."

"Vaguely. Paunchy? With a wild tie?"

"That's the man. Well, no one can figure what he was doing driving north on I-95 after midnight. In a Honda. It wasn't his car. He drove a Caddy."

"Maybe he was drunk."

"Maybe. But what was he *doing* there? In a Honda? The funeral was this morning. What a way to start the day."

"You better have a belt."

"Thank you," he says. Gratefully. "Double gin on the rocks, please. How *are* you?"

She doesn't answer until she brings him the gin. They're in her motel. Two o'clock in the afternoon. She's just in from the pool. Glistening with oil. Wearing a crocheted bikini. Hot pink.

"I'm okay," she says. "I guess."

"What's the problem?"

"That place I work. It's a drag. The money is good, but I can't stand the slobs. Maybe I should move on. Try another city."

"No," he says. "Don't do that."

He is aware of a curious phenomenon. When he is with her—only with *her*—his body chemistry seems to change. His body odor is altered. He feels sweat trickling down his ribs, and the scent is foreign to him. Pheromones? Is he reacting to her bold sexuality?

"How much do you make at the Tipple?"

"On a good week I can clear a thousand."

He is silent.

"I can live on a lot less than that," she offers. "It would be worth it if I didn't have to deal with those slobs."

"Let me think about it," he says. "Maybe we can work something out."

"It would be wonderful. We could spend more time together."

"And I'd end up in Intensive Care."

"No," she says. Laughing. "I wouldn't do that to you. Only as much as you can take. And then just a little bit more. Would you like a matinee? Right now?"

"Thank you, Sally, but I don't think so. I'm still shook from that funeral. God, his wife—his widow couldn't stop crying. And I really should get to the office for a while."

"You've got a few more minutes, haven't you? Come in and talk to me while I shower."

He sits on the closed toilet seat. He watches her naked body behind frosted glass. Water streams. Flesh sparkles. He sees her bend, arch. Golden. It is a fogged dream.

"I'm off tomorrow night," she calls. "Can we do something?"

"Sure. There's a new Italian restaurant on Federal. Supposed to be good. Want to try it?"

"Of course. Whatever you want. It'll give me a chance to dress. You've never seen me all dolled up. You won't be disappointed."

She turns off the water. Slides the door back. Steps out on to the chenille mat. Dripping. Hands him a towel.

"Dry me," she says. "Please."

It's like polishing a statue. He is slow, tender. When he bends to wipe her legs, she puts her hands on his shoulders.

"Everywhere," she says.

He is close to her. So close. Feels her sun warmth. Her palms cradle his face.

"Harry," she says, "I . . ."

"What?"

"Nothing."

"I could call the office," he says. "Tell them I'm not coming in."

"You do that," she says.

Herman K. Tischman is sitting out in the parking lot. In his battered, six-year-old Plymouth. Windows down. But he's sweating. Figures Dancer is good for another hour. At least. What a morning. First the funeral, now this.

A guy comes up on the passenger side. Chunky. Hair cut in a Florida flattop. He's holding an unlighted cigarette.

"Got a match, buddy?" he asks. Gravelly voice.

Tischman digs into his jacket pocket. While he's doing that, the stranger opens the passenger door. Slides in beside him.

"Hi, there," he says.

The investigator bites down on his cold cigar.

"What the hell is this?" he demands. "Get the—"

"You're Herman K. Tischman," the guy says. "Tailing Harry Dancer. Who right now is inside banging a ripe piece named Sally Abaddon."

Tischman takes the cigar out of his face. "Tell me more. Tell me who the hell *you* are."

"The name is Briscoe."

"Yeah? Were you in a black Mercedes the other night?"

"That's right."

"You a PI?"

"Sort of."

"You working this Dancer thing, too?"

"Sure. I think we can do business together."

Tischman is crowded into his corner of the front seat. This hard guy is pressing him. The ex-cop thinks he can take him. But he isn't certain.

"I'm listening," he says.

"You're working for a guy named Glitner," Briscoe says. "I figure you're clipping him for a bill a day. Maybe two. Whatever. No skin off my nose. You keep on working for Glitner just the way you have been. But I'll slip you a hundred a day extra if you report to me first."

"That's unethical," Tischman says.

Briscoe laughs. Not a pleasant sound. "Yeah, isn't it. Also, when you report to me first, there may be some things I won't want you to tell Glitner."

"That's worth more than a hundred."

"Sure it is. But a hundred is all you're getting."

"No deal," Tischman says.

"That's a cute kid you've got," Briscoe says. "What's her name—Mary Jane? Blond curls. Waits on your corner for the school bus every morning. Pretty. And healthy."

"You prick," Tischman says. Fear bubbling.

"Is it a deal?"

The detective doesn't hesitate. "How do I contact you?"

"I'll be in touch," Briscoe says. Climbs out of the car. "Ta-ta."

Briscoe finds a phone booth. Calls the office. Gives his ID number and the day's code word. He finally gets through to the Regional Director.

"I've got Tischman, sir," he reports. "He's ours."

"Good work," the Director says. "And I like the way you handled the Blaine problem. Where is Dancer now?"

"In Sally's motel."

"Then everything's going according to plan."

"So far," Briscoe says.

"You sound a little unsure. Anything wrong?"

"Nothing definite, Director. Just a vague feeling I have about Sally Abaddon. I think she may be weakening."

"Oh? That would be a sad development. I'd hate to lose her after all these years."

"Just the way I feel, sir."

"Well, keep an eye on her, and keep me informed."

"Will do."

The Regional Director hangs up. Turns slowly in his swivel chair. Stares through the darkly tinted picture window at the towers and beacons of Fort Lauderdale. Murky world. Even the sun is muted.

He stands. Paces up and down in his chairman-of-the-board suit. Below him, he knows, computers are humming. Teletypers chattering. Monitors glowing. Machinery of an efficient organization. Information, communications, intelligence, projections, estimates—everything his for the asking.

But all that is nothing. The Department depends for its success on people with the passion and will to carry out its policies and philosophy. And people are not machines. They are frail, imperfect, irrational. They remain loyal only as long as it is in their self-interest.

Take Sally Abaddon, for instance. Faithful. Experienced. Capable. But subject to all the vagaries of humankind. She might desert at any moment. Turn. Put her skills to work for the Corporation. It is possible.

It is even possible, the Director muses, that he himself might defect. He cannot imagine under what circumstances that could conceivably happen. But he is certain his superiors in Cleveland acknowledge the possibility and have devised a contingency plan.

Meanwhile, the Regional Director is running about twenty cases with at least a hundred of the Department's most skilled operatives involved. All those ambitions. Needs. Wants. Greeds. Desires. Vices. And he must be aware of them all. Rewarding the strong. Punishing the weak. Alert always to the potential for betrayal. Even amongst the strongest.

He tugs down his waistcoat. Smooths his jacket. Straightens his rowel-woven tie. He hunches over his desk. Snaps on the intercom.

"Norma," he says, "could you come in for a moment, please."

His secretary enters, pad in hand.

"Close the door," he tells her.

She looks at him. Sees. "Shall I lock it, Director?" she asks.

"Yes," he says. "Lock it."

Anthony Glitner knows that in his business, zeal is never enough. After many years as a field agent, and a decade as a case officer, his fervor has been tempered by recognition of the stubborn recalcitrance of most subjects. Enthusiasm for the Corporation's cause is essential, but rarely sufficient to get the job done.

It is a task calling for patience, subtlety, sympathy for the subject's plight. It sometimes also requires Machiavellian tactics. Many hours of the Corporation's training course are devoted to whether or not, and under what conditions, the end justifies the means.

Glitner's attitude toward that problem is almost wholly pragmatic. Although he would never adopt the methods of the Others—pandering to the subject's coarser instincts—he is willing to take advantage of the subject's weaknesses, faults, and defects to achieve the end that completely justifies all means.

He is aware of Harry Dancer's loneliness. Periods of anomie and despair. Glitner believes Evelyn Heimdall will provide a palliative for those painful anxieties. At the same time, the case officer knows the Department is hard at work. Not to provide its own palliative, but to overwhelm Dancer's miseries by senseless profligacy—in the person of Sally Abaddon.

It is not only a clash of passions and faiths; that exists in all the struggles between Corporation and Department. But in Dancer's case, there is also a battle of techniques: whether appealing to a subject's best or worst impulses is the most effective way of winning.

What the Dancer action comes down to, Anthony Glitner reflects, is a test of the ancient question: Does a human being respond more readily to fear of punishment or promise of reward?

While the case officer is pondering the philosophical implications of his current operation, the subject is suffering a special kind of anguish.

It is true that his grief has frayed around the edges. It is no longer a constant pain that haunts all his hours. Awake or asleep. But his brief bouts of happiness with Evelyn Heimdall and Sally Abaddon have resulted in a fresh affliction. Guilt.

Regret and remorse walk hand in hand. Had he said "I love you" enough times? Had he touched Sylvia enough? Kissed her enough? Done *anything* enough?

He had not.

But now, scarcely two months after her death, he is holding the hands of two strange women. Kissing. Rolling about lubriciously on sweated sheets. He has not yet said, "I love you." But he is *thinking* it.

"What kind of a man are you?" he says aloud. Angrily.

A stiff gin-and-tonic helps. Plasma. Then he prepares for his date with Evelyn Heimdall. Taking as much care as a houri. Bathing, shaving, scenting, dressing. Another gin. Straight this time. And he sallies forth. Humming a merry tune.

She is waiting for him. A knockout! All in white linen. Long skirt sashed in blue. Big picture hat. No makeup, but a glow to her. She looks happy.

"Smashing!" he says. Kisses her cheek.

"Off to the races!" she says. "How handsome you look."

On the drive south, on I-95, he tells her about Jeremy Blaine.

"Oh, Harry," she says. "How awful. Was he a good friend?"

"No. I'm being honest; he wasn't a good friend. But he was my closest neighbor, and you try to get along with your neighbors. I'm not even sure I liked him, but I endured him. He could be coarse at times. And was always calling me 'old buddy.' But I must admit he was very sympathetic and attentive after Sylvia died. Well . . . let's talk about something cheerful. What have you been doing with yourself?"

Chatting easily. Laughing frequently. Listening to music from his tape deck. Recalling lyrics from old songs. She knows all the words to "With a Song in My Heart." Sings them in a pleasing but not strong soprano. They try a duet on "Nice Work If You Can Get It," and give up. Giggling.

Soufflé of a day. Soft and creamy. Pearlescent sky. They drive with the windows down. Smell sweet growing things. Traffic is unexpectedly light. They are at the track before the first race.

"There's a colt in the fourth named Harry's Chance," she says. "I usually don't bet more than two dollars, but I'm going to plunge on Harry's Chance. Ten dollars."

"You'll lose," he tells her.

"I don't think so," she says. Smiling.

She doesn't lose. The horse pays a little more than a hundred.

"I buy dinner," she says.

"No, you don't," he says. "Who do you like in the sixth? Sally's Folly?"

"Oh no. Came up lame last time out."

"I'm going to try five dollars."

"You'll be sorry," Evelyn says.

He is.

They have luncheon in the clubhouse. Caesar salad for both. Bottle of chablis. They don't bet on the last three races. Just sit there. Looking about. Enjoying the scene.

"You're the most beautiful woman here," he says. "Every man who looks at us is envious of me."

She puts a hand on his. "Tell me more," she says. Laughing. "Don't stop now."

They rise after the last race.

"I'm not hungry yet," he says. "Are you?"

"After that lunch? I should say not."

"What say we drive back to Boca and have dinner up there? I know a place with great steaks and a big salad bar."

"Whatever you want."

Which is, he recalls, exactly what Sally Abaddon said to him the last time they were together.

The Kansas City Steak House is on A1A. North of Lighthouse Point. Harry slips Sol, the head-waiter, a pound. They get a corner table. Dim. Secluded.

"Very nice," Evelyn says. Looking around. "Not too bright. Not too noisy. Is that garlic I smell?"

"I hope it isn't the busboy. Do you like daiquiris?"

"Love them."

"They make a marvelous frozen strawberry daiquiri. In a glass as big as a fishbowl. You game?"

"For anything," she says. Looking at him.

Leisurely dinner. Crabmeat cocktail. Rare

mignons. Baked potato skins with sour cream and chives. Fresh spinach with crumbled bacon from the salad bar. Bottle of St.-Emilion. And with the filets, in the Florida style, a thin slice of cold watermelon.

Harry Dancer finds himself relating the story of his life. Indiana farm boy. Purdue. Harvard for an MBA. On to Merrill Lynch in New York. Then to Chemical Bank. Transferred to the trust department in Florida. Decision to strike out on his own. Dancer Investment Management, Inc. A success.

"I met Sylvia at the tennis club in Boca," he says. Finishing. Dabbing lips. Sitting back. "Where you and I played. We were married— what was it—about six months later. Oh God, I must be boring you out of your skull. I'm sorry."

"Don't be silly," she says. Not telling him that she already knows all that. And more. "I like to hear people's histories. Every one of them different."

"What about yours?"

"Oh, no you don't," she says. Laughing. "I'm not ready to confess. Not yet. Besides, it's dull, dull, dull. You know what I'd like to do?"

"What?"

"Have coffee, and then go to the bar. I want to buy you a brandy. After all, I *did* win on Harry's Chance."

"I accept," he says.

The bartender, Cuban, is solicitous. Ice water on the side. Clean ashtray. Little mats for their brandy snifters. He pours Rémy Martin with a flourish. Waits.

"Hokay?" he says.

"Divine," Evelyn Heimdall says.

They sit close together on high stools. Knees touching. Looking into each other's eyes in the silvered mirror behind the bar.

"Want to go on?" Dancer asks. "Music? Dancing?"

"No. Let's go back to my place. Take off our shoes and relax. Have another brandy on the balcony. Listen to what the wild waves are saying."

"Sounds good to me," he says.

In her apartment, she brings small glasses of cognac out to the terrace. Excuses herself.

"I really am going to kick off my shoes," she says.

While she's gone, he takes off his jacket. Tie. Lies contentedly on a lounge. Drink held on his chest. Stares up at the tilting sky. Stars in their dance. He tells himself he is feeling no pain. *No pain*. Wonderful!

She comes back in a loose white terry robe. Buttoned down the front. She is barefoot. Nudges him with a knee.

"Skooch over," she says.

He moves to one side. She lies down on his lounge. Close to him.

"We'll fall off," he warns.

"So?" she says. "Who cares?"

He laughs. Puts his drink down on the tiles. Pulls her closer to him.

"Not if we cuddle," he says. "Do you like to cuddle?"

"I *love* to cuddle. My favorite sport."

"After tennis?"

"*Before* tennis."

He kisses the tip of her nose. Thinking that

sometimes it's grand to be foolish.

"Full moon," he says. "Almost."

"Do you sprout fangs? Thick hair on the backs of your hands? Howl?"

"How did you know?"

She presses closer. They are on their sides. Entwined. Stares locked. Enraptured. Suddenly, without warning, he begins to weep. Silently. Tears plop from his eyes. He tries to pull away. She will not release him.

"Sorry," he says. Voice choked.

"It's all right, Harry," she soothes.

He reaches down for his brandy. Takes a deep belt. Inhales.

"What brought that on?" he asks. "I don't know."

She strokes his face. Wipes away tears with a knuckle.

"I did it all the time," she says. "At first. After a while it stops."

"I feel like an idiot."

"No. Just human. You're not a werewolf after all."

He smiles. Holds her face. Kisses her forehead. Cheeks. Nose. Closed eyes. Her lips.

"Oh . . ." he breathes, "you're so good for me, Ev."

"Yes," she says. "And you for me."

"Partners in sorrow."

"Partners in hope."

He unbuttons the top of her robe. Her breasts are full. Tanned. Pinkish nipples. He bends his head. Tongue busy.

"You don't like the other one?" she asks.

He laughs. "You're too much. I love the other one."

Proves it.

"Harry," she says, "what are you doing with all your clothes on?"

"Out here?" he asks.

"Why not? No one can see."

"Except God," he says. Undressing.

"He'll approve," she says.

In Cleveland, the Department's comptroller, a viperish man, is examining regional vouchers. Sees immediately that the Southeast Region is over budget. Reviews their expenditures. Finds that the Harry Dancer operation accounts for most of the overrun.

He finally locates the Chairman in the War Room. Planted before a national map on a Plexiglass wall. Lights indicate ongoing actions. Operators sit at a battery of consoles, updating intelligence. An oversized digital counter shows number of current campaigns, and daily, weekly, monthly, annual failures and successes.

"A moment of your time, sir," the comptroller says. Bending to whisper.

"What?" the Chairman says. Jerking his leonine head around. "Oh, very well. What is it, Acheron?"

"The Southeast Region is dreadfully over

budget, sir. Mostly due to a single campaign. Harry Dancer."

The Chairman snaps his fingers at the floor supervisor.

"Nick," he calls, "bring me an update on Harry Dancer. Southeast Region."

In a moment the supervisor comes running. Trailing a long computer printout. The Chairman scans it swiftly.

"Progressing well," he says. "Let it run."

"You approve the expenditures, sir?" the comptroller says. Nervously.

The Chairman looks at him. "I approve. Do you wish a written and signed authorization?"

"Oh no, sir, that won't be necessary. I would just like to call the Chairman's attention to our current cash-flow problem."

"Don't tell me we're going broke?"

"Ha-ha," the comptroller tries to laugh. Cracking his face in a bleak smile. "Nothing like that. Our endowment is more than adequate. And current contributions are on target. It's just that we're a bit strapped for cash at the moment."

"That's your problem, isn't it, Acheron?" the Chairman says. "I know I can depend upon you to solve it in your usual efficient manner. I *can* depend on you, can't I?"

"Oh yes, sir. Absolutely, sir. Get on it right away."

The comptroller scuttles off. The Chairman rereads the printout on Harry Dancer. Interesting case. Makes him recall his career as field agent, case officer, and the Department's chief executive officer. Before he rose to his present preeminent position.

There are a few things he might do differently. But generally, he feels, the Regional Director is running a good chase. Eliminating Jeremy Blaine apparently closed the leak. Turning Herman K. Tischman was a real coup. And Sally Abaddon has never failed. Plus Briscoe.

Still, the Chairman is troubled. Something is not quite kosher. He knows that fussy little Chief of Operations in Corporation headquarters. He has fought him before. Knows how dangerous it would be to underestimate him.

He goes back to the printout again. Studies the moves. Countermoves.

The Chairman is a grossly obese man. Sitting in a thronelike chair reinforced with steel braces. He moves as little as possible. He requires assistance to stand up. But no fat around his brain. That is lean, hard, precise.

He beckons the floor supervisor again.

"Nick," he says, "I want to speak to the Director of the Southeast Region. Set it up."

Five minutes later the phone is brought to him.

"The Regional Director is on the line, sir," Nick says.

"Scrambled?"

"Of course, sir."

The Chairman waits until Nick is out of earshot. He trusts no one.

"Director?" he says.

"Here, sir," a tinny voice, scrambled and unscrambled, comes back.

"What did we eat the last time we met?"

"Broiled quail, sir."

"Good," the Chairman says. Fat face creasing with pleasure. "I just wanted to be certain I am not talking to an imposter."

"Very wise, sir."

"Director, you are over budget."

"I am aware of that, sir. I believe the importance of the Dancer operation justifies it."

"I agree. But try to keep your expenditures as modest as possible. You're convinced that the elimination of Jeremy Blaine plugged your leak?"

"I am, Chairman."

"I am not. Humor an old man, Director, but I've been around a long time. I have a feeling we've been blindsided. I want you to try another ploy. Who knows that the Corporation's private detective has been turned?"

"Tischman? Only Briscoe and I know about that, sir."

"Good. I want you to inform all personnel with knowledge of the Dancer operation that Tischman has been turned. Let's see what happens."

Silence.

"Director? Are you still there?"

"I'm here, sir. You feel we may still have a leak?"

"I believe it's possible."

"Very well, sir. I'll do as you suggest."

"Not suggest, Director. Order."

"Yes, sir."

"And watch those expenses," the Chairman says. "Your only justification will be success."

The Regional Director knows a threat when he hears one.

"I understand, sir," he says.

"I don't like that Briscoe," Sally Abaddon says. "He's a sod."

"Well . . . yeah," Shelby Yama says. "He's a heavy. But that's his job. And he's good at it."

"I don't like the way he looks at me. Keep him away from me, Shel."

"I'll try, baby. But the guy swings a lot of weight. He and the Director are buddy-buddy. To tell you the truth, I don't like the way he looks at *me*. I guess it's just his style; he's suspicious of everyone."

"You think he's working for Internal Security?"

"Could be. But we've got nothing to worry about, have we?"

Sally Abaddon has something to worry about. But unless Briscoe is a mind reader, he's never going to find out.

They're in Sally's motel room. Yama is helping her dress for an evening with Harry Dancer.

Her first date with him had been a disaster. She had worn a short, slinky shift of blue-green sequins. Cut low. Pumps with hooker heels. Long blond hair tousled about her shoulders. Thick makeup. She had seen in his eyes that it was all a mistake. After dinner, he drove her home and dropped her. Pleading an early morning business meeting.

"You came on too strong," Yama tells her at the debriefing. "He thinks of you as the nude dancer from the Tipple Inn. A whore. That's okay, he'll go along with that—in private. But in public, he wants a lady. The guy's known around here; he's got a reputation to uphold. What if he meets some of his blue-nosed clients while he's having dinner with an obvious bimbo two months after his wife died? They'd have pulled their accounts the next morning. We've got to dress you like a goody-goody. First, he won't worry about being embarrassed if he's seen with you. Second, he'll remember what's under the Miss Prim costume, and he'll get more excited."

"You know, Shel," she says, "you're not bad."

They spend two hours preparing her. Long hair up in braids. Minimal makeup. Billowy gown of printed chiffon. High at the neck. Loose, flowing skirt. White pantyhose. Demure shoes with low heels.

Yama inspects her.

"Fan-tastic," he says. "You look like you're going to a prom. All you need is a wrist corsage. Baby, you're just right. You'll knock him dead."

"I'll try to bring him back here," she says. Then, casually, "You're going to record tonight?"

"I don't see any point in it," Yama says. "But Briscoe insists on it. We'll be waiting in the parking lot."

"Have fun," she says.

When Dancer shows up in his silver BMW, she looks for his reaction. Sees that Yama is right on target.

"You're beautiful!" Dancer bursts out. "I was going to suggest a rib joint. But not with you dressed like that. Let's go to the club; I want to show you off."

On the drive up to Boca Raton, he keeps talking about how marvelous she looks. How happy he is to be with her. How impressed his friends will be.

"They'll think I'm robbing the cradle," he says. Laughing.

She smiles. Puts a hand on his knee.

The club's dining room is all shadows. Dark wainscoting and red velvet. Lighted candles, fresh flowers on the tables. Hushed chamber with tiptoeing waiters, quiet whisper of voices. "Good evening, Mr. Dancer. Nice to see you again, sir. Yes, Mr. Dancer. Of course, sir. Right this way, please. Is this table satisfactory, Mr. Dancer?"

He waves to several acquaintances. Sally is conscious of the stir she is causing. People turn to stare. Women put on glasses to get a better look.

"We're giving them something to talk about," Dancer says.

"So I notice. Does it bother you, Harry?"

"Bother me? You kidding? I'm *proud* of you."

They order Beefeater martinis, up. Touch rims.

"Here's to—what?" he asks.

"Us," she says.

"I'll drink to that."

They study the menus. Bound in plush with golden cords.

"They have Maine lobster," Dancer says. "Broiled, if you like. Interested?"

"Why don't you order for us, Harry? I like everything."

"What would you say to a steak salad? It's cold, charcoal-grilled sirloin cut into thin slices. With hard-boiled eggs, tomatoes, cukes, radishes, mushrooms, capers, croutons, and a lot of other swell stuff. Bibb lettuce. Want to try it?"

"Sounds devilishly good," she drawls. Imitation of English accent.

He laughs. "Then that's what we'll have. With a bottle of new Beaujolais."

They order. And have another martini. A friend drops by. Dancer introduces Sally Abaddon. Then two men. A couple. Two women. They are all introduced. Chat a moment. Sally is treated cordially.

"You're lovely, child," an elderly lady says.

"Thank you," Sally says. Casting her eyes downward.

"You're a success," Dancer tells her.

"Shall I take off all my clothes and dance naked on our table?"

He rolls his eyes. "Wouldn't that be wicked? What a scene that would be! Want to do it?"

"Later," she says. Groping him under the table. "A private performance only for you."

They stay at the table for almost two hours. Have coffee. Then move to the oak bar. Dancer orders green Chartreuse.

"Try it," he urges.

She sips. "What *is* it?"

"Good for what ails you. It's made by monks."

"Monks? I think I'll skip. Will you finish mine?"

"Sure. What would you like instead?"

"I'd like a Devil's Tail. If the bartender doesn't know how, I'll tell him how to mix it."

She does. Rum, vodka, lime juice, grenadine, and apricot brandy. Blended with crushed ice. Served in a champagne glass with a lime wedge.

"That I've got to taste," Dancer says. Then: "Wow! If I had two of those you'd have to call the paramedics. Where did you hear about it?"

"Oh . . ." she says. "I forget who told me."

They wander out. Holding hands. Valet brings the BMW around. Overcast night. Rumble of thunder to the south. Daggers of lightning.

"I think we're in for it," Harry says. "But it probably won't last long. Just a squall."

"I love storms," Sally says. "Don't you? All that crashing. The world cracking apart."

"You're a strange one. I thought you like hot sun and white beaches."

"I do. But storms are nice, too. I dream of wandering out in a storm naked. Wind against my skin. Getting drenched."

"And getting zapped by a bolt of lightning."

"Not me," she says. "I'm indestructible."

They drive in silence. Rain begins spattering.

"Where to?" he asks.

She considers a moment. Thinking of Yama and Briscoe in the parking lot.

"Not my place," she says. "How about yours? I've never seen it. Okay?"

"Sure," he says. But he isn't sure. In his bed? Sylvia's bed? "Let's go," he says.

By the time they get to his beachfront home the streets are flooded. Lightning is crackling overhead. Thunder snaps a whip all around them. He drives into the carport.

Across A1A, Herman K. Tischman pulls his ratty car onto the spongy verge. Cuts lights and engine. Opens the window a crack. Strips the wrapper from a cheap cigar. Begins to chew. Watching the house.

"Made it," Harry Dancer says. "Just. Another five minutes and we'd have been bogged down. I hope the power isn't out."

"It isn't," she says.

It isn't. He switches on a lamp in the living room. She looks around.

"Beautiful," she says. "I may move in."

"Please do," he says. As lightly as he can. "My wife decorated it. She had good taste."

"She surely did. Where do those glass doors lead to? A swimming pool?"

"No, I don't have a pool. It seems silly when you're a hundred yards from the Atlantic Ocean. That's the patio out there. And the garden."

She presses her nose against the glass. Stares into windswept darkness. Rain rattles against doors.

"Close neighbors?" she asks.

"Not too close. Plenty of privacy. Bushes and dwarf palms on both sides."

"They won't see me then."

"See you what?"

"Prance naked in your garden."

"Oh my God," he says, "you were serious."

"I want to, Harry. Please let me."

"Sure," he says. Not happy about it. "Go ahead. But don't expect me to join you."

"I've got to get out of these clothes. I'm wearing a girdle. Can you believe it? And it's killing me."

She begins taking down her hair. He goes into the kitchen. Takes the Tanqueray bottle from the freezer. Pours himself a stiff jolt. Sips it standing at the sink. Wondering what is happening to him. Doubting what he is doing.

Brings the remainder of his drink back to the living room. She is at the glass doors, fumbling with the lock. Blond hair cascading down her muscled back. Naked, she looks twice as large. Everything about her vital and bursting.

He works the lock for her. Slides back the door. She darts into the storm. Yelping. He closes the door. Stares out. All he can see is a cavorting wraith. Hair streaming in the wind. Pale specter in the black. She is here, there, everywhere. Then gone.

A crack of thunder makes him start. Howitzer shot right over his home. His garden. In the following stab of lightning he sees her planted. Arms outstretched. Face raised to the downpour.

"Nut," he says. Aloud.

Goes into the downstairs bathroom. Gets towels and Sylvia's heavy terry robe. Monogram SD on the pocket. He comes back to the glass doors and waits.

She finally dashes across the patio. He slides the door open for her. She comes in. Squealing with delight. Hair sodden. Body dripping. He wraps towels about her. Begins to rub her dry. Then gets her into the robe. She uses a towel on her hair.

"Cold?" he asks her.

"It was super," she says. Still bubbling. "Just super. The rain felt like pins and needles."

"You better have a drink," he says. "Brandy?"

"Whatever."

He pours her a small Courvoisier. And another gin for himself. When he brings the drinks back to the living room, she is seated on the floor. Bare legs spread. Still tousling her hair. He sits on the couch near her. Holding their drinks.

"You're a wild one," he says.

"An hour ago you called me a strange one."

"So you are. Strange and wild."

"I guess I was," she says. Grinning up at him. "When I was young."

"When you were young? Ho-ho. And what are you now—ancient?"

"You'd be surprised," she says.

She rises. Tosses the towel aside. Curls up on the couch close to him. Takes her drink. The robe falls open. He looks down.

"Nice?" she asks.

"Very nice," he says. Sliding an arm about her shoulders.

"Harry, have you been thinking about it?"

"About what?" he says. Knowing.

"Taking me out of the Tipple Inn."

"I can't go for a thousand a week, Sally."

"I didn't expect you to. Five hundred?"

Looking down at her . . .

"All right," he says, "let's try it. Either of us can cancel at any time without giving any reason. Okay?"

"Sure," she says, "I'll go along with that. You want me to move in here?"

"No," he says. "It wouldn't look right. Stay where you are."

"But I can stop over here, can't I? Occasionally."

"Of course."

"Like tonight?"

Her ashy scent is stronger. Sweet char.

"Yes," he says. "Like tonight."

"Good brandy," she says. Sipping. "Want a taste?"

She dips a forefinger into her glass. Smears her nipples. Pulls his head down.

"Taste," she commands.

He obeys.

"What's upstairs?" she asks.

"Bedrooms."

"Well?"

They go up the stairs slowly. Hand in hand. He pulls blanket and sheet down on his bed. Sylvia's bed. Then closes the blinds.

"Leave the light on," she says. "I like to watch." Then: "Let me do the work tonight. All right?"

"No, I want to do the work."

"We'll both do the work."

"Me first," he says. Laughing.

"No, *me* first," she says.

She crouches over him. Drifts her damp hair back and forth over his body. Feathering him. Watching his reaction. He reaches up for her. Pulls her down atop him. Unexpectedly she kisses him on the lips. Soft. Tender. Then moves away.

"Harry," she says, "I think I've got a problem."

"What's that?"

"I love you."

The Corporation's Chief of Operations has a private chamber adjoining his office. Not much larger than a walk-in closet. Austere. Furnished only with an antique prie-dieu. It is rumored he naps in there.

He does not. But within that soundproofed

hidey-hole, he meditates. Plays chess games in his
mind. Planning moves to keep him ahead of the
Others. Sometimes, checkmated, he accepts defeat. Or settles for a draw.

But not in the case of Harry Dancer. Not yet.

Latest intelligence has been puzzling. Norma
Gravesend reports that all personnel assigned to
the Dancer operation have been informed that
Herman K. Tischman, the Corporation's muscle,
has been turned.

In his closet, kneeling painfully, the Chief
ponders the significance of that. He can understand the twisting of Tischman. It makes sense to
double one of your opponent's players. But why
announce the corruption publicly? Such victories
are usually revealed only on a "need to know"
basis.

The Chief tries to put himself into the devious
mind of the fat Chairman of the Department.
What is that evil elephant up to? What does he
hope to gain by informing so many people of
Tischman's defection?

Of course! The Chairman is not satisfied that
the leak in his Southeast Region has been closed
with the elimination of Jeremy Blaine. He is setting a trap. Now, if Tischman is taken out, the
Chairman will know a traitor still exists in
Regional headquarters. Their Interior Security
will take up the search again.

So, to protect Norma Gravesend, it will be
necessary for the Chief to ensure that Herman K.
Tischman continues to function. How to do that?
The answer seems obvious: Tischman has been
turned once; he can be turned again. Double and
triple-agents are not all that uncommon. When a

man has defected once, he can be whirled like a windmill. Revolving to the strongest pressure.

He summons Anthony Glitner to Washington. The case officer is shocked to hear of Tischman's betrayal. The two men discuss how to handle the private investigator.

"Let's dump him," Glitner suggests. "His reports on Dancer's activities are valuable, but if he's been taken, we can't trust him. He may be feeding us disinformation."

"Undoubtedly," the Chief agrees. "But if we eliminate him, we endanger our mole in the Department. How do you think they turned Tischman?"

"Money," the case officer says. "The man is greedy."

"I suspect you're right. But our budget is stretched thin as it is; we can't afford to keep upping the ante."

"Well, then . . . ?"

"Does this Tischman have a family?"

"Yes, sir. Wife and little girl. About twelve years old. Mary Jane."

The Chief fumbles with a roll of Tums. Trying to tear it open. "There is a ploy we've used in the past on cases like this. High success rate. It's called Fatal Illness. Have you ever worked it?"

"No, Chief. I don't know what it is."

"I'll explain. You may think it cruel, even immoral. But no one gets hurt. Although there is a certain amount of, ah, discomfort. I think it may bring Mr. Tischman back into the fold."

He outlines to Glitner exactly how Fatal Illness is played. The case officer takes notes.

When the Chief finishes, Glitner snaps his notebook shut. "As you say, sir, it is a little on the scurvy side. But I'm willing to give it a try."

"Could one of your people act the healer?"

"Willoughby, our communications man, could do it. He's been asking for a more active role. I think he could handle it."

"Fine. Tell him if he does well on this, it will go on his record. He wants to be a field agent?"

"That's his ambition."

"Here's his chance. Get the scenario rolling as soon as you return to Florida. Tony, are you satisfied with Evelyn Heimdall's performance?"

"Absolutely, Chief."

"Good. Keep me informed. I want to win this one."

"So do I, sir."

Sylvia's death has left him numb. Feelings jumbled. Thoughts fleeting. He believes himself a rational man and resolves to make no determinations concerning his personal life while pain corrodes and emotions churn. He knows he is temporarily incapable of linear thinking, of even imagining what his future might be like.

But now Sally Abaddon and Evelyn Heimdall have appeared. He does not believe that only loneliness is driving him to embrace them. It is true they are a refuge. But they are also escape. And a challenge to reflect on how he wishes to order his remaining years.

It is not a decision, he feels, that must be made

immediately. He cautions himself to wait, consider, ponder, judge. To *think*.

At the same time, a worm of doubt gnaws. Is the temporizing because of fear? Fear that another close, personal, permanent relationship might end as tragically as his love for Sylvia? At 3:00 A.M., wide awake, he listens to the waves turning on the strand and wonders if he is burned-out. Emotions depleted. Unable ever again to feel deeply.

He tries to hint something of this to Sally Abaddon.

She looks at him. "You've got the jimjams," she says. "The willies. You spend too much time alone. Brooding. Harry, you've got to start living. Having fun. I know just what you need."

She is practiced in all the sensual arts. Which buttons to press. Which triggers to pull. Slowly, patiently, she leads him into a netherworld of delights. He follows gladly. For there are no doubts there. No questions. Just physical exhaustion and blessed oblivion.

He doesn't know if it is pleasure or pain. Sometimes her passion seems excessive. Verging on hysteria. He can't believe she is faking it, playing her whore's trick. Whores don't dissolve in tears and cling desperately. He tries to understand her, but cannot.

When he mentions his inner confusion to Evelyn Heimdall, she listens attentively. But prescribes no quick fix.

"Don't judge yourself too harshly," she advises. "You are going through a very difficult period of readjustment. Right now you don't know what you want. Or who you are, for that matter."

"I can't seem to get my act together," he says. "I don't want to whine, but I'm at sixes and sevens. Nothing definite. No foundation."

"You'll come out of it," she says. "I really believe that. Remember what I said about faith? It does help, Harry."

"How do I get started?" he asks. With a foolish laugh.

"Let's take a walk on the beach. It's such a lovely evening. We'll just talk."

"All right," he says. "Maybe it'll help me unwind."

She is steady, thoughtful. What she tells him makes sense. He had always thought of faith as blind acceptance.

"It's a game, Harry," she says. "Or, if you wish, it's theater. A part to play. Faith is like civility. Make-believe. It's very difficult to be polite and courteous to strangers. Or to people you dislike and can't respect. But without civility, life becomes vile and brutish. And without faith it becomes nothing. Meaningless. Just putting in your time. Like a prison sentence."

"I don't think I could pretend a faith. In anything."

She smiles. "You'd be surprised. It becomes a habit. Like breathing. Unconscious. Automatic. After a while, when you stop questioning, you just accept. Then it's always there."

"Are you proselyting me?"

"I guess you could call it that. You're obviously unhappy. I want you to be happy. Is that so awful?"

"Of course it's not awful," he says. Taking her hand. "I appreciate what you're trying to do, but

I don't think I'm ready for it yet.''

"I'm going to keep nagging you," she warns.

"Do that. You're the sweetest nagger I've ever met. Getting tired? Shall we turn back?"

"I think so."

"We can have a cold drink on the patio," he offers.

"And then?"

"We'll let nature take its course."

"Excellent idea," she says. "Would you like me to stay over?"

"Please. I don't want to be alone tonight."

"You won't be. Ever."

The debriefing goes badly. Briscoe is a pit bull; he keeps snapping.

"Why did you go to his place?" he asks Sally Abaddon. For the third time. "Why didn't you take him to your motel? You knew Yama and I were waiting in the parking lot. We wanted it all on tape."

"I told you," she says. "He insisted we go to his home. If I had fought him, the evening would have come to a screeching halt right then."

"That makes sense," Shelby Yama says.

"No," Briscoe says, "it does not make sense. Sally, you claim that you've got Dancer hooked, that he'll follow your lead. So?"

"What difference does it make?" Sally says. "He wanted to go back to his place. We went. I fucked his brains out. And got a commitment from him to take me out of the Tipple Inn. Keep me. Five hundred a week. That's what you wanted, isn't it?''

Briscoe stares at her. "If Tischman hadn't reported, we wouldn't have known where you were. We'd have been sitting in that damned parking lot all night. From now on, you obey orders—exactly."

She throws him a mock salute. "Yes, *sir!*" she says. Then: "I'm seeing him tonight, and I've got to get dressed. Can I leave now?"

Briscoe lets her go. He sits there, scrubbing his scalp with his knuckles. "I don't like it," he tells Yama. "She's lying. I think she may be getting personally involved."

"Sally?" the case officer says. "Never! You know her record. How long she's been in the field. She hasn't failed yet."

"There's always a first time," Briscoe says. "There's a lot riding on this, Yama; we can't be too careful. I want you to—" He stops suddenly. "No," he says, "that's all right; I'll handle it myself."

He finds Herman K. Tischman in his office. The private detective is on the phone. He hangs up. Turns to Briscoe. Face blanched.

"My little girl is sick," he says. "Very high fever. That was my wife on the phone. She says the doctor wants to put Mary Jane in the hospital."

"Tough," Briscoe says. "Where's Dancer?"

"In his office. He never leaves before six."

"You'll pick him up then?"

"Well, uh, I want to get over to the hospital. For a while. But yeah, I'll pick him up at six."

"Okay. Now, two things . . . First, when you report to Glitner, I don't want you to say anything about Sally Abaddon. As far as you're concerned, Dancer isn't seeing her anymore."

The PI peels cellophane from a fresh cigar. Bites down on it. "Won't Glitner think that's funny?"

"What's funny about it? He'll figure Abaddon is a tramp. Dancer had a few one-night stands with her, and then gave her the brush. It makes sense."

"What the *hell* is going on here?" Tischman cries.

Briscoe glares at him. "You like the money, don't you? You need the money—your little girl in the hospital and all. So don't ask questions. The second thing is this: I want Dancer's home wired. Bugs in the phones that'll pick up calls and interior conversations. Especially the bedroom. You know any techs who could do that?"

"Well, yeah, I know a couple of guys. But it'll cost."

"I didn't figure on getting it free. I want it as soon as possible. Like tomorrow."

"I'll try," Tischman says.

"You'll have to do better than that," Briscoe says. "Get it done."

Two days later, the condition of Mary Jane Tischman has worsened. She isn't responding to antibiotics. She is aflame with fever. She is packed in ice, but doctors cannot control the fire. They no longer say: "Serious." Now they say: "Critical."

Anthony Glitner arrives at Tischman's office just as the investigator is leaving.

"I can't talk to you now," the detective says.

"I've got to get to the hospital."

"The hospital? What's wrong?"

"My little girl. She's very sick."

"I'm sorry to hear that. What is it?"

"You think anyone knows?" Tischman says. "Those smart high-priced doctors, they can't do a thing. She's dying, and all they can say is, Let's try this or let's try that. Nothing works. Jesus! Mary Jane is twelve years old. If she goes, my wife's life is down the drain. And mine, too."

"That's terrible," Glitner says. "Listen, if the doctors give up on your little girl, give me a call. I know a man who's had amazing success with cases like that."

"No kidding? A doctor?"

"Not exactly. He doesn't have a degree. Can't practice medicine. He calls himself a healer. A faith healer. But it really works."

"What does he do?"

"He'll just put a hand on Mary Jane's forehead and say a prayer. I know it doesn't sound like much, but it *works*. Besides, what have you got to lose?"

"Yeah, you're right. Let me talk to my wife about it. This guy charges?"

"Not much. You'll be able to handle it. Easily."

Next morning, Glitner gets a frantic call from Herman K. Tischman. The investigator is weeping.

"She's going," he reports. "In a coma. My Mary Jane. The docs can't do nothing. Could you bring that guy of yours around? The healer?"

"We'll be right there," Glitner promises.

Willoughby is a tall man. Thin. Gangling.

Lumpy Adam's apple. Wearing black suit, white shirt, black string tie. Carries a Bible under his arm. He smells faintly of incense.

"Let him in," the resident physician says. "Let them all in. Whatever gives them comfort."

Tischman, his wife, Glitner, Willoughby—all cluster about Mary Jane's bed. Staring down at that still form. The healer places his palm against the child's forehead.

"Lord God," he intones, "listen to my prayer."

His lips move. They all stand silently. Heads bowed. After a few moments, Willoughby takes his hand away. Lowers the Bible to press it against Mary Jane's parched lips.

"It is done," he says.

Glitner and Willoughby sit patiently in the waiting room. One hour. Almost two. Then Herman K. Tischman comes rushing in. Face alight.

"Her temperature's down!" he shouts. "She's going to make it." He grabs up their hands. Won't let go. Then he embraces Willoughby. Begins crying. "She's all right. The docs say she's going to be all right. The fever has broken. Thank you, thank you, thank you. How can I ever repay you?"

"I'll tell you," Anthony Glitner says.

The Chairman of the Department, in Cleveland headquarters, follows developments in the Harry Dancer case with intense interest. Tischman is still on the job. So the Chairman assumes the leak in the Southeast Region really has been plugged by the elimination of Jeremy Blaine.

That is good. What is bad is Briscoe's uncertainty about Sally Abaddon. The Chairman knows full well the importance of the field agent. He or she is the essential pivot on which the whole operation turns. If Sally has been compromised— by the Corporation or her own weakness—the Dancer campaign is lost.

The Chairman approves the expenditure for the bugging of Dancer's home. Smart move. It should prove or disprove the validity of Briscoe's doubts. Apparently all is going well. But the fat man cannot rid himself of the irritating suspicion that he is being outmaneuvered by that belching bastard in Corporation headquarters.

He is angered by his distance from the scene of action. Having been in the field so many years himself, he knows how often operational reports are falsified, exaggerated, or just incomplete. The agent knows what is happening. The case officer learns a portion of that. And headquarters is informed of a part of *that*. Intelligence dribbles away as it moves up the chain of command.

The Chairman, seated before the war map in his reinforced throne, pulls at his rubbery lips and ponders the case of Harry Dancer. Then he snaps his fingers for the floor supervisor.

He sends a coded message to the Director of the Southeast Region. He requests a report on anything unusual, puzzling, or unexpected in the personal lives of people involved in the Dancer action.

It is not much, the Chairman acknowledges.

But it is all he can do at the moment to calm his fears. Cover all bases. If he is to lose, it will not be from lack of trying. He does not wish to report failure, due to inaction, to his superiors. He knows the consequences.

If Harry Dancer cannot understand Sally Abaddon, he has company: she cannot understand herself.

She recognizes what she is risking. Eternal youth. Beauty. The excitement of evil. But something is stirring. A want she can't define. Vague longing. A wish for—what?

She searches Dancer's face. Trying to find the answer there. He is handsome. But she has known handsomer men. He is a good lover. But she has known better. He is kind, gentle, considerate. She has corrupted a hundred men with the same qualities. So what *is* it?

She doesn't know. Can't label it. Gives up trying. But the chemistry is there. Seducing her. Warm softness. A hint of something better. Not thrilling, but satisfying. And dangerous.

She wonders if it may be just boredom. Weariness with the sameness of her life. Perhaps, before endangering herself, she should ask for a transfer. Even a vacation. Would that renew her resolve? She doubts it. She is conscious of slow, deep movement. A fault slipping. And then the earthquake. A holiday could not stop it.

She is aware of Briscoe's doubts. That cold man suspects something is happening to her. She takes precautions. In bed at the motel, she puts her mouth close to Harry Dancer's ear, whispers, "I love you." Knowing it will not be overheard and recorded by those voyeurs in the parking lot.

"I love you," she whispers. And when he starts to respond, she puts a soft finger on his lips.

The scenario calls for his sexual enslavement. Old plot. High success rate. But this time she finds the script offensive. Not so much what his total subjugation will do to him, but what it will do to *her*. Crushing the thing she feels growing, moving.

But then fear arises. If she tempers her passion, can she hold him? Keep him? Not for the Department, but for herself. For the first time in her long life she is unsure. Riven. Sex has always been her weapon. Now it becomes a snare.

"I love you," she whispers. Running a palm over his naked body. Feeling pound of heart. Surge of blood. Touching muscle. Probing secret, shadowed corners. She would like to be *in* him. Completely. Enveloped and gone. Disappeared in his tissue. A part of him.

She sits astride. Bends to stare into his eyes. Her hair falls around. A tent. She holds his face within her hands.

"Darling," she whispers. "Sweetheart. I love you."

Treachery. She knows it.

The Fatal Illness ploy is a complete success. Herman K. Tischman is tripled. Anthony Glitner reports that the PI, in gratitude for the life of his daughter, agrees to inform the Corporation of Harry Dancer's activities before telling Briscoe. And will censor the intelligence passed to the Department as Glitner dictates.

Tischman's first revelation is that Dancer is now keeping Sally Abaddon. Seeing her two or three times a week. And the Department has wired Dancer's home. With the capability of overhearing and recording telephone calls and interior conversations.

The Chief of Operations is pleased with the turning of Tischman. He is not so pleased to learn of Dancer's closer relationship with Sally Abaddon. And he is puzzled by the bugging of the subject's home. With the Department apparently succeeding in the debauching of Harry Dancer, what is the need? The Chief doesn't know.

He makes certain case officer Glitner informs his agent of this new development. That whatever she says, and does, in Dancer's house will be shared by the Department. Then the Chief retires to his hideaway. Kneels at his antique prie-dieu. Prays for enlightenment.

Evelyn Heimdall, being informed, cajoles Harry Dancer into coming back to her apartment after a sinfully fattening dinner of grilled sweetbreads and bratwurst with bacon.

"We could go to my place," he offers.

"Not after that dinner," she says. "I must have gained five pounds. I want to get into something loose and flowing before I start popping buttons."

"It *was* good, wasn't it? We should have skipped the Key lime pie, but I couldn't resist it."

They sit on the balcony. Groaning with content. Watch a shimmering moon track. And far out, bobbing lights of fishing boats.

"This place is like a travel poster," she says. "And I'm right in the middle of it."

"Glad you came here, Ev?"

"I never want to live anywhere else."

"I'm happy to hear that. Some people can't adjust. The tropical heat. The indolence. The mañana philosophy. They think it's corrupting."

"Do you think it is?"

"Lord, no! I work as hard down here as I did in Manhattan. But I relax more—when I get the chance."

They lie on adjoining couches. She reaches for his hand.

"Maybe I feel a teensy-weensy bit of corruption," she says. "But I prefer to think of it as thawing. It's as if I'm learning what pleasure and joy are like—after all these years."

"You never felt pleasure or joy before?"

"Of course I did. But it was planned. Structured. We'll go to a Broadway play on Thursday night. We'll have a picnic on Saturday. We'll drive to the shore on Sunday. That was pleasure and joy—usually. But they were brief incidents. Here it becomes your whole life. You begin to understand that you can be continually happy. I don't mean there aren't disappointments and aggravations. But they seem so minor, really meaningless, compared to the sun, sand, sea. Or a night like this. Am I making any sense at all, Harry?"

"Sure you are. You're well on your way to becoming a lotus-eater."

"Oh, Harry!"

"I recognize the symptoms," he says. "I live on the beach; I see what happens. Women come down here from up north, and for the first six months they wear a one-piece bathing suit with ruffles and a skirt. Then they switch to a two-piece suit. Navel covered, of course. Within a year they're wearing the tiniest bikini they can find."

She laughs. "I bought one today. I'm afraid to wear it in public."

"You'll wear it," he assures her. "My friend, Jeremy Blaine, died recently. Since then his widow has been wearing nothing but black bikinis. Florida mourning. But the size of your bathing suit is just an outward indication of what's going on inside. As you said, a thawing. A more animal approach to life. Learning to loosen up. Completely. Taste food. Enjoy drinks. And discovering how to avoid hassles. Or ignore them."

"Did all that happen to you?"

"Sure it did. Until Sylvia died, and I was jerked back into the real world."

"I don't know . . ." she says. "I'm getting to the point where I'm not sure what the real world is. Is it sorrow and pain and suffering, or is it what we have right now?"

"Good question. I wish I had the answer, but I don't."

"I just feel sexier," she says. "Does that shock you?"

"Of course not. Delighted to hear it."

She is silent. Realizing she isn't following the scenario. Tony Glitner will be furious. But at the moment her case officer's anger seems unimportant. She just doesn't want to proselytize. Suddenly faith is a foreign language.

"I have the makings of a brandy stinger," she says.

"That'll do it. You'll never get me out of here."

"That's the idea."

In her bed, she leans over him and says, "You are a nice man. A nice, nice man."

"That's the stinger talking."

"No, that's me talking."

She is a robust woman. Sturdy. Heavy breasts. Narrow waist. Hips flowing like a lyre. Strong, tapering legs. A scent to her flesh like incense. Dressed, she resembles his wife. Naked, she is totally different.

She is engrossed with his body.

"Men have nipples, too," she says. "Don't they?"

"That's right. Two of them."

"Your skin is like suede, Harry."

"Good or bad?"

"Good. So good. Close your eyes and pretend to sleep. Let me do things."

He closes his eyes. Feels her mouth. Lips. Tongue.

"Ev . . ." he says.

"Shh. I'm thawing. What you said—a more animal approach to life. I do believe I'm becoming an animal."

"Does it bother you?"

"I don't know," she says. Troubled. "I don't know how to handle it."

"You want to let go? Surrender?"

"Yes," she says, "that's what I want. To let go. Do everything."

She explores him with wonder. He is part of a new world she is just beginning to glimpse. She forgets limits. Not forgets, but disregards. It lures her. She thinks he will be her passage. All things are possible. Complete freedom. Liberty.

"Enough," he says. "Please."

"More," she begs. Listening to herself. Not believing.

At the debriefing, she says, "I think it's going well, Tony. We had a long talk into the wee hours of the morning. I really think he's coming around."

"Fine," Glitner says. "Now tell me what he said, and what you said."

She concocts the whole thing. Cleverly. Faltering at times. Not too glib. Spinning a tale of the conversion of Harry Dancer. She admits they made love; that is sanctified. But she comes down hard on Dancer's doubts, her answers, his equivocation, her insistence.

"Sounds good," the case officer says. "But don't press him too hard. We don't want to scare him away. Slow and easy. We know what the Others are doing. We want to offer Dancer a more attractive alternative. You've got to be steady, positive, absolutely sure. You've done this before; you know the drill. I can do so much. Headquarters can do so much. But essentially it's up to you, Ev. We're depending on you."

When she is alone, she wanders onto the balcony. Grips the railing. Looks out at a roily sea stretching to nowhere. Wants to weep but cannot. Squinches her eyes shut. Sees suede skin. Tastes it. Remembers what they did. Shudders with bliss.

Harry Dancer admits he has become a weather vane. He twists in the wind. Adopts the opinions and philosophy of the last person he speaks to. Seems incapable of independent judgment. But in his confusion, he can recognize the confusion of others. It takes one to know one.

He cannot understand Sally Abaddon. She has made no pretense of being anything but a venal woman. Her body purchasable—if the price is right. Now she talks of love. Hinting she seeks a deeper, more permanent relationship. He recognizes her dissatisfaction, but can't define it.

He cannot understand Evelyn Heimdall. That strong, faithful, steady woman is becoming wildly passionate. With an appetite for the spiced and exotic. She acts like one throwing off shackles. Everything about her—speech, dress, actions—signifies a new freedom. Self-indulgence.

And Harry Dancer cannot understand himself. He had thought his affairs with Sally and Evelyn would soothe the pain of Sylvia's death. Turn him toward the future rather than the past. Exorcise, finally, those haunting memories.

It has not happened. Instead, the intimacy with both women has, somehow, re-created Sylvia. Texture of their skin. Warm breath. The sweetness of the secret places of their bodies. All the glories of physical love recall vanished splendors.

The way Ev shakes her head to fling her short hair into place. The way Sally soaps her breasts: serious and intent. Both painting toenails. Shaving legs. Touching him. Curling up to sleep. Trimming wisps of pubic hair. Padding about in bare feet. Wearing his shirts—and nothing else.

All these intimate physical details recall for him a life that was, and is no longer. Sylvia did all those things. He remembers, and can see her plainer every day. How to account for that—new loves reviving an old? They are resurrecting something he thought dead and gone.

He cannot comprehend. Is it that love exists by itself? Is all love one—a generic feeling needing no special object? Would any man or any woman do as well as any other? With only the emotion itself having meaning? Like patriotism. What difference does the nation make? Only the devotion is significant.

All this puzzles him. Troubles him. He feels caught up in a struggle he cannot identify.

"What's going on?" he asks aloud. And realizes, with a pang, he is not talking to himself. He is speaking to Sylvia.

Plot—counterplot . . .

The Chief of Operations summons Anthony Glitner to Washington. They confer in the safe room.

"That business about wiring Dancer's home . . ." he says to the case officer. "What do you think the Department is up to?"

"The usual, I suppose," Glitner says. "Raw material for blackmail—if it's ever needed."

"Perhaps," the Chief says. Chewing on a

Tums. "But I believe there may be another reason. I'm guessing they don't trust their own agent."

The case officer is startled. Then considers. "It's possible, sir. A way to check up on her when she's with Dancer. Yes, that makes sense. Chief, you don't think we could turn her, do you? What a coup that would be!"

"I asked Intelligence for a complete dossier on Sally Abaddon. She's been with the Department a long, *long* time. A splendid record—from their point of view. Remember that Secretary of State we lost? She's the one who debased him. There's not a single hint in her file of the slightest infidelity of the Others' creed. But this bugging of Dancer's home is curious. Maybe she's burning out—or perhaps just bored. It could be a number of things. But we'd be remiss not to follow up on it. Give her a nudge—if she's really thinking of defecting."

"How do we do that, sir?"

"You know, Tony, sometimes we try to be too clever by far. We neglect the simple and obvious solutions. In this case, I believe the most effective thing we can do at the moment is to make an anonymous telephone call to Sally Abaddon. Just tell her that Harry Dancer's home is bugged, and hang up. If she's still true-blue to the Department, it won't mean a thing to her. If she's beginning to doubt, she'll change her way of operating. You'll have to put someone on her to observe. How about Willoughby? He did a good job acting the faith healer."

"I think he can handle it," Glitner says. "You want her followed?"

"As closely as possible. When you get back to Florida, brief Willoughby, and then make that phone call to Abaddon. Let's see what happens."

At the same time, the Chairman of the Department, in Cleveland, is reviewing a report from the Director of the Southeast Region. This is the intelligence he requested on anything unusual, puzzling, or unexpected in the personal lives of people involved in the Dancer action.

The Chairman finds what he's looking for in a short paragraph on Herman K. Tischman. It states that the detective's daughter suffered a sudden and inexplicable illness. Was given up by attending doctors. Staged a miraculous recovery, and is now in good health.

Miraculous indeed! the Chairman thinks. And immediately recognizes what has happened: the Department's hireling has been switched.

He puts through a call to the Regional Director on a scrambler line.

"You fool!" he says. "You've been duped. That private detective of yours has been turned. His daughter's illness was staged."

The Director begins stammering.

"Shut up!" the Chairman says. "Briscoe recruited him, didn't he? Then let Briscoe clean up the mess. Feed this Tischman disinformation. If the Corporation reacts, you'll know I'm right. Then let Briscoe take it from there. I expect results within forty-eight hours."

The Director calls in Briscoe. Repeats the Chairman's orders.

"Son of a bitch," Briscoe says. "I thought I had that idiot in my hip pocket. The guy's a whirling dervish. You mean his daughter's fever was a

Corporation scam? That was smart. And it cost them nothing."

"I'm not interested in how smart the Corporation is," the Director says. "You have forty-eight hours to take care of this. The Chairman wants it proved out before we take extreme action. I think it would be best for both of us if you deliver."

They stare at each other.

"Yes, sir," Briscoe says.

He concocts a complex plot. It contains elements of truth he is unaware of. He will tell Tischman that Harry Dancer has become sexually obsessed with Evelyn Heimdall. The two are planning to leave the country together. To live in sin in some foreign place.

Briscoe reckons that if Tischman has been tripled, he will inform the Corporation of this development. And the Corporation will pull Heimdall off the case and assign a new field agent.

But before Briscoe has a chance to put this outlandish scheme into operation, he receives evidence of the detective's guilt from another source. A voice-actuated tape recorder in Sally Abaddon's motel picks up an anonymous phone call.

"Miss Abaddon?"

"Yes. Who is this?"

"Let's just say a friend. I think you should know that Harry Dancer's home is wired. All the phones are bugged, picking up and recording phone calls and interior conversations. For the benefit of your employers."

"What did you say?"

"You heard me, Miss Abaddon."

"Who *are* you?"

Click!

Briscoe listens to this tape twice. Then considers
. . . Only he, the Director, Tischman, and the
techs who installed the bugs know of the electronic
surveillance of Dancer's home. But the techs have
no knowledge of Sally Abaddon. And, of course,
Briscoe eliminates the Director and himself. That
leaves Herman K. Tischman.

The Chairman is right; the detective has been
twisted. He snitched to the Corporation, who set
up the anonymous call. Briscoe tells the Director.

"Terminate him, sir?" he asks. "Extreme prejudice?"

"Yes," the Director says. "Immediately. An
accident."

"Of course," Briscoe says. Miffed because the
Director thinks it necessary to tell him how to do
his job.

At 6:00 P.M. that evening he finds Tischman.
The detective is slouched in his rusted Plymouth
outside Harry Dancer's office. Briscoe parks his
own car. Gets out. Strolls over to the PI's heap.
Leans down to speak through the opened window.

"Any action?" he asks.

"He had lunch with the Heimdall dame,"
Tischman reports. "Then they went to her place.
Long enough for a matinee. That's all."

"You and I have got to talk."

"About what?" Tischman says. Chewing on a
wet cigar.

"A new assignment. More bucks. You can use
the loot, can't you? The hospital bills for your
little girl and all."

"Well, yeah, sure. Climb in, and we'll talk."

"Not here. Too public. Knock off early tonight.
I'll see you at your office at nine. Okay?"

"You're the boss."

"That's right," Briscoe says.

He gets to Tischman's office a half-hour early. Parks a block away. Walks back. Carrying two liters of cheap vodka in a brown paper bag. He uses a surgeon's scalpel on the door lock and presses with his knee. Door pops open. He goes in. Closes the door. Switches on a desk lamp.

He pours a liter of vodka into the littered wastebasket. Over the upholstery of a garish couch. The rug. He wets the drapes. Rolls the empty bottle under the desk. Uses half of the second bottle to make a puddle beneath Tischman's swivel chair. Then he waits. Sitting.

Tischman shows up a little after nine o'clock. He is shocked to see Briscoe behind his desk.

"How the hell did you get in?" he demands.

"The door was open," Briscoe says. Rising.

"Bull*shit* it was. I always make sure to lock up. My God, this place smells like a brewery."

"I've been having a few," Briscoe says. Grinning. Holding up the half-empty bottle. "Want a shot?"

"What *is* this?" the detective says. "The place is soaked."

"Yeah," Briscoe says. "And look at that."

He points a thick forefinger at the wastebasket. It bursts into fire. Blue flames flicker upward.

"My God!" Herman K. Tischman cries. "What's going—"

"And that," Briscoe says. Aiming his forefinger at the drapes. Couch. Rug. "And that. And that."

The office roars. Conflagration spreads. The detective turns to flee. Briscoe grapples him with heavy arms. Flings him into the swivel chair. Tischman's clothing ignites. Body lurches upward. Briscoe slams him down. Pours the remaining vodka over him.

The office is an inferno. Flame. Smoke. Crackling. Things snapping. Tischman, mouth wide, writhes slowly. Hands opening and closing. Eyes melting. Clothes burning away. Flesh charring.

Briscoe waits patiently. Standing amidst the fire. Untouched. Then, when he sees Tischman is still, a black crisp, he walks out of the office calmly. He sees people running toward the blazing office. But he saunters back to his parked car. Fresh air is an offense. He relishes the scent of burning things. And ash.

Sally Abaddon is no dummy. She reports the anonymous phone call to Shelby Yama and Briscoe.

"What the hell is going on?" she asks.

"Nothing," Briscoe says. "Forget it."

"Is Dancer's home really bugged?"

"You have no need to know," Briscoe says.

Later, when they're alone, Yama asks him, "What is this? You checking up on her?"

"Yeah," Briscoe says. Staring at the case officer. "Any objections?"

"No, no," Yama says. "Can't be too careful."

"Uh-huh," Briscoe says. Giving him a wisenheimer grin.

It limits Sally. She knows her place is tapped.

And now Harry's home is covered. She considers what she might do: Rent another motel room without informing the Department. Or take Dancer to a different hot-pillow joint every time she sees him.

She realizes neither will work. Briscoe will demand to know where she went with the subject. What they said. What they did. And why wasn't it on tape?

She and Dancer go to the jai alai matches at Dania. Lose a few bucks. Then have dinner at a funky rib joint on Federal Highway. Drive home through thin traffic. The season is over; snowbirds have gone.

"You feel like a little tender, loving care?" she asks him.

"Why not?" he says. "Where?"

"Your place. Outside. On the patio or beach. I want to look at the stars. How many are there?"

He has no shame at repeating a good line.

"Six hundred million," he says, "four hundred and thirty-one thousand, eight hundred and fourteen."

She laughs. Puts a hand on his thigh. "You're crazy," she says.

"True."

They take cans of Michelob encased in plastic foam coolers. Start walking south on the beach. Few people about. Lovers. Jogger. Woman searching for shells with a flashlight. Man surfcasting. Patiently. Hopelessly.

There are no stars. A thick night roofed with clouds. Air is still, heavy. Far to the south, around Pompano, they see lightning flickering. Dimly.

But the fishing boats are out. In a cluster of lights.

"Something must be running," Dancer says. "Is it season for blues?"

"Blues?"

"Bluefish. You ever go fishing?"

"No," she says. Thinking that is not strictly accurate. "I did once, but didn't catch anything and got an awful sunburn. My nose peeled for days."

"There's so little I know about you," Dancer says. "I know you're not from Florida. At least you don't talk like a native."

"New England," she says. "Originally. Salem, Massachusetts."

"Oh-ho! Where the witches come from."

"That's right."

"Are you a witch?"

"I try," she says. Laughing.

"Well, you succeed. You've bewitched me."

"Have I? Have I really, Harry?"

They stroll with linked hands. Sometimes dashing up onto dry sand when a big wave comes in, white froth clawing for them.

"How long did you live in Salem?" he asks her.

"Not long. My father was a traveling salesman. We were always moving around the country as he got transferred from one region to another."

"Oh? What did he sell?"

"Fire insurance. Mostly to farmers. He never got rich at it, but he made a good living."

"And I suppose you got switched from one school to another."

"That's right. More than I can remember. I finally graduated from high school in Hadesville, Texas. You know where that is?"

"No."

"You're lucky. Harry, let's turn back. This soft sand is tough to walk in."

They plod back to Dancer's home.

"Then what?" he asks her. "After high school."

"I went to New York. I was runner-up in a beauty contest and thought I could become a fashion model. But I just wasn't the type. Too big all over."

"Not for me. Did you ever do any nude modeling? For men's magazines?"

"Why do you ask that?"

"You have the body for it; I thought you might have."

"As a matter of fact I did. But it's a sleazy business and doesn't pay all that much. Then I sort of drifted—here, there, and everywhere. And ended up in Florida."

"Lucky me," Harry Dancer says. "Well, here we are. Tired?"

"A little. Can we sit on the patio?"

"Of course. Another beer?"

"That would be nice."

He brings out cold beers. Closes the sliding glass door to the living room to preserve the air conditioning. Sally can't believe the Department's mikes will pick up voices on the patio.

"Do we need that light?" she asks.

"It's supposed to keep bugs away," he says, "but I'll turn it off if you like."

"Please," she says. "The darkness is nicer. More intimate."

"Intimate," he repeats. Tinny laugh. "I'm not sure I'm ready for that yet."

"I don't understand. I thought you and I were as intimate as a man and woman can get."

"We are. Physically. Sexually. I don't think I've ever been more intimate with a woman. In that way."

"But . . . ?"

"But the other day I was wondering if I'm capable of anything more than that. Since my wife died, I seem to have a fear of intimacy. Of really getting close to someone. It scares me."

Sally Abaddon sets her beer aside. Rises. Comes over to perch on the edge of Dancer's lounge. Puts a cool palm to his flushed face.

"Harry," she says, "are you talking about love? Is that what you mean?"

"I guess so. I guess that's what I mean. Fun in bed is one thing. I like that—as you well know. But I don't know if I can handle anything more."

"You're trying to tell me something, aren't you? Warn me off?"

"Oh no, darling," he says. Lifting her hand from his cheek to kiss the palm. "I just want you to know that right now you're dealing with an emotional cripple. Don't expect too much. Lately I've been getting the feeling that the games we play aren't enough for you. That you're looking for something else. A more—a more permanent relationship. More meaningful. Am I right?"

"Yes," she says. Low voice. "You're right. I feel it. I didn't know it showed."

"It does to me. Sally, I just don't want you to get hurt. I'm being as honest as I can. I'm disturbed that you might become too—too *intense.*"

"That's not your problem," she says. "It's my problem. I haven't asked for anything from you, have I? Other than the five bills a week for fun and games. But have I asked for any emotional commitment from you?''

"No," he admits, "you haven't. What I'm trying to tell you is that right now I'm not capable or willing to make any commitment.''

"Don't worry it, Harry. I'm a big girl, and I've been around the block twice. If I make mistakes, they'll be *my* mistakes. I won't blame you. Except for being such an adorable shithead.''

They both laugh, and it's all right.

He pulls her close. "What happened to that tender, loving care you promised?''

"Whatever you want, Harry. You call it.''

"Should we go upstairs?''

"Let's stay out here," she whispers. "It's dark. No one will see.''

"We're liable to get rained on.''

"I'd love it. Wouldn't you?''

Giggling, they undress. He bundles up their clothing, shoes, takes them into the living room. Then stealthily returns, sliding the glass door slowly so it won't squeak. He finds her lying on the patio tiles. Shining up at him. He lies down alongside.

"We'll get dusty," he warns. "Plus bruises.''

"Do you care?''

"Not really.''

She moves closer. Insinuates a knee between his thighs. Nudges. Gently. "Harry, what we were talking about before. Love. What is it?''

"All kinds and varieties. Affection. Friendship. Devotion. Attraction. Physical love. Emotional love. Intellectual love. Admiration. Loyalty. Religious love. Passion or tenderness. I could go on and on. It's like a big thermometer. Different degrees."

"So I can love you in one way, and you can love me in another?"

"Yes, that's possible. Probable, in fact."

"That's all right then. I accept that. Don't you?"

"Of course."

"We each do our thing."

"Well . . ." he says, "it doesn't always work out so neatly. The lover usually wants the same degree of love in return. Or more. And when he or she doesn't get it, there's trouble in paradise."

"Not in our paradise," she says. "I'll take what I can get—whatever you give me—and be happy."

He doubts it, but says nothing. He kisses her closed eyes. Nibbles ears. Draws an eager tongue down her neck. The hollow. Shoulder. Presses one of her breasts into his eye.

"Blind me," he says.

She stirs on the hard tile. Tugging him tight.

"What do you want me to do?" she asks. "Tell me."

"Just be you."

He is all over her. Voracious.

"Shh," he whispers. "Shh. The neighbors . . ."

They feel a light spattering. Rain drips, drizzles, drives. Big drops. Warm. Tile slickens. They skid. Slow motion. Laughing through their kisses. There is lattice overhead, but the rain comes through. Drenching.

Harry Dancer rolls away. Thrusts his erection at the glowering night sky.

"You were right," he says. "Pins and needles. Wonderful!"

They play with each other. Wet puppies. Rolling. Sliding on the skim. Rain streams from them.
They do nothing. He does not penetrate her; she
does not envelop him. But they cleave in joy.

"You told me," she says. "All kinds of love."

"Oh yes," he says. "Oh my, yes!"

Rain lasts for ten minutes. Maybe fifteen. They
lie supine. Opening mouths to drink it in. Spreading legs wide to feel it. Rolling. Biting. Licking.

It mists away. They are left spread-eagled on the
wet. Fingertips touching. Through the lattice they
see scudding clouds. Patch of clear.

"A star!" Sally Abaddon cries. "I saw a star.
And there's another one!"

"You and me," Dancer says. "One for each of
us."

She turns onto her side to bend over him. Sodden hair falls onto his face. He does not brush it
away.

"Let me love you, Harry," she says. "The way
I want to. And you love me in your way."

"Yes," he says. "All right. That's fair."

Both sides disregard budgets and assign addi-
tional personnel to the Harry Dancer action. The
Corporation, having lost Tischman, brings in an
operative to tail the subject while Willoughby
follows Sally Abaddon. The Department counters
with agents ordered to cover Dancer and Evelyn
Heimdall.

The two case officers coordinate the activities of

their staffs. Arrange schedules. Devise codes and passwords. Collate intelligence. Submit daily reports to their superiors. Always optimistic.

The wild card in this farrago of espionage and counterespionage is Briscoe. He is running two campaigns: trying to thwart the Corporation and to search out any evidence of chicanery in Department personnel. He believes Shelby Yama is stupid and inept. But not a traitor. Briscoe is not so certain of Sally Abaddon.

She claims that Dancer wants to couple on his patio, the beach, in his car. All places beyond electronic surveillance. Briscoe doesn't like it. He tells the Director of his suspicions.

"She says that Dancer insists on this and insists on that," he reports. "But she's supposed to be doing the insisting; that's her job. She swears she's got him hooked. I'm not so sure."

"I can't believe she's softening," the Director says. "She's an old hand at this game. She's never been anything but one hundred percent loyal."

"I know all that, sir, and I admit I have no hard evidence that she's thinking of defecting. But I'm an old hand, too, and I tell you something doesn't smell right here."

"What do you suggest? Shall I talk to her? Remind her of the penalties for betrayal?"

"No, Director, not yet. I don't want her to know we're suspicious. Let me see if I can devise some kind of test. See how she reacts."

"All right, do it your way. Incidentally, according to Yama's most recent report, the man assigned to Evelyn Heimdall says she is acting, quote, In an erratic manner for a Corporation agent, unquote. I'm not quite sure what he means by that, but I've contacted Intelligence in Cleveland, requesting a complete dossier on Heimdall.''

They look at each other.

"Yes, Briscoe," the Director says, "I know what you're thinking. We may have two field agents here who are considering turning. A very chancy situation. I would love to switch one of the Corporation's best. But not at the expense of losing one of ours. There's no profit in an equal trade. Move very cautiously on Abaddon. I'd hate to lose her and get nothing in return. Meanwhile, talk to the man covering Heimdall and see if you can find out why he thinks she's acting erratically. If he's correct, we might be able to push her a bit.''

Evelyn Heimdall comes off the court, sweating and laughing. Slides into a chair at Harry Dancer's table. Under a big, fringed umbrella. He has a vodka gimlet waiting for her.

"Well done," he says. "You creamed her.''

"It wasn't that easy. She was lobbing me crazy. You're not playing today?''

"Woke up this morning feeling a mite peakish." Gestures at his Bloody Mary. "But after two of those I'm bright-eyed and bushy-tailed.''

"Glad to hear it. You look beautiful. You should wear white more often. By the way, I'm taking you to lunch.''

"You are? What's the occasion?''

"No occasion," she says. Secret smile. "I just feel reckless."

He looks down at her smooth, tanned legs. "And where are you taking me to lunch?"

"My place," she says. "I have a Caesar salad already made. And a cold bottle of Frascati."

"I'm your man."

"I hope so," she says. "I think it's called a matinee. Or is it called an orgy?"

"Can two people have an orgy?" he asks.

"We can try," she says.

While he's setting the table and opening the wine, Evelyn goes in to shower. After she's soaped and rinsed, washed her hair, she stands under the lukewarm spray. Looks down at her streaming body. Rivulets and rivers. Bikini tan marks. Lower half of her breasts white. And a shoestring band across her hips.

She is seeing a new body. Or seeing her body in a new way. Something vibrant. Full of promise. Excitingly sensitive. Now so tender that she responds physically to colors, scents. The lilt of Harry's laugh.

"I just feel reckless." Had she said that? She had. She tries to estimate the limits of her novel adventurousness. Then, with a shiver of fearful delight, acknowledges there are no limits.

"Hey," Harry Dancer calls, "are you drowning in there?"

Yes, she is drowning.

She dries, pulls on her white terry robe. Dancer is wearing white linen, white shirt, white bucks. They lunch at a white table set with white. Cobwebby white drapes billow in from the opened balcony door. White light suffuses the room. They float in a globe of milk.

There is easy talk, teasing, laughter. Evelyn Heimdall is conscious of the delicate mood of the moment. And the insubstantial bond between her and this resplendent man. More, she knows suddenly the evanescence of life. Brightening, brightening, and then lost in opaque whiteness.

Dancer is telling her an amusing story of a client who erred on the name of a security he insisted on buying, and made a bundle. She listens, smiling, nodding.

But not really hearing. Devouring him with her eyes. Tanned hands. The slow, purposeful way he moves. Rugged features. Blue, pained eyes. Crow's-feet of paled laugh lines. Jut of jaw. Graying, sun-bleached hair. The masculine solidity of him. She sees his naked body. Suede skin. And between his legs . . .

She realizes he has stopped talking. "That's marvelous," she says. "It should only happen to me. More salad?"

He laughs, jerks his chin at the empty salad bowl.

"Oh . . ." she says. Confused. "I can mix some more."

"Don't you dare. That was just right."

"There's some of your Frangelico left," she says. "I could pour it over ice cream."

"Maybe later," he says. "I'm satisfied right now."

"Are you?" she says. "Completely?" And marvels at her boldness.

"I must pay for my lunch?" he asks. Mock-solemn.

"You must," she says. Surrendering to the new her.

In bed, naked, he touches the marks of her bikini tan.

"I told you so," he says.

"Yes. So you did. I thought people would stare. But they don't—which is worse. Would you like me all chocolate, or chocolate and vanilla? I can go down to the pool or tan on the balcony."

"Whatever pleases you."

"No, Harry. Whatever pleases *you*."

She has fantasized about this midafternoon scene. It will be insane, passionate, and lustful. Spiced by the searching light of the sun. There is nothing they will not do: he to her, she to him.

But now, the time arrived, she feels a curious lassitude. Warm languor. She is bundled, swathed in light and the heat of her own inchoate want. She floats. Realizing, mistily, that if he is to strangle her at that moment, she will offer no resistance. But might bend her head to kiss his tensed knuckles.

"Whatever . . ." she murmurs.

She is conscious of his hands. Mouth. Total surrender is a blessing. She is in a white dream. Drifting. Until the glow begins. At first no larger than the flicker of a match. Deep within her. Then a flame that crimsons the white.

Conflagration grows. Concentrating her mind, her energies. She begins to tremble. Twisting in the fire. Consumed and vitalized at once. The man says something, but she does not hear. She listens only to the roaring of the holocaust within her. And sobs in welcome.

She cannot know how long it lasts. Until the

flames begin to dwindle. Bloodred fades. Pales. White returns. Sun. Light. She is alive. Unconsumed. And stirs. Except, except down inside a flame still flutters.

"Pilot light," she says. Aloud.

"What?" Harry Dancer says. "You said, 'Pilot light.' What on earth does that mean?"

"Nothing on earth," she says. Smiling. Turning on her side to touch him. "Are we still in Florida? I thought it might be another planet."

"Still Florida. Are you all right, Ev?"

"I'm fine. Marvelous. Super."

"Your eyes are wet. You haven't been crying, have you?"

"If I have, it's from gratitude. Thank you, darling."

He laughs. "Did I pay for my lunch?"

"Overpaid."

"If you're willing to wait a little while, I could leave a tip."

"Oh yes," she says, "you must give me a tip. Better yet, let me take it."

Later, they lie listless and content. Mesmerized by the radiant light. Hands covering each other's secrets.

"I feel guilty," he announces.

"Guilty? Whatever for?"

"I don't know. Just a vague feeling."

"Well, don't feel it. I'm an adult female. You didn't seduce me with wild promises."

"I know. But still . . ."

"Harry, let me tell you what you've done for me. Are doing. Escape. That's the word. To another world."

"I don't understand."

"I've been so—so structured. Definite. Sure. Disciplined, you could say. But all that's changing. I know it."

"Florida," he tells her. "Blue skies. Hot sun. Beach. Ocean. I said you were going native."

"That's part of it, I suppose." Turns onto her hip to embrace him. "And you're part of it. Initiation rites into a new life."

"Hey," he says, "wait a minute. I make no claim to being a demon lover. You've been with men before."

"Yes. I have. But you're you, and it's different. I don't want you feeling guilty. No obligations whatsoever. What's happening is happening to *me*. You didn't plan it. As a matter of fact, I didn't either. But it *is* happening. I'll never ask you for anything, Harry. Never! Except to keep seeing you. Spending afternoons and nights like this. Am I shameless for saying that? Yes, I'm shameless. I don't care."

"Ev, do you know what you're doing?"

"I know. More than you can ever guess. I'm shedding an old skin, Harry."

"Like a snake?"

She nods. "Just like a snake."

He ponders. "You tell me I have no obligations. But that's really my decision to make, isn't it? If I feel a debt . . ."

"All right," she says, "if it will make you feel any better, if it wasn't you, it would be another man. And if you leave me, I'll find another. There. Does that soothe your conscience?"

"Soothes my conscience and deflates my ego."

She strokes his cheek. "I'm just trying to convince you that you're blameless. I take full responsibility. For everything."

"And what do you get out of it?"

"You," she says. Rolling atop him.

Tony Glitner, in his role as case officer, has run a number of field agents over the years. He understands the pressures they endure. Skittish people, for the most part. Prima donnas. They must be coddled, nursed. Given confidence. Their faith in what they are doing constantly reinforced.

He has had failed agents. But never lost one to the Others. He has no intention of ruining that record. He does not like to imagine the consequences.

Evelyn Heimdall has become a problem. Her debriefings are unsatisfactory. With no hard evidence, Glitner senses that the Heimdall-Dancer relationship has changed. It is not as the agent describes it. She is holding back intelligence that Glitner must know if he is to do his job. She may not be lying, but she is dissembling.

He is aware of a new lightness about her. Almost frivolity. He notes it in little things: brighter clothing, more frequent laughter, heavier make-up, a looser way of moving. When she sits, she makes no effort to conceal her good legs. She greets her case officer with a kiss. Departs with a kiss.

Everything about her now suggests self-indulgence. She claims to appreciate the importance of what they are trying to do. But Glitner sees shocking levity. Irresponsibility. She is no longer serious about their assignment. Makes jokes and cynical asides.

These the case officer omits from his daily reports to the Chief of Operations. He wants to be sure before he condemns her. Because her expulsion from the Corporation will be his failure.

He mentions his suspicions to no one on his team. But takes it upon himself to conduct a personal investigation. Follows her from her apartment on Saturday morning to the Boca tennis club. Sees her play. Watches her join Harry Dancer. Tails them back to her apartment. Glitner waits several hours, but Dancer doesn't appear.

At the debriefing, he says, "How did you make out on Saturday?"

"Not so good," Evelyn Heimdall says. "Harry wasn't feeling well. Hangover, I think. Anyway, he drove me back to my place and then split. No hits, no runs, no errors."

"Uh-huh," the case officer says. "When are you going to see him again?"

"We left it open. He'll call me or I'll call him."

Glitner lets her go. He doesn't know how to handle this. He's losing her—that's evident. But is she beyond reclamation? The thought occurs to him that possibly the Department is trying to debase her. Just as the Corporation hopes to elevate Sally Abaddon.

He decides that, in his own self-interest, he can no longer withhold this development from the

Chief of Operations. He calls Washington to set up an appointment. But the Chief is at a Board of Directors meeting in New York.

Now convinced that the situation cannot be allowed to deteriorate further, Glitner calls New York. Finally locates the Chief. Asks permission to fly up to discuss a matter of the "utmost urgency."

He hears a small belch on the other end of the line.

"All right," the Chief says. "Come ahead. I can give you an hour. No more."

The two men meet in a lavish suite at the Helmsley Palace.

"The Corporation takes care of its own," the Chief says. Wry smile. "Whatever happened to the sanctity of poverty? Well . . . never mind. What's the problem, Tony?"

Glitner spells it out. Admitting he has nothing that would hold up at an official hearing. But there is Heimdall's new persona. Her failure to submit a complete report on her activities with the subject on Saturday afternoon.

"It's just my opinion," the case officer says. "My impressions really. But I think we're losing her."

The Chief sighs. "I trust your judgment, Tony, but she has a fine record. No suggestion of backsliding."

"I know that, sir. This is as big a shock to me as it is to you. And I like the woman. She's warm, personable, and—I thought—steady and dependable. The perfect agent to bring Dancer around. I'm afraid it's not going to work out that way."

The Chief goes into the bathroom. Takes a swig

of Maalox from the bottle. Comes out again. Wiping his lips.

"Let's consider our options," he says. "We don't have enough evidence even to justify a reprimand. Let alone an official hearing. You can keep tailing her, hoping to get something solid. Or we can pull her off the case immediately, and assign another agent."

"Then all the time we've put in would be wasted," Glitner says. "We'd have to start over from square one. Making contact with the subject, and so forth. The Department is ahead of us already. A new agent is a prescription for disaster."

"I concur," the Chief says. "I think the first step is to prove out Heimdall, one way or another. Following her around won't do it. As you said, all you have are impressions."

"Then what's the solution?"

"It's obvious, isn't it? Nasty, but obvious. I'm returning to Washington tomorrow afternoon. I'll talk to Tommy Salvo in Counterintelligence. I think he better assign a man to Evelyn Heimdall. A devil's advocate, so to speak. He'll operate completely outside your team. You won't even know who he is. You recognize the need for that, don't you?"

"Yes, sir. He'll be reporting directly to Counterintelligence?"

"That's correct. And through them to me."

"But you'll keep me in the picture, Chief?"

"Of course. As much as you need to know."

Next day the Chief of Operations meets with Tommy Salvo. Man who wears tweed jackets, flannel slacks, and smokes a yellowed meerschaum pipe. The Chief explains the problem.

Salvo puffs thoughtfully: college professor without tenure.

"Yes," he says. Making that one word sound pontifical. "I believe I grasp the situation. You're looking for an agent provocateur. Am I correct?"

"No," the Chief says, "you are not correct. We have no desire to entrap this woman. We wish only to make certain of her loyalty. It is a test. Not a deliberate attempt to seduce her. Is that distinction clear?"

"Oh yes. Yes, yes, yes. I understand completely. I think I have just the man for you. Young, handsome, virile. Excellent record. Completely trustworthy. His name is Martin Frey."

"All right," the Chief says. "Brief him, and get him down to Florida as soon as possible. I have no idea how he'll make contact with Evelyn Heimdall."

"Martin will know how," Tommy Salvo says. Smiling.

Harry Dancer, confused, trying to find meaning in his life, turns back to memory.

He knows he is sometimes a dour man. With a taste for solitude. Not gloomy, but reflective. Silent moods. Sylvia could jolly him out. That woman was everything he is not: light, capricious, with a love of laughter and a zest for whims. She was the yeast in his life.

He can only remember the good times. Happiness recalled grows stronger. It seems to him now that they never exchanged a cross word, sulked, or barked at each other. He knows that cannot be true, but his memory allows only sunshine in. If there was pain and hurt, he refuses to acknowledge it.

Sally Abaddon and Evelyn Heimdall are disorder. They jumble him; he cannot think straight. What are they to him? What is he to them? He rummages, but can find no answers. Only the memory of his dead wife is simple, neat, clean. She was his touchstone.

His marriage was a better time. He had a role to play then. He knew his lines. He knew who he was.

Sally Abaddon's physical beauty is as much curse as blessing. Her roguish father spelled it out for her before she was sixteen.

"You're going to break a lot of hearts," he told her. "You can make a career of it—if that's what you want. I know you've got a good brain. The question is: Do you want to use it? You can become a rich man's darling or a poor man's slave —and wither away from boredom and the realization of lost opportunities and a wasted life."

"Then what shall I do? Tell me."

He looked at her speculatively. Head cocked to one side. "You might think about joining my company. Important work, and the rewards can be enormous."

"But I've had no experience."

"They'll teach you, Sal," her father said.

It turned out to be an exciting world. Filled with mystery and delight. Travel. Meeting new people. Becoming an expert at what she was trained to do. And as her father had said, the benefits were tremendous. The only catch was that you had to be perfect at your job; failures were not tolerated. Her father had found out. He was gone now.

Her successful career went on. And on and on. With never a qualm or doubt. She was convinced she had enlisted in a service for which she was uniquely qualified. She was, as the Department had promised, supremely satisfied. Then she was assigned to the Harry Dancer case.

Now qualms and doubts assail her. She struggles to understand what is happening. She tells herself it is not Dancer himself, the physical man. It is what he represents. Verities that were anathema to her. But which have suddenly become alluring, partly because they are forbidden to Department personnel.

She has always been an addicted risk-taker. More danger, more pleasure. But now she is courting the greatest peril of her life. Knows it, and cannot resist.

"Harry," she says, "tell me the story of your life. What you did when you were a kid and growing up and where you lived and everything."

"That would take a month of Sundays."

"I want to know."

They are driving up the coast to have dinner at Palm Beach. She is wearing her tailored suit of ashy linen, with a single strand of black pearls. Her hair is up, and she is not using the approved scent. She is turned sideways in the passenger seat so she can look at him as he speaks.

He tells her some things, trying to keep it light and amusing. But she is not appeased. Keeps asking questions about his parents, schools, church, girlfriends, loves, hobbies, habits. His marriage to Sylvia.

"It sounds like a wonderful life," she says.

"Yes," he says, surprised. "I guess it was. Maybe not wonderful, but a good life. Ordinary. Nothing very dramatic about it. But now that I look back, I realize how satisfying it was."

"Was? It's not over, Harry."

"I know that, but since Sylvia's death, things have changed. I can see how lucky I was. I don't know what's going to happen now."

"You'll still be lucky. *We'll* be lucky."

A moment later, they stop for a traffic light. Black Mercedes pulls up alongside. Sally glances, sees Briscoe and Shelby Yama staring at her. She looks away.

"What I'd like to do," she tells Dancer, "is to forget about dinner and just keep driving and driving."

"Where to?"

"The ends of the earth," she says.

He laughs. "Great idea. But I've got to get back to work."

"Yes," she is about to say, "so do I." But she says nothing.

They have a leisurely dinner at the Breakers. Window-shop along the Via Mizner. Stop at a tiny outdoor cafe. Have a champagne kir.

"You're awfully quiet tonight, Sal," he says. Taking her hand.

"Bored?"

"Lord, no. I'm never bored when I'm with you.
But it seems to me I've been doing all the talking.
You've hardly said a word."

"I've been thinking."

"Deep, deep thoughts?" he asks.

"*Very* deep," she says. Turning to him with a
smile. "Can we go back to my place?"

"Sure, but I'll have to leave early."

"Whatever you say. You're the boss."

"Am I?" he says. Looking at her strangely.
"Sometimes I wonder."

On the return trip, she turns briefly to glance
out the rear window. Black Mercedes two cars
back. She is suddenly fearful. Not of failing the
Department so much as losing Dancer if she
doesn't continue to play her assigned role. But
that would represent a personal betrayal.

In the parking lot, she puts a hand on his arm to
stay him. "You know what I'd like to do tonight?
Just for kicks? Keep all the lights off. Lower the
venetian blinds. We'll make love in complete
darkness. You'll love it."

"I said you were a wild one."

"Trust me," she says.

In the blacked-out motel suite they move cautiously. Trying not to stumble. Undress awk-
wardly. Find the bed. She gropes, finds him.
Presses his shoulders. Makes him sit on the edge.
Kneels in front of him.

"What are you doing?" he asks.

"Let me, Harry," she says. "Please."

He bends to peer. Touches. Discovers her hair is
down. Feels her cool fingers on him. Both are
silent in the darkness.

"Slowly," she whispers.

"I wish I could see you, Sal."

"Later. Just lie back."

He does as she orders. Stares up into the black. Clenches his fists as she begins.

"Something new," she says. "You like?"

"You *are* a witch," he says. Gasping.

She falters. Then continues. Bringing him along.

"Lover," she says, "am I good for you?"

He doesn't answer. Can't answer.

"Just let me love you," she murmurs. "My way. You promised."

He reaches down. Entwines his fingers in her hair. Clutches tightly.

"Pull," she says. "Hard."

He cannot understand what she wants. Feels her sharp teeth and wonders if she means to devour him. Mouth. Lips. Tongue. And prying fingers. She turns him upside down and inside out.

He lurches. Sobs. Pumps. Releases her hair to hold her face. Wetness. But whether it is her tears or his juices, he does not know. And, at the moment, does not care.

They lie in the darkness. Holding each other.

"Call the paramedics," he says. "Tell them to bring stimulants and oxygen. Oh, Sal . . . That was too much."

"No," she says. "Not enough. Let's do it again."

"In about five years. I should be recovered by then."

"I told you that you'd like it in the darkness."

"I did. You were disembodied. Weird sensation. Where did you learn these tricks?"

She doesn't reply. But snuggles closer. Hugging him.

"I want to do everything for you," she says. "Everything."

"You just did."

"No, not that. I mean I want to be the kind of woman you want me to be."

"You are, darling."

"And you love me? In your way?"

"I do."

"Say it."

"I love you, Sal. In my way."

"That's all right then," she says. Contented. "Don't ever stop."

At the debriefing, Briscoe is furious. "Why didn't you turn on the lights? The cameras got nothing."

Sally Abaddon has prepared for this. "Look, this is a very conservative man. A real square. He wanted the lights off. What am I supposed to do—argue with him?"

"Well, what did you do?"

"We went to bed, he got his jollies, and left. You saw him go, didn't you?"

"Did he ball you?" Shelby Yama asks. "Or did you ball him?"

"He made love to me. That's the way he likes it."

"Well, what did he say?" Briscoe demands.

"The two of you were whispering so much the mikes hardly picked up a word."

"Mostly he kept saying, 'I love you, I love you, I love you.' "

"That's great," Yama enthuses. "It's going according to the script. We better start thinking about closing the deal and signing him on."

"No," Briscoe says, "not yet. I want this guy so befuddled he doesn't know which way is up. Have you tried the drugs?"

"I tried," Sally lies. "He's not interested. I told you—a very conventional man. Especially sex-wise. Kinky stuff turns him off."

"Your job is to turn him on," Briscoe says. "This thing is taking too much time. He should be signed, sealed, and delivered by now."

"I don't want to spook him," Sally says. "You'll have to let me do it my way."

Briscoe is not convinced. Abaddon continues to worry him. He senses weakness there. If she becomes unmoored, the Dancer case could be a debacle for the Department.

He meets with the Director and Ted Charon, head of Internal Security. At Briscoe's request, case officer Shelby Yama is not asked to attend.

"I tell you Abaddon is becoming unglued," Briscoe argues.

"You mentioned these suspicions before," the Director says. "But you have no hard evidence?"

"No, sir. Just a lot of little things. Feelings. Impressions. I believe she's thinking of going over."

"That would be a disaster," the Director says. "After all our work. The funds expended. Any ideas, Ted?"

"We could test her," Charon says. "Bring in an agent provocateur. Briscoe, does Sally have any close women friends?"

"Not that I know of."

"Well, I've got a woman in my section who specializes in assignments like this. Her name's Angela Bliss. Isn't that a great name for a Department operative? Anyway, she works out of Chicago. I don't believe she's ever served with Abaddon, but we can ask Cleveland to check the records and make sure."

"You want to sic this Angela Bliss onto Sally?" the Director asks. "Get close to her and try to find out it she's thinking of turning?"

"Not exactly, sir. Angela plays a more active role than that. She deliberately tries to switch the agent. A devil's advocate, so to speak."

"Briscoe," the Director says, "what do you think?"

"Let's do it. I haven't been able to come up with anything better."

"All right. But hold off, Ted, until I get a go-ahead from the Chairman. He has to approve all transfers of personnel from one region to another."

"This Angela Bliss," Briscoe says to Charon, "is she good at her job?"

"The best," he says.

S hoofly agents of the Corporation (Martin Frey) and the Department (Angela Bliss) arrive in

Fort Lauderdale on the same day. Both are briefed, given their assignments. It is understood that Frey will report to Tommy Salvo, head of Counterintelligence in Washington. Bliss will report to Ted Charon in Southeast Region headquarters.

Frey rents a small apartment in the beachfront complex where Evelyn Heimdall lives. Tony Glitner drives him to the tennis club in Boca. Points out Evelyn, taking a lesson from the pro.

"There's your target," he tells Frey.

The agent stares. "All right, I've got her. Does she swim in the ocean or use that pool at the apartment house?"

"Usually the pool."

"Fine. I'll try to make contact there."

Glitner starts to say something, then stops. He doesn't like what they're doing to Evelyn. But recognizes the need.

An hour later, Martin Frey is lying on a padded redwood lounge on the lawn surrounding the apartment house pool. He is wearing shiny black briefs. Body of a swimmer. Wide shoulders, long muscles. Olive-skinned. Jetty hair combed straight back from smooth brow. He could have Indian blood—or south Italian. Fierceness there.

He is in and out of the water several times. Easily doing fifty laps in the short pool. Pulls himself out with an effortless heave of arms and shoulders. Shakes his long black hair like a dog. Combs it back with his fingers.

There is one middle-aged couple. An older man by himself. Two nymphets come by for a quick dunk. Splashing and giggling. Then run down to the beach. Frey watches tanned legs flashing in the sunlight.

He is about to give up for the day. But Evelyn Heimdall comes out of the back door. She is wearing a white lace coverup, gladiator sandals. Carrying a yellow beach bag. Frey lies back, clasps hands on his chest. Watches her through half-closed eyes.

She takes a lounge at the other end of the pool. Spreads a big towel on the pad. Takes off sandals, coverup. Wearing a yellow string bikini. She begins to oil herself. There is something about the way she does it. Caressing, Frey decides.

He stands, surface dives, begins to glide back and forth in an easy crawl. As he makes his turn at her end of the pool, he notes that she is watching him as she anoints her legs with oil.

He comes out of the water. Shakes himself. Dries off. He looks about uncertainly. Then he walks toward her, bouncing lightly. She is wearing sunglasses now, tinted lens turned to him.

"I beg your pardon," he says. Dazzling smile. White teeth gleaming against dark skin. "I'm new here. Could you tell me if there's anyplace I can get a cold drink?"

"I'm afraid not," Evelyn Heimdall says. "You must bring your own. But no bottles or glasses allowed in the pool area. That means cans and plastic cups."

"Oh," he says, "next time I'll know. Thank you."

"You swim beautifully," she says.

It's that easy.

Angela Bliss has no greater trouble, in almost identical circumstances. Briscoe rents a room for her in Sally Abaddon's motel. Helps her move in. Gives her the number of Sally's suite.

"You can't miss her," he says. "Tall blonde. Big all over. Long hair. You've seen her ID photo?"

"Yes."

"Then you'll have no problem. She usually works on her tan every afternoon. You can watch the pool area from your bedroom window."

"Good enough," Bliss says. "I'll take it from here."

She bolts the door after he leaves. Undresses, dons a conservative white maillot. She puts on reading glasses, goes over Sally Abaddon's dossier again. Woman sounds straight—but you never know.

Angela Bliss is thin, bony. A board, without discernible bosom or hips. Russet hair in a boy's cut. Eyes a milky blue. Knife nose and hard lips. Everything about her is sharp, cleaving. Her only vanity is her hands: long, supple, beautifully shaped. Nails are painted bloodred.

She goes into the bedroom several times to peer out the window. Finally she sees Sally Abaddon spreading a towel on a plastic web chair. It is placed in the sun, near a metal table with a wide beach umbrella. Abaddon is wearing a flesh-colored diaper suit. Nothing between her legs but a narrow strip. She looks naked.

Bliss inspects the pool area. There are two other umbrella tables, both occupied. She puts on a voile coverup, sandals, wide-brimmed hat. Hangs a canvas beach bag from her shoulder.

Steps outside her living room door. Walks around to the pool. Abaddon is smoothing lotion onto her shoulders and arms. Bliss glances about, then walks hesitatingly up to the target.

"I beg your pardon," she says. Timid smile. "I wonder if I might share your table."

"Help yourself," Sally says. Laughs. "I can only sit in one chair at a time."

"Thank you," Angela Bliss says. "What a beautiful, beautiful tan you have."

"I spend a lot of time on it."

"I'm so pale. But I'm determined to get some color. Just to prove to the folks back home that I've been in Florida. Will you tell me what suntan lotion to use?"

"Be glad to."

"My name is Angela," Bliss says. "What's yours?"

The Chairman, seated in his thronelike chair in the Department's Cleveland War Room, reads through the latest intelligence on current actions. It is the daily computer printout. A final summary gives the previous day's score: fourteen successes, twelve failures. Too close for comfort, the Chairman decides.

He turns back to the Harry Dancer campaign. Its complexity fascinates him. He is happy to see the Internal Security agent has made contact with Sally Abaddon. That should effectively thwart the possibility of betrayal by that lady.

But he's bemused by the report of the Department's agent assigned to observe the activities of Evelyn Heimdall. Apparently she has made a new friend. Young man. Handsome. The agent has observed them together on several occasions. Talking. Laughing. Swimming. Walking the beach. The man's name is Martin Frey.

In the Chairman's world, things rarely happen by chance. He summons the floor supervisor, requests an Intelligence rummage on Martin Frey. He waits patiently. About twenty minutes later, a printout is brought. He scans it swiftly. Frey is a Corporation agent attached to Counterintelligence.

The Chairman pulls at his rubbery lower lip. Deliberating. It is possible, of course, that Heimdall knows who Frey is, and the Counterintelligence agent has been assigned to her as backup or bodyguard. But the Chairman doesn't think so.

He believes the Corporation is worried about Heimdall's loyalty. Martin Frey has been assigned to test her. The same reason Angela Bliss was sicced onto Sally Abaddon. The Department and the Corporation are making similar operational moves. Their secret war demands it.

The Corporation's Chief of Operations has come to the same conclusion. Anthony Glitner reports that Willoughby, assigned to cover Sally Abaddon, says that the Department's agent has a new friend. A woman living in her motel. Name: Angela Bliss. Physical description is given.

The Chief runs the name through the computer. Within minutes he has the answer: Angela Bliss is an agent provocateur. Working in the Department's Internal Security Section. Home base: Chicago. So the Department is as concerned about its field agent as the Corporation is about theirs.

Chairman and Chief ponder their next moves. In this struggle, inaction is tantamount to defeat. Both men believe their basic strategies are sound, but tactics must be revised to take into account the presence and activities of the new players.

Each begins to plot how he might best take advantage of the other's weakness. And, as not infrequently happens in the world of espionage and counterespionage, unwittingly the primary purpose of the campaign takes second place to the stimulation and intellectual challenge of opposing game plans.

Harry Dancer is going through a curious metamorphosis. His intimacy with Evelyn Heimdall and Sally Abaddon, instead of dimming recollections of his deceased wife, has sharpened memories. They have moved into the present tense.

Sylvia and he bed together several times before she proposes. He accepts. They spend an inebriated evening planning the wedding (small) and the honeymoon (grand). Suddenly Harry stops grinning, sobers, stares at her.

"Syl," he says, "I'm scared."

"Why so?"

"Marriage is new. You know? Something different. Something I've never done before."

"I haven't either, but I'm not scared. You want to back out so soon?"

"Oh no. No. Syl, do you think it will change things?"

"What things?"

"Between us."

She considers that. "Probably," she decides. "So far it's all been fun and games—right? Now a preacher says a few words, and we sign a contract. Sure, things will change between us. Got to. But I think we can hack it. Don't you?"

"I'm going to give it the old college try. I swear to God I am."

"Me, too. You're right, Harry; it's not going to be easy. We've both lived alone a long, long time. Adjustments . . ."

He nods. "A lot of little things. Toothpaste tubes squeezed in the middle or the end. Toilet paper coming off the roll over or under. Dishes in the sink. Stupid things. Not important. Not worth fighting about. We'll be able to laugh them all away. What bothers me is our love for each other. Will that fade when we're married? We've never been together for more than, oh, maybe twenty-four hours. What happens when we live in the same house? Together—until death do us part?"

"Don't look for trouble," she advises. "We're not a couple of teenagers. We've both been around. It'll be give and take, won't it? The way I see it, Harry, we'll both be making a sacrifice. Giving up a piece of ourselves. But in return we get a third entity. There will be you, me, and our marriage. With work and a little bit o' luck, the marriage will become more important to us than our own selves."

"That's a happy thought," he says. Taking her into his arms. "You're going to be good for me, Syl; I just know it."

"I'm going to love you to death," she says. "You'll see."

The wedding ceremony is decorous and moving. Dancer is shocked at Sylvia's beauty. It is not only the shimmering white gown, the veil. It is her luminescence. She is a stranger to him. Ethereal. He kisses a wraith, fearing she may dissolve.

The reception at the club is a rowdy lark. All that booze. Suggestive jokes. Nudges and smirks. They move through it all. Smiling, smiling. Then, hand in hand, duck out the back door. Drive to the Lauderdale airport. In time to catch their flight to LaGuardia.

"Congratulations!" the stewardess says.

"Who told you?" Sylvia demands.

"No one. You just have that look."

When she moves away, Sylvia asks him: "What look is that?"

"Stupefied," he says.

They have a suite high up in the New York Hilton. Harry has arranged for flowers and champagne. He doesn't neglect to carry her over the threshold.

"Instant hernia," he says.

They stand at the window, clasping each other's waist. Look down at the glittering city.

"Want it?" Harry says. "It's yours."

"Nah," she says. "Too small. I want you."

"I'd like you to know that I realize this is your wedding night, and I promise to be ever so tender and gentle and understanding."

"Go fuck yourself," she says.

They go out for dinner at a steak joint on the East Side. Take a carriage ride through Central Park. Stop at the Oak Bar at the Plaza for a brandy stinger. Then cab back to the hotel.

"I'm wiped out," Sylvia says. "It's been a long day."

"Oh-ho. First night, and you've got a head-ache."

She laughs. "I could have convulsions, and I wouldn't miss this. How often does a girl get shtupped on her wedding night?"

Still dressed, they come close. He tries to tell her how he felt when he saw her floating down the aisle to him.

"I knew then," he says, "*knew* it, that we were doing absolutely the right thing. We can't miss, babe."

"I love you, Harry."

"I love you, Sylvia."

They shower together. First time they had ever done that.

"Hey," she says, "how long has this been going on? It's great."

"I invented it," he tells her. "Syl, if I can't get it up tonight, I'm going right out the window."

"Don't give it a second thought," she says. Then adds: "Just concentrate on the first."

She is right: it had been a long day. With a heavy emotional charge. They lie naked in each other's arms. Talking, talking. The wedding. Reception. How guests looked. What they said. And did you see . . . ? And did you hear . . . ?

Suddenly—blackout. They are both asleep. Clinging. Dancer wakes first. Groggy. It takes a half-minute before he remembers who he is, where he is, who this woman is, what he has done. He glances at their travel clock. Almost four-thirty in the morning. He slides carefully out of bed. When he returns from the bathroom, she is awake.

"Wasn't that great?" he asks her. "Wasn't that the most marvelous lovemaking you've ever had?"

"Beast," she says. Reaching for him with bare arms.

It is an idyll. Lighthearted and without care. They come together in joy. Nuzzling.

"Gosh, Mommy," she says, "now I've got someone to play with. This is keen."

Her body is tanned. Hard. Muscle under satin. He touches her with wonder. Realizing she is suddenly new to him.

"Sweetheart . . ." he says.

"What?"

"Nothing. Just sweetheart. Do you like that?"

"No, I do not. And I'll give you exactly three hours to stop."

"Nut," he says. Laughing. "I've married a nut."

"Mr. and Mrs. Nut," she says. "Doesn't it sound nice?"

"Back rub?" he asks.

"Yes. Please."

She rolls prone. He straddles her. Begins softly massaging her neck and shoulders.

"Magic fingers," she murmurs.

He kneads her back. Gently rubs the stones of her spine.

"Got to fatten you up," he says.

"Whatever."

He bends to drift lips and tongue. Kisses ribs.

Hunches to nibble her rounded tush.

"Ooh . . ." she says. "You never did that before."

"I've never been married before. Want to sleep?"

"You've got to be kidding."

She rolls over. They embrace with smiling delight. Their love is airy. No strain, no pain. Then, flesh fevered, the easy joining. Slick slide.

"I do," she says. Repeating her marriage vow. "I do, I do, I do. Oh lordy, do I ever do."

It is a memorable week in Manhattan. Filled with odd charms. Unexpected incidents. Good food. A crazy session at a roller skating rink. One good Broadway play. They eat raw fish for the first time. See an Ingres at the Metropolitan that makes Sylvia weep with pleasure. Take a yacht trip around the island. Buy pretzels from a man on stilts.

Then they are back in Florida. Settling into their beachfront home. Dancer goes back to work. Sylvia gets busy redecorating the house. Moving her things in. And trying not to call him every hour to say, "I love you."

Routine and habit grow. There are minor clashes—as they expected. Little, stupid things, they agree. All smoothed over. But their marriage grows. Blooms. Until they rather spend an evening alone together than to endure the company of friendly strangers.

"We've got to stop this," Sylvia says. "The honeymoon is over."

But it is not.

What saves them from cloying happiness, despicable to acquaintances, is the clash of their personalities. She so light, breezy. A sprite, really. He so heavy, introspective. And sometimes, when the mood is on him, silent and lachrymose. This disparity is the cause of psychic pushings, pullings, a covert and occasionally overt warfare that leaves them shaken and depressed.

Until, three years wed, they realize that this tension is pepper to their lives, and their marriage would not survive without it. Then they accept each other as is. Their relationship deepens to become one of respect and understanding as much as love.

Martin Frey, trained Romeo, learns early on that small flattery is no flattery at all.

"You're the most beautiful woman I've ever met," he tells Evelyn Heimdall.

She smiles. Lazy as a cat. Rolling softly on her lounge at poolside. Toasting the flesh. Opening the body to that penetrating sun.

"You're a sweet boy," she says. "A sweet, *young* boy."

"Does that make a difference?"

She lowers her sunglasses to stare at him. "No, it doesn't."

"You only live once."

"So I'm learning," she says.

"I'd like to take you to dinner tonight," Frey says. "May I?"

"Sorry. I have a date."

"A cocktail? Before your date?"

She thinks about it. "All right. One drink. Then I'll have to run. Will you settle for that?"

"I'll settle for anything. Would you like to stop by my place? Say around five o'clock?"

"Make it six. I'll stay for an hour. No more. Now are you going to give me a swimming lesson?"

"Of course."

"What are you going to teach me today?"

"The breast stroke," he says. Grinning.

"You're awful," she says. Takes his hand so he can help her rise. They move to the pool together.

"Let's try the flutter kick again," he says.

They go into the shallow end. She grasps the gutter. Floats facedown.

"All right," he says, "start kicking. From the hips. Slowly at first."

She tries.

"No, no," he says. "You're kicking from the knee. Here, keep your legs straight."

He puts his hands on her. Makes her lock her knees. His fingers are silk under water.

"Point your toes," he commands. "Keep your legs stiff. Try it again."

Her long legs scissor. From the hips. Knees locked. Toes pointed. She beats the water to froth.

"Good," he says. "You're doing great. Now turn around. Float facedown. Push off and flutter kick across the pool. Take a deep breath and keep your face in the water. Arms extended. Don't try to stroke. Just kick to the other side."

She pushes off. Almost makes it. But then has to raise her face from the water to take a breath. It breaks the rhythm of her kick.

"Okay," he calls, "you did fine. Now come

back the same way. Just take it slow and easy. Put all your strength into your thighs."

She extends her arms. Takes a deep breath. Puts her face in the water. Pushes off. She kicks to him. He moves so that her grasping hands touch his tight briefs. She raises her head. Gasping for breath.

"Well done," he says. "Do it a few more times. Tomorrow we'll try the length of the pool and see how far you can go."

She kicks across the width of the pool several more times. When she comes back to where he stands in shallow water, her hands reach to touch him. Lingeringly. A ballet.

"You're doing great," he tells her.

"Am I?"

"Just keep those beautiful legs locked, and move from the hips."

"I'll remember," she says.

When she shows up at his apartment at six o'clock, she is wearing a loose chemise of lavender linen. Cut high in front. Plunging almost to her waist in back. Tanned skin gleams.

"You look smashing," Frey says. "Lucky man you're meeting tonight. What would you like to drink? I have vodka, rum, scotch, white wine. That's about it."

"A white wine would be nice. You know, Martin, I'm beginning to feel all that kicking in my legs. My thighs and calves ache."

"You'll work it out tomorrow. After awhile your muscles will get toned, and you won't feel a thing."

He is barefoot, wearing tight white short-shorts and a khaki tank top. She sees tufts of soft black hair protruding from his armpits. She looks away. Oddly excited.

"Good wine," she says. "Thank you. How is the job-hunting coming?"

"Another interview tomorrow," he says. "I'm not discouraged. The jobs are there, but the salaries aren't so great."

"I know very little about computers," she confesses.

"It's not as difficult as you think. If I can do it, anyone can do it."

They sit side by side on his couch: a rattan monstrosity covered with an orange batik print. Frey puts his palm lightly on her bare back.

"Hot," he says. "You're not getting too much sun, are you?"

"I don't think so. I use a sun-screen lotion."

"Good. Or you'll be peeling like an onion. Ev, if your date is over early, or even if it isn't, and you'd like to stop back here for a nightcap, I'd love to see you."

His fingertips glide over her back. Feathers. She shivers.

"I don't think I could do that," she says.

"Why not?"

"A small matter of morality."

"Morality?" he says. Fierce grin. "What's that? If you're not hurting anyone, where's the harm?"

She doesn't know the answer.

"Well," he says, "you think about it. I don't get to bed until two in the morning, so you won't be disturbing me."

"I'll think about it," she says. Feeling his hard fingers caressing.

"You're obviously not wearing a bra, are you?"

"Obviously I'm not."

"I'll give you my phone number," he says.

Evelyn Heimdall and Harry Dancer go to a new French restaurant on Las Olas. They have escargot, veal, and a Grand Marnier soufflé. A corky chablis. Dancer is in one of his moods. It's a subdued dinner.

"I'm sorry," he says. Putting his hand on hers. "I'm grumpy tonight, and I know it. Please forgive me."

"What *is* it, Harry?"

"Oh, I go through these things periodically. Not depression, exactly, but a kind of sulking. I'm ashamed of myself, but I can't help it."

"I don't believe you ever sulk."

"Solemn rumination then. Will you settle for that? It only lasts a day or two, but while it's on me I know I'm lousy company."

"I have a confession to make, too," she says. "It's that time of month for me. Sorry about that, chief. But maybe we're lucky our inactive moods coincide. In a few days we'll be swinging from the chandelier again."

That elicits his first laugh of the evening.

"You better believe it," he says. "I'll get you home early, and we'll both dream of better things to come."

On the drive back to her apartment house, she

says: "By the way, I have a new boyfriend."

"Good for you," Dancer says.

"Jealous?"

"Madly."

"I find that hard to believe. He moved into my apartment house. Very nice, but a little too young for me. But he's teaching me how to swim."

"You mean you can't swim? Good lord, you should have told me. I'd have taught you."

"Too late," she says. "I've got a teacher."

"What's his name?"

"Martin Frey. He's from somewhere in New Jersey. Trying to get a job down here working with computers."

"Is he handsome?"

"Very."

"Now I *am* jealous."

She laughs. Pokes his arm. "Harry, you don't have a thing to worry about."

It is a little after ten o'clock when she is home, alone, in her own apartment. Turns out all the lights. Undresses slowly. Goes out onto the balcony, naked. Lies on a lounge. The cool breeze has lips. She closes her eyes against the moonglow.

How comforting to submit to a discipline. Army, state, religion—whatever. Accepts myths, dreams, illusions. Give yourself over. Oh, to be rid of choice! Those damned decisions. Sign on, and you're free. Is tyranny a kind of liberty?

She stirs. Opens her eyes wide to stare at the star-flecked sky. That means freedom is painful. Hurt and suffering. Take responsibility for your own destiny, and you're in trouble, Charlie. The question is . . . The question is . . .

"What is the question?" she asks. Aloud.

That pilot light within her flickers hotter. She swears to herself, solemnly, it is not only physical desire. It is a want to breathe free. Take the world to bed and note what happens. She sees doors opening. Windows flung up. Intoxication. Wild fantasies come clamoring. She is aswoon.

Rises shakily. Pads into the living room. Phones Dancer.

"Harry? You got home all right?"

"I did indeed. Sorry I was such a grump at dinner."

"You're entitled. We all have moods. I was sorry I wasn't, ah, physically capable of making you forget your troubles."

He laughs. "Tomorrow's another day, Ev."

"So it is. I love you, Harry. Sleep well."

"You too, dear. Thank you for calling."

She goes back to her balcony lounge. Happy she phoned. But still dissatisfied. Harry seems part of a past life. Discipline, myths, dreams, illusions. He is behind closed doors. Windows down. No seductive breeze there, tanged with salt, to stir and excite.

She touches herself. Confused by myriad "What ifs?" She is a tot, wandering into a garden. All those blooms, smells, sensations. She has never had to choose between alternatives. Doesn't know how. Sign on, and your preferences are dictated. How can she wear red when white is prescribed?

Lies back. Throws her arms wide. Lifts her knees. Spreads her thighs.

"Fuck me, moon," she says aloud. Giggling.

Madness! She doesn't know its source. But knows it is evil. And exciting. And cannot with-

stand its allure. To be all things! Know all things!
No standards, morals, laws. Not a one. No desire
for reward. No fear of punishment. Then how
grand a life might be!

She is not ready for that. Yet. But glimpses the
enticement. It is, she tells herself, akin to prison
doors unlocked, swinging wide. The prisoner
looks in disbelief. Amazement. Takes one hesitant
step. Another. Another. And then, released, trots,
runs, sprints. Laughing. Weeping.

Evelyn Heimdall is burning with that vision.
Returns again to the living room. Switches on a
table lamp to search through her purse. Finally
finds his number.

"Martin?" she says. "Good evening. This is
Evelyn."

"Hi," Frey says. "How was the date?"

"It was okay. I'm home. Does that invitation
for a nightcap still stand?"

"Of course. Come on down."

"No," she says. "You come up here."

Sally Abaddon has forgotten what it is like to
have a close woman friend. All her assignments
are men. All her associates are male. Now here is
Angela Bliss. Friendly. Generous. Eager to please.
Sally enjoys having a confidante.

The two women spend hours together. Usually
in the mornings and afternoons. And those evenings Sally doesn't see Harry Dancer. They laze at
poolside or on the beach. Shop at malls. Search

out amusing restaurants. Take a boat trip along the Intracoastal Waterway.

Physically unalike, they have some things in common. The experience of hard work and long careers. Independence. Both with lives centered around men. In Angela's case, it's an invalid husband confined to a nursing home. She says.

"I feel guilty about leaving him," she confesses. "But I had to get away, if only for a few weeks. At home, I speak to him every day and visit him three or four times a week. It's a drain."

"I should think so," Sally says. "There's no hope he'll get better?"

"No. None. It's a degenerative nerve disorder. The doctors say he could live for years, getting progressively worse."

"How awful."

"Sometimes I feel like just taking off. You know? And never coming back. But I can't do that."

"Why not?"

"Well, I really do love him, and he's completely dependent on me. Also, I'm a very religious woman, and I know that deserting him just wouldn't be right. I don't know what I'd do without my faith and my church. They give me strength to go on."

Sally Abaddon makes no reply.

They are having breakfast at a Howard Johnson on Briny Avenue. Outside, a rainsquall drives spatters against the windows. But behind it is blue sky, promise of a steamy day.

"It'll blow over," Sally says. "We'll have some tanning time. You're getting good color."

"I'll never be as dark as you," Angela says.

"But you're not really dark; more of an apricot shade."

"Apricot?" Sally says. Laughing. "Thanks a lot!"

"You know what I mean. You're really a very beautiful woman. I wish I had your figure."

"You do all right," Sally assures her. "But I think you could do a lot more with yourself than you do. A padded bra would help, for starters. Or maybe cosmetic surgery. They can do wonders these days."

"Oh no," Angela says. "I could never do that. My church teaches that vanity is a sin. I'll just have to live with what I am."

Sky clearing. Sun beginning to glow redder. They walk slowly back to their motel.

"We could go out to the Pompano Fashion Square," Sally suggests. "Jordan Marsh is having a sale on swimsuits."

"Maybe later," Angela says. "I'd like to get some sun before it gets too hot. Then I have to write some letters."

"To your husband?"

"My husband, my priest, other people."

"Your church really means a lot to you, doesn't it, Angela?"

"A lot? It means everything. I don't know what I'd do without it. It keeps me going. You're not religious, are you?"

"No, not really. I just wasn't brought up that way."

"Well, I never try to convert anyone. What you believe or don't believe is your business. But I wish you'd come to church with me on Sunday morning. It's so beautiful. So comforting."

"I'll think about it," Sally Abaddon says.

She lies prone on a beach towel spread on the lawn. Unfastens the bra strap of her bikini. Angela sits beside her. Rubs suntan lotion onto her shoulders. Her back. Soft, caressing strokes.

"That feels so good," Sally murmurs.

"Let me do the backs of your legs," Angela says.

That night, at Harry Dancer's home, Sally tells him about her new friend.

"It must be nice to believe in something as strongly as she does," she says. "With a bedridden husband who's dying, she'd have every reason *not* to believe."

"Does she work?" he asks.

"Yes. In the loan department of a Chicago bank."

"Well, I hope her husband has good medical insurance. Or maybe he's on disability. Those long illnesses can wipe you out."

"She didn't mention how they were paying for it, and of course I didn't ask. Do you go to church, Harry?"

"Haven't since Sylvia's funeral. We used to go occasionally. Easter and Christmas. Some other times. But not regularly."

He has made a big salad of shrimp and lobster chunks. With crusty garlic toast. And a jug of chilled Rhine wine. Informal meal. Informal dress. They are both wearing jeans. Sally with one of Harry's old shirts. Tails knotted. Showing tanned midriff.

"Ooh, that was good," she says. Sitting back. "You can cook for me any day."

"What cooking? It was all cold. Except for the

garlic toast, and I just heated that up in the oven. What would you like to do—take a walk on the beach?''

''Not really. Let's take the rest of the wine upstairs with us.''

''Splendid idea,'' he says.

She performs. Knowing their pillow talk and sounds of their lovemaking are being overheard and recorded. She says things and elicits responses from Dancer she thinks will please Shelby Yama and Briscoe.

Later, Dancer goes into the bathroom to shower. Sally lies alone in the big bed, on sweated sheets. Puts a forearm across her eyes.

What she feels, she decides, is a peculiar kind of loneliness. Not for someone, but for some *thing*. A new surety. Her future, that had once seemed bright with the promise of endless joys, now appears drab and lifeless.

Harry Dancer's recollections of his life with Sylvia have given her a glimpse of a foreign land of love and solid civility. She would like to live in that world of sweet reasonableness. Day after day exactly like that passed and that to come. Continuity and meaning. With a steady faith like that of Angela's.

She cannot hope for marriage to Harry Dancer. She has played her part too well; he thinks of her as an exotic, a wild boff. But not as a mate to love and cherish as he did Sylvia. And if she suggested such a thing, the Department would discipline her. In ways she'd rather not imagine.

She hears him come out of the bathroom. Takes her arm away from wet eyes. Watches him move about the room, dressing. A sweet, sturdy man, worthy of love. The best, probably, of all her victims. Somehow, in ways unknown to him, and to her, he has taught her guilt.

She showers. Dresses. He drives her back to the motel. Kisses her goodnight. She goes into her garish suite. Looks around, grimacing. She showers again. For reasons she cannot comprehend. Tries a book. Radio. TV. Nothing works for her. Emptiness roars.

She pulls on shorts, a T-shirt. Goes outside. Sees a light burning in the room occupied by Angela Bliss. Knocks. Is admitted.

"That church of yours," Sally Abaddon says. "On Sunday." Tries a laugh. "What time does the show go on?"

Spymasters sit in the center of webs, awaiting tremors. The Corporation's Chief of Operations believes he has planned well. All his players are in place. He has done what he can to forestall betrayal. Now he must wait. Putting his faith in the talent and resolve of employees hundreds of miles away.

But he faces an implacable enemy. The treachery of the night code-clerk has been uncovered; the poor fellow has been shipped off to a rehabilitation center. But who knows how many other moles have been implanted in the Corporation's bureaucracy. And what damage they have done. Are doing.

The Chief idly touches the keyboard of his desktop computer. He is surrounded by state-of-the-art technology. There is no hardware he lacks to make him more effective at his job. His superiors allow him wide latitude in setting strategy and tactics. He can have no excuse for failure.

But, he knows, his machines, files, percentage tables and probability ratios—all are meaningless compared to the belief and will of the agents involved. They, being human, are the big gamble. And being human, can be weak, vacillating, even disloyal. They are not interchangeable machine parts, but vulnerable, sentient beings with incalculable defects and strengths.

He jots notes on his featured actors:

Anthony Glitner: Case officer. Earnest. Hard-working. Determined. But does this man have the verve and imagination to honcho a complex assignment? Does he, perhaps, lack the moral steel needed? In fact, is he strong enough to bulldoze his way, if necessary, to victory?

Evelyn Heimdall: Field agent. Warm, attractive woman. Excellent record with no evidence of backsliding. But now exhibiting troubling signs of weakening resolve and a penchant for self-indulgence. Her moral frailty could endanger the entire Dancer campaign.

Martin Frey: Counterintelligence agent. Professional gigolo. But does he comprehend that his assignment is merely to *test* Evelyn Heimdall, not actively lure her into betraying her vows? Has he the perception to understand this fine distinction?

Reading over his notes, the Chief acknowledges that defects on the part of any of his three main protagonists could mean defeat. He reaches for a roll of antacid tablets. Rises, begins to pace about his office. Hand pressed against his diaphragm.

He realizes, suddenly, that in his brief analyses of personae on the Dancer team, he has neglected the personality and character of the most important player: Harry Dancer himself. Operational problems of the action have made him slight the goal.

But it is Dancer who, unwittingly, will reveal the strengths and weaknesses of the Corporation agents sent to win him. They cannot fail but react to him, his likes and dislikes, prejudices, joys. His moods.

In a queer sort of way, in campaigns of this sort, the target becomes the spymaster. Unknown to himself, he runs the team assigned to him. Determines their moves. Makes them revise their tactics. Drives them to despair or offers enough hints so they may happily plot how, eventually, he is to be taken.

But what kind of man *is* Harry Dancer? Looking at the thick file of reports on his desk (submitted by Tony Glitner), the Chief of Operations concedes that he has no clear conception of the target. He is this, he is that. Voluble and taciturn. Happy and disconsolate. Sensuous and puritan.

In other words, the Chief admits, a human being. Incomprehensible. An enigma.

H arry Dancer on a night beach. Dreaming . . .

"Hey there, grumps," Sylvia calls. Prancing in. Carrying rackets and tennis bag. "I won, I won, I won! I'm in the semis on Saturday.''

"Good for you," Harry says. Smiling. "You'll go to the finals and take the brass ring."

"Nah," Syl says. "That Laurie Christopher will cream me. She's got a serve you can't even see. I'm lucky to make the semis."

"Don't talk like that. I want you to turn pro and hit the circuit so I can retire."

"That'll be the day," his wife says. Flopping into an armchair. "Mix me something tall and cool, will you, hon? I'm bushed."

He brings her a big vodka and cranberry juice with a lot of ice. She kisses the back of his hand gratefully.

"Seven sets," she says. "I'm wiped out. I'm going to soak in a hot tub for a least an hour. We're not going out tonight, are we?"

"Hadn't planned on it. There's a barbecued chicken, salad makings, and half a honeydew."

"Sounds divine. But you may have to feed me. I haven't the strength to lift a fork."

"That I've got to see."

She examines him. "You look a little ragged around the edges, professor. Tough day?"

"They're all tough. I don't know how the idea got around that it's fun to play with OPM—Other People's Money. I don't get any fun out of it. Just aggravation and worries."

"Try to forget it for tonight. After I revive, I'm going to bang your socks off."

"Promises, promises," he says.

"Have I ever disappointed?"

"No," he admits, "never."

She sits sprawled. Bare, brown legs thrust out. Those crazy little fluff balls hanging outside the heels of her tennis shoes. White shorts hiked up. T-shirt showing wide shoulders, strong arms. Short hair spiking up. Face aglow. Healthy, vibrant woman. Juicy. She makes him feel old. Drained.

"Like what you see?" she asks him.

"Love it."

"You'll see more later."

"Go take your bath before I rape you right here on the rug. I'll make the salad. Eat in an hour—okay?"

"You're the boss," she says.

"Since when?"

He sets the table, carves the chicken, mixes the salad. He also makes another gin martini for himself and a vodka gimlet for Sylvia. He carries the drinks upstairs. She is still lolling in a frothy tub. Bathroom is steamy. Scented.

He sits on the closed toilet seat. Hands her the gimlet.

"Plasma," he says.

"Thanks, dear. Harry, Blanche and Jeremy Blaine want us for dinner on Friday night. It's their turn. I told her I'd check with you first."

"Whatever you want."

It is the fourth year of their marriage. He knows she is trying to enlarge their lives. Entertain more. Go down to Miami and up to Palm Beach to catch touring Broadway plays. Take cruises. Visit art galleries. Plan a European vacation. Left to himself, his world would be scrunched down to office and home.

"What would you like to do, hon?"

"Sure," he says, "let's go. He'll do his W. C.

Fields imitation, and she'll complain about how hard it is to get good help. But I can endure it for five hours or so."

She sits up in the tub. Soapy water streams from her elegant breasts. She bends a forefinger, flicks suds at him. He ducks.

"My old grumps," she says. "You're in a real mood tonight. Grouty?"

"Not really. Just subdued. I'll recover."

"You always have. Otherwise I'd have traded you in for a new model a long time ago."

She opens the tub drain. Hands him her glass. Stands. He looks at her shimmering body. Slender. Taut. She pulls the curtain. Begins to shower away soap and bath oil film. He goes into the bedroom. Slouches in a little cretonne-covered armchair.

He is coming out of it. Feels it. Spirits lifting. It's not the martinis; it's her. She has that effect. Blessed gift.

Nothing momentous has happened since she entered the house. Their talk has been banal, their gentle chivying a routine. It is nothing she has said or done. It is *her*. Her presence. Warm closeness. He belongs to her, she belongs to him. Two against the world. She had it right; the third entity, their marriage, has conquered.

He cannot conceive what this evening would have been like if she had not come home. If she did not exist. Solace from a bottle, he supposes. Or just hopelessness. Yearning and not finding. In a way it frightens him. His dependence. He is still fearful of investing everything in her. Benefits are enormous. But the risk . . .

She comes out of the bathroom in her big, white terry robe. Toweling her hair. Takes her drink from him and drains it.

"You smell nice," he says.

"Sure I do," she agrees. "I put a drop of this and that here and there. Hey, when do we eat?"

"Right now," he says. Rising. "Everything's ready. Hungry?"

"Famished," she says. Suddenly swoops. Hugs him. Kisses. "For you. Feeling better?"

"How did you know?"

"I can tell."

She eats ravenously. Twirling chicken legs in her sharp teeth. Gobbling salad. When she slows down, he gets her talking about the tennis match. She relives it, set by set. He isn't all that interested, but he wants to hear her voice. See the animation in her face.

She is *alive*. And by some curious process of emotional osmosis yields to him some of her own vitality. She invigorates him. He can only pray it is not a one-way flow. That she is getting something from him—whatever it may be.

They finish the melon. (Mealy.) Take iced coffees laced with Kahlua out onto the patio. Lie on lounges. Stare up. A nothing sky. No moon, no stars. But they don't care.

"I love you, Syl," he says. Suddenly.

She turns her head to look at him. "Sweet. And I love you, Harry. But what brought that on?"

"It just occurred to me that I don't say it often enough."

"You show it."

"Do I? I hope so. But I've got to learn to verbalize my feelings more. I can't go through life ex-

pecting you or anyone else to know how I feel.
Actions speak louder than words? Bull*shit* they
do! Actions are just as open to misinterpretation
as words. You've got to combine the two. There's
a synergism working there. The whole is more
than the sum of its parts.''

"Thank you, professor," she says. "I'm just
sorry I'm not taking notes."

He cracks up. "I deserved that. I can always depend on you to bring me back to earth."

They lie then in silence. Sipping their drinks.

"Want to adopt?" she asks.

"What?"

"Adopt. It doesn't look like you and I are going
to be able to make a little bi-bee. Should we
adopt? What do you think?"

"I don't know," he says. "It bothers me. Self-
ish reasons. Competition. I want all your love.
That's lousy, I know, but it's the way I feel. You
want to adopt? If you insist, I'll go along."

"I don't know what I want, Harry. Sometimes I
think, Oh Jesus, yes, I want a smelly little brat
running around the house. Patter of tiny feet—
and all that. Other times it scares me. The responsibility. So if I'm not sure, that means I'm not
ready for it yet—right?"

"I guess so. When you make up your mind,
may I be the first to know?"

"Absolutely. And then, also, I feel the way you
do. You and I have got such a great thing going
here, why take the chance of ruining it? Or changing it. And a kid would be a hell of a change.
Maybe for the better, maybe for the worse. But
I'm scared of the risk."

"Well, we don't have to decide this minute, Syl.

We're not *that* old. Let's think about it, talk it over again.''

"You and I can talk about *anything*, can't we, Harry?"

"I hope so. Wouldn't be much of a marriage if we couldn't."

"Hon, I'm so sleepy I'm practically unconscious."

"We can't talk about that," he says. Laughing.

He gets her to her feet. Supporting with a strong arm about her waist. They stumble up the stairs. Singing their favorite song softly together: "I'll Be Seeing You." He seats her on the edge of the bed. Props her up with one hand while he turns down coverlet, blanket, top sheet.

Her eyes are closed. But she murmurs—a child's burbling—when he wrestles her robe off. He gets her into bed, straightens out her legs. Pulls sheet and blanket up to her chin. Tucks her in. She sighs. Turns onto her side.

He turns on the air conditioner. Switches off the light. Closes the door gently. Goes back downstairs and cleans up the kitchen. Trying not to make too much clatter. Then he does the rounds, checking locks on doors and windows.

It is silent in the house. Dim. Empty without her bouncy presence. He pours himself a small cognac. Carries it up to the bedroom, entering cautiously. He finds his way to the little armchair. Sits there, sipping the brandy slowly. Listening to his wife breathing. He feels complete again.

If there is one law in his business, financial investing, it is: Diversify! Never put all your eggs in one basket. He wonders now, hearing Sylvia sleep, if the same holds true for emotional investing. Is it wise to put all your love in one security? If that fails, where are you?

But of course money grows, assets increase, allowing for more diversification. But does love grow? Or are we all granted a finite amount to invest as we wish: splurge, gamble or husband. Knowing that when it is gone, it is completely depleted. Nothing left.

He is not so sure of that. It may be that love requited is love replenished. The principal, wisely committed, earns dividends, compounded. Why, in a lifetime one's capacity to love might double. It is possible.

Another of life's insoluble problems, he mournfully admits. Diversify or concentrate your emotional capital? Choose well; you'll never get a second chance. But meanwhile his investment of love in that sleeping beauty is returning benefits beyond reckoning. It is silly to worry that she is his total portfolio.

Sylvia rouses. Calls drowsily. "Harry?"

"I'm here, love," he says.

In a moment she is asleep again. Secure and content.

The Chairman is restive. Shifting enormous bulk on his throne in the Department's War Room. That damned Dancer thing is beginning to obsess him. What started out as a simple seduction has evolved into a twist of wills and cunning with the Chief of Operations in the Corporation's Washington headquarters.

The Chairman is impatient. He wants results. From someone. Anyone. Reports trickle in. He tries to make sense of what's going on. But there's little logic to it. No string he can follow to its inevitable end. Unless that frail thread is all stupidity and betrayal.

It is not his strategy that is at fault. He is certain of that. It is the incompetence of his employees on the scene that frustrates him. They have denied him a quick, smashing conquest.

Director of the Southeast Region: Magisterial man. With swollen amour propre. Good on routine, but lacking the imagination to run a complex operation. Strictly middle management. If rumors are true, the dolt's a slave to his baser instincts.

Shelby Yama: Case officer. Hollywood type, but without the necessary grittiness. Lightweight bossing his first important assignment. He sees it as theatre. Drama. Would he be more successful at farce?

Sally Abaddon: Field agent. Fantastic record of wins—but is she burning out? Recent reports indicate slackening resolve. But she is the linchpin of the operation. If she weakens, the whole campaign to win Harry Dancer collapses.

Briscoe: Special agent. Dark, violent man. Thuggish. Too free with the Special Powers. Suspicious. But he does get results. In a position of more power, he might prove dangerous. Use him, but recognize his limitations.

Angela Bliss: Internal security agent. A ferret. Everything in her file attests to an almost demoniac loyalty. But is there an element of hysteria? The Department is wary of fanatics. Employees like Bliss don't bend; they break.

Reviewing his dramatis personae, the Chairman concedes they are not the best team he could have fielded. Neither are they the worst. A mixed bag at best. He is aware of their pressures and tensions. He doubts if they recognize his.

Occasional frailty of Department personnel has long been a matter of wonder and puzzlement. These people have been promised the world. And paid. Why then should they surrender treasure for dross? The Chairman doesn't know. But it happens.

It is something to be guarded against. Backsliding is a constant peril. Treachery lurks. He feels he has done all he can to prevent it. But the action is miles away. He can direct, but he cannot control.

The key, of course, is the subject himself: Harry Dancer. Odd that the victim should dictate the crime—but it has always been so. The Chairman wishes he knew more about this man Dancer. Then he might mold his tactics to fit the profile.

But not knowing, exactly, he can only go by past experience. Converts are won by appealing to their lust, their greed, fear. Any and all of human weaknesses. But what is Harry Dancer's chink?

Why, it might even be love. As many targets are converted through their virtues as through their vices.

She calls him at his office late in the afternoon.

"Harry," Evelyn Heimdall says, "about our date tonight—I hope I can make it. I feel awful."

"What's wrong?"

"I think I've got a cold. Is it possible to catch a cold in Florida?"

"Sure it's possible. And it takes a week or two to get rid of the damned thing. You want to cancel tonight?"

"Not really," she says. "But I'm not in the mood for getting all gussied up and going to some fancy joint where the air conditioning is turned down so low you turn blue. That I don't need."

"Well, you've got to eat. Tell you what: Suppose I pick up a couple of thick New York strips and maybe some frozen hash browns. You drive over to my place, and we'll eat about seven or so. Then you can take off early, go home and get into bed. If you've got a cold, sleep is the best cure."

"You're sure you won't mind?"

"Of course not."

"Harry, you're an absolute darling."

"I agree."

"I'll see you about seven then. And I'll try not to sneeze in your face."

He pan-broils the steaks, sprinkles the potatoes liberally with garlic salt and paprika before popping them in the oven. Makes a small salad of romaine and onion slices with a dressing of sour cream and Dijon mustard. Puts out a jug of chilled California chablis.

"Marry me," Evelyn Heimdall says. Rolling her eyes. "If you can cook like this, I *need* you."

"Stop by tomorrow night," he says. "Bologna

sandwiches and kosher dills. How's the cold?''

"Forgot all about it, the food's so good. But I do feel feverish.''

He puts a palm to her forehead. "A little warm. Before you leave, have a brandy. It couldn't hurt.''

He is attentive. Solicitous. Is the steak tender enough? Potatoes too highly spiced? Air conditioning too cold? He hovers over her. Serves her. Makes her eat everything. Brews coffee. Brings out the brandy bottle. Pours them snifters.

"You really are a darling," she says. "What would I do without you?''

"What *have* you been doing? More swimming lessons.''

"Not today—I felt so miserable.''

"Did he ever get a computer job? That friend of yours—what's his name?''

"Martin Frey. No, he hasn't landed anything.''

"I'll ask around if you like. I know a few outfits that might need someone.''

She looks at him strangely. "That's kind of you, Harry. I know he'll appreciate it.''

Dancer makes her finish her brandy. Then, because she admits she has none at home, he insists she take the bottle along with her. It's about half-full. He puts it in a brown paper bag.

"Now I'm brown-bagging it," she says. "Harry, thank you so much for tonight. I can't tell you what you've done for my morale. The next time I see you I'll be all healthy again and hot to trot.''

"You just take care of yourself," he admonishes. "Get plenty of sleep. Drink a lot of liquids, especially fruit juices. Get yourself some hefty vitamin C tablets. Stay out of the pool and ocean for a few days. And make sure your air conditioner isn't blowing directly on you.''

"Yes, professor,'' she says. Then: "Harry, what is it? Did I say something wrong?''

"No. Nothing wrong. But you called me professor. I haven't been called that in a while.''

"Sylvia?'' she asks.

He nods.

"I'm sorry I brought up old memories.''

"No, no. They're good memories. It's all right.''

She drives home. Thinking what a dear, sweet man he is. Then fabricating the dialogue she will repeat to Tony Glitner at the debriefing: about belief, faith, the need for devotion, and the promise of eternal reward.

"I really think he was impressed,'' she'll tell Glitner. "He's looking for something. A truth. He's close to a decision.''

In her apartment, she takes off her shirtwaist dress. Puts on cutoff jeans. Removes her bra. Pulls on a T-shirt that has GO FOR IT printed on the front. Then phones Martin Frey.

"I'm home, honey,'' she says. "Shall I come down?''

"Give me fifteen minutes,'' he says. "I was just heading for the shower. I haven't got much to drink, Ev.''

"Don't worry about it. I've got half a bottle of brandy. I'll bring it along.''

Martin Frey is not a stupido; he knows what has happened to him. You play a role long enough, and it ceases to be a part. You become what you

play. All actors and politicians suffer from that
syndrome: after a while the curtain never comes
down.

Take this Heimdall assignment . . . He comes
down to Florida thnking it's just another temptation job. You dangle your lure (some lure!), the
fish gobbles, and you haul in the victim-traitor.
Frey has done it many times before; he doesn't
take seriously his superiors' fine moral distinction
between "testing" and "seducing."

But Evelyn is something new. Maybe ten years
older than he. But with a young body. Ripe.
Handsome woman. Easy to meet, easy to get
along with. Good sense of humor. Not too demanding. And a lot smarter than his usual targets.

What puzzles Martin, what troubles him, is
something he senses in her. Wildness. Like a kid
suddenly turned loose in the world's largest toy
store and told, "Take what you want." She acts
like she's been freed. All restraints gone. Sometimes it scares her, this novel liberty. But she is intent on exploring it.

The Counterintelligence agent knows he should
have reported all this to Washington. But he has
not. Serious dereliction of duty. He tells himself it
is because Ev's libertinism may be a temporary
aberration, and she will soon straighten out. Then
it would prove a cruel injury to her and her career
to have turned her in as a backslider.

But Frey knows that is not the real reason for
his failure to do his job. The truth is that he is
drawn to this woman. In ways he cannot totally
comprehend. Perhaps it is the simple joy she takes
in physical contact. Even a touch. Maybe it's her

fantastical moods. Her eagerness to race to the furthest limits. She acts like an untamed beast released from a cage.

When she arrives, he is wearing a sashed silk happy-coat. Back embroidered with a fire-spewing dragon. She embraces him. Laughing. She is splitting with vigor. Skin flushed. Flesh swollen. Hard nipples poking. She presses a knee between his thighs.

He holds her away, reads the legend on her T-shirt. "Go for it? What does that mean?"

"I'm not sure," she confesses. "Yield to temptation, I suppose. Try everything. Don't hold back."

"I didn't intend to," he says. Automatically. Playing his role.

They take brandy-and-sodas out onto his balcony. Much smaller than hers. Room for only two chairs, a cocktail table.

Brilliant night. Black sky punched with starholes. Wisps of clouds no larger than beards. Glaucous moon, not full but fat enough. Northeastern wind with a slight edge. Sea is up; they hear thrumming of the surf. Everything is close. Wrapped around them.

"On a night like this," she says, "I feel like I'm going to live forever. But there's not much chance of that, is there?"

He answers cautiously. "Not physically, no. Preachers talk about life eternal. Of the spirit, you know. But I don't believe that. Do you?"

She is silent a moment. Then: "I don't know. But it's not important."

There it is, he thinks. Proof positive of her perfidy.

"Just to be alive," she continues. "To see, hear, smell. To *feel*. What a joy that is! Since I moved to Florida, I've started to grow again."

He laughs.

"It's true," she insists. "I was like one of those bonzai trees. They keep cutting them back. Wiring the branches to make then grow in strange shapes. Keeping them miniatures. That's what I was—a miniature. But in the last month I've been sprouting."

"All over the place."

It's her turn to laugh. "Well, why not? Even bonzais die. Eventually. But while they live, they're poor, frustrated things. Never allowed to achieve their potential. I don't want that."

"What do you want, Ev?"

"Just to be. To *do*. And not to hurt anyone in the process. Does that sound so bad?"

"Of course not."

"Martin, do you think I'm a wicked woman?"

He cannot throw away his script as agent provocateur. "Come on, Ev. We're all going to be dead a long time. We've got to grab every minute."

"That's the way I feel," she says.

If he had doubts before, he has none now. She is gone from the fold. This is no temporary aberration. It is a seismic change. Until she is rehabilitated—if that is possible—she is no longer of use or value to the Corporation. And Harry Dancer is lost.

"Have you had enough foretalk?" she asks. Turning her head to stare at him. "I have."

In bed, his professionalism drops away, and he is frightened. Thinking this woman may destroy him. Burn him down to a cinder. She thinks anything is possible. Is not content with his bag of tricks. Hovers on the edge of hysteria. Crying, "More!" And he retains just enough wit to wonder how much of her emotional and physical excess is due to guilt.

He contains her paroxysms as best he can. Grappling her slickness. Trying to act the *danseur noble* in this violent ballet. Until, reason fled, he enters her mad, choked world of raw sensation. Then he is as desperate as she. The two helpless and insensible. Clinging in a crimson haze. Flames consuming flesh. They smell the ash.

He lies torpid. Feeling the diminishing crunch of his heart. Heaving gasps calming. Sweat drying. His tightened muscles pulling loose. She is asleep—or has passed out. He doesn't know, and doesn't care. He glances at her once to reassure himself: her bruised breasts are rising, falling . . .

She tears him wide open. Not only with magnified pleasure. But cracks what he *is*. All his beliefs, faith, his education and training—like a slow motion film of a tall building being dynamited and demolished. He can almost feel the crumble, the destruction. Almost hear it. Thunderous roar of broken beams and falling masonry.

And in its place—what? Verdant park or arid desert?

Temptation gnaws. To join in her new world. Break all shackles. Deny everything, and seek the limits of bliss. The enticement frightens and excites. He tries to imagine a self-serving life devoted only to sin. But it would not be sin, of course. He would have put that concept behind him. Joy would eliminate sin.

Does he have the courage to make that turn? He wonders, and admires the resolve of this robust woman who has decided to smash out to unprincipled freedom.

He is still debating, his mind a stew, when she rouses. Looks at him. Smiles wickedly. Reaches for him with strong, brown arms. Mouth open and waiting.

Discipline shreds. One night can do no harm. Brief visit to that forbidden land. Roam wild, and let whim dictate his destiny. He knows all his hidden desires and throttled fantasies. Now to be uncovered, exhibited, exposed without shame. Until he is stripped of mind and body. Becomes a single naked nerve. Fluttering.

Briscoe survives in a world where everyone fears him and no one respects him. He succeeds through cunning and duplicity. But he is brainy enough to use brute force as a shortcut when ordinary procedures would take too much time—or simply bore him. Violence is just another method. Special Powers make it easy.

He is capable of juggling several plots at once. And would be a top-level executive if he could govern or conceal his rage. Ambition fuels him. He deserves, he feels, a regional directorship. At least. And then on to Cleveland headquarters.

But meanwhile, he is forced to follow the orders of cautious and frequently inept supervisors. And although he has permission to overrule Shelby

Yama's decisions, it is Yama who has the title of Case Officer in an action that Briscoe is running. If Harry Dancer is subverted, the case officer will get the kudos.

In addition to trying to win Dancer, Briscoe is also countering the Corporation's machinations and keeping a close, suspicious eye on Sally Abaddon's loyalty. But in the dark watches of the night, it is his own aspirations that thump his thoughts. Pleasure does not woo him. Power does.

He schemes logically. It seems to him the first step is to rid himself of the irritating presence of Shelby Yama. That effete, ineffective man. Disgrace to the Department. Once Yama is out of the way, Briscoe will naturally be granted the title of Case Officer. Only right since he is already performing the duties.

So he turns his devious mind to the elimination of Shelby Yama. Inter-Departmental assassinations are rare—and even more rarely countenanced by headquarters. Yama must be made to indict himself. Failing that, his removal must be proved to have been at the hands of an enemy agent.

Briscoe likes the last possibility. Killing two birds with one stone, so to speak. Eradicate Shelby Yama, and then terminate the Corporation agent apparently responsible for Yama's demise. There is a neatness to that intrigue that Briscoe finds satisfying. He sets to work . . .

A few days later he reports to Shelby Yama:

"I think the Corporation's got a guy on Sally Abaddon. Tailing her. A tall, skinny gink. I better check him out."

"Sure," Yama says. "You do that."

A day later:

"That man following Sally—I tailed him back to his motel and slipped the room clerk a couple of bucks. He says the guy's name is Willoughby. You think I should run him through records in Cleveland?"

Yama, portentous, considers. "Yes, Briscoe, I think that would be smart. We've got to keep up on these things."

Two days later:

"Yama, that guy Willoughby I told you about is in the files at headquarters. He's Corporation all right. Mostly communications. This must be his first field assignment."

"Oh wow," the case officer says. "What do you think we should do now?"

"He's a clear and present danger," Briscoe says. "We've got to put someone on him."

"Another operator?" Yama says. "The Director will never go for it. We're over budget as it is."

"I know," Briscoe says. "We'll just have to make do. Listen, I have my hands full, what with checking on Dancer, transcribing the tapes, and so forth. Why don't you get on this Willoughby personally? He sounds like an amateur. Maybe you can turn him. It would be a real feather in your cap if you could get him sending disinformation to the Corporation."

"Hey," Shelby Yama says, "you're right. Another nail in Dancer's coffin, you might say."

"Correct. I'll give you the guy's address, and I'll try to get a telephoto of him so you can identify him. Also, he goes to a church in Deerfield.

Maybe you can make contact there."

"Good deal," the case officer says. "This is exciting!"

Three days later:

"You were right about that Willoughby," Yama tells Briscoe. "He's definitely following Sally. Also, I've made contact!"

"No kidding? That's great. You really know your way around."

"Well, I was a successful field agent for many years. You never forget the old tricks."

"And you're buddy-buddy with him now?"

"Uhh . . . not exactly. But getting there. The guy goes to that church two or three times a week. Sunday service, Wednesday night prayer meeting, choir practice, and so forth. I'm getting close to him. Slowly."

"You think he can be turned?"

"At this stage I just don't know. He acts like a real believer. But yes, I think I can budge him."

"Keep at it," Briscoe advises. "What a coup it would be for you!"

The next day, Briscoe has a private meet with Ted Charon, Chief of Internal Security.

"Look," he says, "I don't want to condemn a man out of hand, so I'm dumping it in your lap. I don't like the way Shelby Yama has been acting lately. He disappears on Sunday around noon, on Wednesday night, and a couple of other evenings. I ask him where he's been, and he fobs me off."

"You think I should put someone on him?" Charon asks.

"It wouldn't do any harm," Briscoe says.

Angela Bliss is not bedeviled by semantic sub-
tleties, by the fine distinction between "testing"
and "entrapment." Her orders are quite clear:
She is to run a sting operation on Sally Abaddon.
Attempt to turn her. If Sally succumbs, she is
doomed.

Angela has been following orders all her life. In
her career as Internal Security agent, she has uncovered treachery in lowly file clerks and in
members of the headquarters hierarchy. It is all
the same to Angela. Treason is treason, wherever
it lurks, and must be rooted out.

She is a solitary woman. No friends, and no
enemies worthy of her. The Department is her life.
It gives meaning to her often arduous and painful
labors. She can endure the tragic fate of her victims only by loyalty to the higher good—the wel-
fare of the Department.

But she has never before been assigned a target
like Sally Abaddon. The field agent's beauty over-
whelms. She seems to radiate. About her is an
aura of ripe sensuality. She is of another race en-
tirely: larger, healthier, with higher color, unflag-
ging vigor, and movements that create kinetic
sculpture in space.

In addition, there is a soft vulnerability that
Angela finds troubling. Sometimes Sally reminds
her of a little girl dressed up like a woman: picture
hat, smear of lipstick, oversized gown, dan-
gling pearls. Teetering along on high heels. The
image touches and saddens.

They come from poolside to cool off in
Angela's grungy motel room. To share a pitcher
of iced tea. Angela slouches in a clumsy armchair.

Shoulder straps of her maillot flop loosely. Sally sprawls on the bed. Wearing a bikini cut high on the thighs. Hair bound up with a vermilion scarf.

Venetian blinds are closed. Room is dusky. Air conditioner whirs. Outside sounds muted. Faraway. Inside is chilled quiet. Thoughtful closeness.

"Date tonight?" Angela asks.

"Maybe. He has to work late. But if it's not too late, he'll call, and we'll have dinner."

"So you'll want to wait for his call. I thought you might like to take in a movie, but we can make it another time."

"Tomorrow night," Sally says. "Okay? He's going up to Orlando tomorrow to see some clients."

Silence. Then . . .

"You love him, Sally?"

"He pays the bills."

"But do you love him?"

The field agent turns her face to the wall. "Yes," she says. So low Angela can hardly hear. "So much. But it's not really him. It's what he represents."

"I don't understand."

Sally whirls onto her back. Clasps hands behind her head. Stares at the crazed ceiling. "I don't either. I'm all fucked up. Excuse the language."

"I've heard worse," Angela says. Puts her iced tea aside. Comes over to sit on the edge of the bed. "Sally, what *is* it?"

"I don't know. I really don't. I just feel my life is coming apart. I don't mean I'm cracking up or anything like that. But I'm changing. I feel it. I want something better. More satisfying. But I don't know what it is."

Angela puts a cool palm to the other woman's hot forehead. Shocked by her own tenderness. "Don't worry it. I hate to see you unhappy. You're so beautiful. And you're such a *nice* person. Oh, don't cry, Sally. Please don't."

Swoops suddenly. Embraces. Holding that sun-surged body in her arms. Feeling powerful pulse. The life force of her! Sweet scents. Flesh blood-flushed. She holds Sally. Rocking her gently. Crooning softly. Job, career, loyalty, Department —all wither and grow dim. In the warmth and dearness of this woman.

What's happening? she thinks dully. To me? Gray woman, cold woman, suddenly suffused and throbbing. Cataclysm.

Darling, she says. Trying it. But not aloud. To herself. Darling. Strange word. Has she ever uttered it? No.

"Sally," she says aloud, "if your boyfriend is too late to have dinner with you, why don't you stop by here? We can go out together."

"All right."

"Your skin feels so hot. I hope you're not going to peel. Let me rub in some moisturizer."

"All right."

"Do you want me to shave your legs?"

"All right."

Angela waits through that evening. Trembling. Peering from her window. Finally sees a silver BMW pull up. Sally runs out. Whisked away. Her golden girl. Gone.

She paces. Hugging her elbows. Trying to comprehend what's happening. What she is feeling. Turmoil. Her life has been all logic. But if the thesis is faulty, everything that follows falls into

disrepair. Independent thought comes hard. New
language.

How could a lifetime of discipline melt so
rapidly? In the hot Florida sun. She cannot imagine the consequences. Refuses to acknowledge
them. All she feels is the onset of passion. Rising
flood. Sweeping her away.

The phone rings.

"Hi. Ted Charon here. Any developments?"

"No," Angela Bliss says. "Nothing new."

Problems pile up for Anthony Glitner. The case
officer senses that the Corporation's campaign to
win Harry Dancer is not going well. Yet he feels
powerless to influence the course of events. Not
events so much as people.

Coded messages from the Chief of Operations
in Washington state that counterintelligence agent
Martin Frey has, so far, given a clean bill of health
to Evelyn Heimdall. Frey reports that the field
agent is apparently operating in an active and effective manner. He can discern no hint of weakening resolve, no possibility of defection.

But Heimdall's debriefings continue to baffle
Glitner. There is something in her that did not
exist before. A breeziness. Almost a high. If he
didn't know better, he would say she was on something. An intoxicant. Booze, speed, cocaine. Her
eyes are too bright. Speech too rapid.

And she has become coquettish. Almost seductive.

Glitner cannot understand why Martin Frey has not observed and reported on these changes. The only way he can account for it is that Frey was not acquainted with Heimdall previous to his assignment. So, of course, he would not be aware of alterations in her personality.

But the case officer is conscious of the modifications. They worry him. The scenario calls for a steady, sober woman offering tenets of the Corporation as a way to redemption and life everlasting. But the new Evelyn Heimdall no longer seems to Glitner to be playing that role.

"Are you all right, Ev?" he asks her.

"I'm fine."

"No problems? Nothing you want to discuss?"

"Can't think of anything," she says. Smiling brightly. "I'm seeing Harry a couple of times a week and speak to him on the phone almost every day. He's coming around. Tony, you worry too much. We'll take this one."

But Tony is not convinced. A case officer running a field agent must not only dictate the agent's tactics, as precisely as possible, but must be privy to the agent's thoughts, fears, impressions. Glitner has the sense of being shut out. Heimdall is no longer open. She has closed up.

Another problem is intelligence supplied by Willoughby. He reports that on several occasions, at the Deerfield church he attends, he has been approached by a man giving his name as Shelby Yama who acts in a manner Willoughby describes as "suspiciously friendly."

Glitner runs the name and physical description through the Washington computers. Learns that Yama is a Department employee. He then asks the

Chief of Operations to query his mole at Southeast Region headquarters. He is subsequently informed that Shelby Yama is the Department's case officer on the Harry Dancer action.

"What do you suppose he's up to?" he asks Willoughby. "Trying to turn you?"

"That must be it, sir. I was probably spotted tailing Sally Abaddon, and they did some checking and ID'd me. How should I handle it? Cut him off?"

"No," Glitner says, "don't do that. There's another possibility. He may be thinking of defecting, and is trying to set up a sympathetic contact. Play him along for a while. See if you can find out what's on his mind. But be very, very careful. That odious Briscoe is on the scene, and it could get dicey."

"I'll watch my back," Willoughby promises.

Tony Glitner's third problem concerns his relations with headquarters. Apparently the conversion rate for the past month was down almost five percent from the corresponding month of the previous year. As a result, the Chief of Operations is under heavy pressure from his superiors to boost Corporation conquests.

The only way the Chief can do that is to lean on his case officers in the field. Glitner gets a constant stream of complaints, exhortations, completely impractical suggestions. Each of these messages ends, "Reply soonest." As a result, the case officer is engulfed in a swamp of paperwork. All of which means extra labor that does nothing to further the winning of Harry Dancer.

Finally, Glitner flies to Washington and has a tense confrontation with the Chief. Anthony says, in effect, "Get off my case." He demands the right of independent initiative, without second-guessing.

"If you don't like the way I'm running things, sir," he says, "then take me off. But I can't operate with you looking over my shoulder and breathing down my neck. I recognize that you have problems, but I have them, too. You've got to let me decide tactics. I'm on the scene and, with all due respect, I think I know more of what's going on than you do."

The Chief swigs Maalox from the bottle. "All right, Tony, you do it your way. I'll cut out the memos. In return, I expect to be informed immediately of any significant developments."

"I promise you that, sir."

"Incidentally," the Chief says, "Counterintelligence informs me that the most recent message from Martin Frey repeats that Heimdall is clean. So apparently your suspicions were unjustified."

Glitner doesn't reply. But he is not persuaded, despite Frey's reports. On the flight back to Fort Lauderdale he reflects on the fragility of trust. Ponders how he might personally prove or disprove his doubts of Evelyn Heimdall's loyalty.

There is one way. But he isn't certain he has the moral courage to try it.

For a period after his wife's death, Harry Dancer finds his memories of their life together blocked. He envisions the thick wall of a great dam. Holding back a flood. Recollections, big and small, of events, scenes, shared habits and secret smiles—all contained.

Intimacies with Sally Abaddon and Evelyn Heimdall breach the wall. First a tiny crack; a rivulet. Widening. Then a fissure; a stream. Growing. He cannot understand how loving Sally and Ev has broken the barrier. Is it true that if you love one woman, you love all women?

Memories grow stronger. Details become vivid. Colors. Scents. Tunes and talk. Sylvia begins to live again. He can see her. Feel the texture of her skin. He recites their duologues. Almost word for word. A film, in color, he can play over and over. Never tiring. Laughing at the jokes. Weeping at the sad parts.

Sits alone in his darkened home. Untouched gin martini on the table beside him. Ice melting. Laces his fingers across his chest. Closes his eyes. Starts the projector. A Harry Dancer Production . . .

Hot August afternoon. Searing sun. Pearly sky with a few stretched clouds like chalk marks. Sea is calm. Ripples splashing onto the sand.

They bob a hundred yards offshore in an inflatable plastic float. Not as large as a rubber dinghy, but big enough to accommodate both of them. With two ridiculously short aluminum oars. Swimmers are closer to the beach. Boats farther out. The ocean is theirs. Alone.

They lie facing each other. Legs entwined. Sylvia takes off the top of her bikini. Spreads arms wide. Reclines with a contented groan.

"If there's anything I hate," Harry says, "it's peeling boobs. And that's what you're going to get if you're not careful."

"Just for a little while," she says. "Fifteen

minutes, no more. Just to get a little color. Who wants white tits?''

"I do," he says. "Yours."

Little craft nods gently. Seemingly anchored in one spot. They close their eyes against the glare. Feel oven heat melting their bones.

"What more can life hold?" she asks.

"A cold drink," he answers. "We must hire a swimming butler. By the way, I was at the library yesterday, looking for a legal dictionary, and I came across a book that gives the meaning of names. You know what 'Sylvia' means?"

" 'Forest maiden.' "

"You knew all along and never told me? All right, my smart-ass forest maiden, what about 'Harry'?"

"That I don't know."

"It means 'grumpy professor.' "

She opens her eyes. Laughs. Lifts a knee, prods his ribs with her toes. "Silly. I'm going into the water."

"Topless?"

"Why not? There's no one around."

"I'm around. And God."

"You both love me, I know."

"Well, be careful getting out. Don't tip us over."

She slides over the gunwale. Hardly makes a splash. Swims a few yards away. Dog-paddles, turning to face him. He looks at her. Smiling. Seeing sleek white breasts. Brown legs kicking. Strong arms stroking.

"Harry," she calls, "you've got to come in. It's like warm milk."

He rolls into the sea. Surface dives. Touches

sandy bottom with fingertips. Kicks powerfully.
Comes plunging up.

"Beautiful," he says. Swimming to her side.
"Very sexy."

"What is?"

"The ocean."

He comes close.

"I'm drowning," she says, "and you must res-
cue me."

"Nut!"

She floats on her back. He paddles alongside.
Puts an arm across her chest. Grabs one of her
slick breasts.

"Handy handle," he says. "Now what do I
do?"

"A little mouth-to-mouth would be nice."

She rotates lazily in the sea. Comes into his
arms. Cool, salty kiss. She looks around. No one
near them. She pushes away from him. Begins
swimming slowly back to their float.

"Now what?" he calls. Watching her.

She threshes in the water. Goes under a moment. When she pops up, she is holding the bottom part of her bikini. Waves it triumphantly.
Then slings it into the float. Beckons to him.

"Madness!" he howls. But swims to her side.
Skins off his trunks. Tosses them into the float.
Naked, she comes between his legs.

"This is better," she says. "Isn't this better,
Harry?"

"Not better," he says. "Best."

They need to rub wet skin. Grapple and hold.
Dive together. Beneath pellucid water they touch,
feel, grasp. Hair swirling. Explore. Come floating
up. Gasping.

"Can we?" she asks.

"We can try," he says.

Sitting alone in his darkened home, Harry Dancer remembers that day. It still has the power to bedazzle. Recalling, he is sick with longing. Could it have been that perfect? Or was memory playing its usual trick: good times endure; bad times fade.

He reaches for his gin martini. Ice melted, but drink still cold. Lifts the glass. Suddenly realizes he has an erection. My God, can memory do that? Oh yes. He had an erection in the sea.

"What I don't need now," he had said, "is a hungry barracuda."

Or was it, he thinks, a fantasy. Did it really happen?

"Of course it happened," he says aloud to the empty room.

Details are so distinct. Green of the water. Blue of the float. Sun burning. Sea calm. No one around. She did. He did. They did. Azure sky. Everything as he remembers.

Unless . . . Unless . . . He is imagining. Dreaming an idyllic life that never was. Creating joy out of sorrow.

He mocks himself. Playing the part of a toothless gaffer.

"Oh my yes," he says. Aloud. In a cracked, trembling voice. "Those were the good old days. We screwed in the sea. Yes, we did. Bare-assed naked we was. Took off every stitch. No one around to see. I mean it! We had some high old times. I could tell you . . ."

Finds himself weeping softly. At this precognition of what his life to come may be. All remem-

brances of things past. Mixed with dreams and
fancies. The whole of an old man's wanderings.
And nothing between real and chimera.

Rises. Switches on a table lamp. Calls Sally
Abaddon. No answer. Calls Evelyn Heimdall. No
answer. Ashamed of his weakness. Goes into the
kitchen to mix another drink. Stops abruptly.

It *did* happen. Exactly as he recalled. Sylvia was
wearing a tiny purple bikini. He goes charging up
the stairs. Flicks on lights. Frantically paws
through her bureau. Her clothing. Things he
hasn't had the courage to give away or throw
away.

He finds a purple bikini. Stands, holding it.
Stroking it. Sniffing it.

Tiny purple bikini . . . That proves it, doesn't
it? Or does it?

They meet in the Director's conference room.
Sitting at one end of the enormous table.

"Here's what we've got," Ted Charon says.
Looking down at a sheaf of notes. "It appears
that—"

"Wait a minute," the Director says. Hoisting
a pink palm. "Does this involve possible dis-
ciplinary action, Ted?"

"Yes, sir, it does."

"Then I think we better have a record of this
meeting. In case questions are asked later. Would
either of you gentlemen object if I ask Norma

Gravesend to sit in and take shorthand notes of
the proceedings?"

Ted Charon and Briscoe state they have no objections. Gravesend is brought in with her pad, in-
structed to take down everything that is said.

"It doesn't have to be word for word, dear,"
the Director says kindly. "If you just get the gist
of it, that will be sufficient."

"I could bring in a tape recorder, Director,"
she offers.

He considers that. Comparing the difficulty of
editing an audio tape versus the ease of censoring
his secretary's shorthand account.

"Oh, I don't think that's necessary," he says.
"This is really a preliminary, informal meeting.
Ted, will you start again, please."

"It appears," Charon begins, "that case officer
Shelby Yama has engaged in and is engaging in a
continuing series of meetings with an individual
who has been identified as a Corporation employee. Code name: Willoughby. He is in our files
as a communications man, but apparently has
become an active agent in the Harry Dancer campaign."

"He's tailing Sally Abaddon," Briscoe says. "I
know it for a fact."

Ted Charon consults his notes. "Yama has been
making contact several times a week at a Deerfield
church that Willoughby attends. My operative
hasn't been able to get close enough to overhear
any of their conversations. But he reports that in
the past week, Yama and Willoughby have apparently become closer. They have been observed
on two occasions eating together at a fast-food

joint near the church. The first thing that must be
established is this: Is Shelby Yama authorized to
make such contacts with a Corporation agent?''

"Not by me,'' the Director says immediately.
"Briscoe, were you aware of this?''

"No, sir. I got suspicious of Yama's unex-
plained absences, but I had no idea what he was
doing. I asked him but never got a direct answer.
It worried me. So I turned it over to Charon,
figuring it was a matter for Internal Security.''

"You did exactly right,'' the Director says.
"Eternal vigilance. We must have it.''

He sits erect in his armchair. Fingers making a
steeple under his heavy chin. As usual, he is im-
peccably clad. High white collar starched and
creaseless. He sits in silence. Staring off into the
middle distance.

"Well . . .'' he says. Finally. "I don't think this
is a matter for Cleveland. Yet. But I believe it
should be treated seriously as a subject of utmost
importance. Involving, as it does, a possible
breach of security and potential treason. Norma,
are you getting all this?''

"Yes, Director. I'm caught up.''

"Thank you, dear. If we go too fast for you,
just tell us to slow down. Well, gentlemen, as I see
it, our next step is to bring Shelby Yama in for
questioning and ask him to state exactly what he's
been up to. It may be a tactical initiative on his
part. In that case, his only error would be in not
informing me prior to instigating the action. But it
may be more serious than that. In which case, dis-
ciplinary action will be called for. Do you gentlemen concur?''

"Before we bring him in, sir,'' Ted Charon

says, "could I have a few more days? A week at
the most? What I'd like to do is keep Yama under
very close surveillance. If my people can observe
him passing documents, or anything at all to Willoughby, our case will be a lot stronger."

"A week?" the Director asks. "That seems reasonable. Briscoe, how do you feel about it?"

"I agree. Give him a chance to hang himself."

"All right, Ted," the Director says. "We'll
meet again in a week and decide on our next step.
And while we're discussing the Harry Dancer action, what do you hear from Angela Bliss?"

"No new developments, sir. She says that so far
Sally Abaddon has exhibited no deviations. Apparently she's going by the book."

"Briscoe?"

"I don't believe it," the dark man says. "Abaddon is turning. If not today, then tomorrow."

"Oh my," the Director says. Shaking his leonine head. "You suspect everyone."

"That's right," Briscoe says. Looking at him.

Evelyn Heimdall knows the clichés describing
her current mood. Off the deep end. Caution to
the winds. Couldn't care less. All denoting rash-
ness. She is aware of her temerity and doesn't
care.

Recklessness is a state of mind. Deliberate disregard of danger. But these days, Evelyn acknowledges, she is not governed by her mind. Her body
possesses her and dictates.

"My brain's in my snatch," she tells Martin Frey. And when he laughs, she wonders if she might repeat the comment to Harry Dancer. Decides not to.

It is a fever. Being obsessed by the physical. Now she can understand why the Others remain faithful to their creed. If she were promised endless years of carnal joys, might she not renounce her vows and switch sides in this everlasting duel?

Everything in the corporeal world is a new delight. Colors stronger. Scents fresher. Sounds more musical. She feels she has been in a lifetime coma. Suddenly awakened. Looks about and sees a shining globe. She is intoxicated with sensation.

"More!" she cries to Martin Frey. That becomes her rebel yell: *More!*

She tries to explain to Harry Dancer how she feels. He listens. Looks at her gravely. Nods.

"I tried to tell you, Ev," he says. "It's the sun, the heat, the physicality of this place. It affects all of us, to one degree or another."

"Florida's part of it," she agrees. "Flowering. That's just the way I feel. Bursting out all over. But part of it's the way I lived before. Tight and disciplined."

"I was wondering . . ." he says. "What happened to those things you spoke to me about. The need for faith. Devotion. Spiritual foundation."

"I still believe in all that. There's no contradiction between believing and what I feel now. Is there?"

"Not if you don't think so."

"Think? Oh Harry, I haven't thought in weeks!"

He is, she decides, a nice, sincere man. But lacking in wildness. He just will not let go. She wants him as free and passionately eager as she. Barbaric. But there is a reserve in him. Something held back and guarded. She cannot get through.

They are in her apartment. Saturday morning before a tennis date.

"We have time," she says. Looking at him. "I could ball you until your teeth rattle."

"And have me collapse on the court?" he says. Smiling. "Let's save it till tonight."

"I don't want to save," she says. "Spend, spend, spend!"

"Tonight," he promises.

"Super," she says.

But the night is not super. Satisfying enough. Pleasurable. But she dreams of love as strong and strange as primitive art. Seeks the savage and finds the civilized. Fakes her response. Tells him how much she loves him.

"I've never felt like this before," she says.

The moment he is out the door, she is on the phone to Martin Frey. He doesn't answer. She keeps calling. Gets that maddening *"Buzz, buzz, buzz."* Defeated, she sits slumped on the edge of her bed. Too late to go out? Too late to drive to a bar, anywhere, and find a fierce stranger? A brute.

Ringing of the phone saves her. She grabs it up.

"Hi," Martin Frey says. "How are you?"

"Where *were* you?" she wails. "I've been calling and calling."

"Well, I knew you were busy tonight. I went to the dog track."

"Why are we talking on the phone?" she demands. "Why aren't you *here?*"

"Will be," he says. "Five minutes."

She doesn't shower. Doesn't make the bed. This night she wants Dancer in her, Frey in her, the world in her. Surrender to the storm she feels. Capable of anything and everything.

Suddenly, with no thought, flops to her bare knees at bedside. Clasps her hands. Closes her eyes. Prays for help and forgiveness. But in the middle of her supplication, the doorbell rings. She rushes to greet Frey. Naked and with wet eyes. Trembling with guilty delight.

He is becoming as insensate as she. Their love-making is not courtship, but a violent struggle. They war and call it joy. Hurt is bliss. Teeth. Claws. Plunge into the jungle with roars, shrieks, caws. Both in unholy rut. Sobbing. Slavering. Faith vanquished, conviction lost.

Then they lie battered and dulled. Slackened.

"I've got something to tell you," Frey says. Voice without timbre. Droning. "A confession."

"Oh?" she says. "Serious?"

"Yes. Very. I'm with the Corporation. Counterintelligence."

She jerks upright. Stares down at him. Eyes wide.

"No!"

"Yes."

"Then they know about me," she says. "I'm finished."

"They know nothing," he says. "About you. About me. About us. I've been filing fake reports."

She flings herself down. Stares at the ceiling. Gnaws a knuckle. "Why were you assigned to me? Who tipped them off?"

"I don't know all the details. But I gather your case officer felt things weren't right with you. That you were changing."

"Tony Glitner," she says. "A sensitive man. I should have known I couldn't con him. So you were sent down to test me?"

"Something like that."

She is not bitter. Just resigned. "Well, you got what you came for."

"I told you, I haven't reported anything. As far as Washington is concerned, you're clean. Which makes me an accessory, doesn't it?"

She kisses him frantically. "Partners in crime," she breathes. "Why didn't you turn me in?"

"You know why. I'm as guilty as you."

"Not guilty, darling. Happy."

"Yes. Happy."

They lie quietly. Then clasp fingers.

"What should we do?" she asks.

"I don't see why we have to do anything. You keep working on Harry Dancer. Tell your case officer it's taking longer than you expected. I'll keep filing affirmative loyalty reports."

She shakes her head. "It won't work. Not for long. Headquarters wants results. And Glitner can't be stalled forever. He already senses what's going on."

"What's the worst that can happen? You'll be pulled off the Dancer case and reassigned."

"And what will happen to you, Martin?"

"Same thing. Reassignment."

"Then we'll be apart. Maybe a world apart. Do you want that?"

"No," he says. "Do you?"

"Never!" she cries.

Fear of separation spurs them. They embrace tightly. Clinging.

"Could we go away together?" she asks. "Just take off? The two of us?"

"Are you wealthy?"

"Don't be silly."

"I'm not either. Maybe the two of us could manage a year. Then what?"

"Get jobs. Both of us."

"Doing what? With our training, what else are we suited for? Besides, they'd find us. You know that. Then the pressures would begin. We'd end up in rehab centers."

"Oh God. What are we going to *do*?"

He turns in bed. Begins to lave her with his febrile tongue. Then they are mindless again. Fears fled. Ignited by their sense of sin. Pleasure heightened by surrender to treasonous evil. They deny all and find a new heaven. A more rousing hell.

Until anguished flesh can endure no more. Rubbed raw and aching, they pull apart to glare. Maddened by excess. Skin abraded with scrapes and bites. Punctures and scratches. Taste of blood. Smell of ash.

She grips his face. Bends nose to nose. Stares into his widened eyes.

"We could go over," she says. Whispering.

"To the Others?"

"Yes."

Norma Gravesend makes a transcription of shorthand notes taken during the conference on the activities and future of Shelby Yama. This report is given to the Director. That night, a photocopy is passed along to Norma's contact, Leonard. He codes the report and radios it to Washington. A decoded version is brought to the Chief of Operations.

He finds the contents disturbing. He immediately alerts case officer Anthony Glitner that agent Willoughby may be in peril. He suggests to Glitner, but does not order, that Willoughby break off all contacts with Shelby Yama.

The case officer, studying this intelligence, feels the Chief is unduly alarmed. It appears to Glitner that if the Department is suspicious of Yama's activities, not authorized by higher authority, then there is a very good chance that he, Glitner, made a correct guess that Shelby Yama is thinking of defecting and trying to establish a friendly contact.

"Work on him," he tells Willoughby. "If he hints that he wants to come over, let him know that he'll need to establish his bona fides before we grant him sanctuary. Ask him to deliver a complete personnel roster of the Department's Harry Dancer team."

At almost the same time, Shelby Yama is reporting enthusiastically to Briscoe that he is making progress in turning Willoughby.

"He's a farmerish guy," Yama says. "Not too sophisticated. I've been telling him some wild stories about the way I live, and he's swallowing them all. I can tell he's excited. It's *Rain* all over

again. I'm playing Sadie Thompson to his David-
son."

Briscoe pretends to give the matter deep
thought. "If you've got him hooked, why don't
you slip him some of our recruiting brochures.
And maybe a copy of our employment contract."

Yama is doubtful. "I don't think he's ready to
make the switch yet. And I don't want to scare
him off by going too far too fast."

"You're probably right," Briscoe says.
"You've had a lot more experience than I have,
and I trust your judgment. Forget about the contract. But it wouldn't do any harm to pass him the
recruiting booklet. The new four-color job on
slick paper with the centerfold. That'll open his
eyes."

"And give him ideas," the case officer says.
Laughing. "Yeah, maybe I'll do that. Show him
how the other half lives."

Two nights later, exiting from the Deerfield
church, Shelby Yama hands Willoughby a manila
envelope. This action is observed by Ted Charon's
Internal Security operative.

I've known so many men," Sally Abaddon
says. "All sizes, shapes, colors. I can't even remember them all. I don't even try."

"Recreational sex," Angela Bliss says.

"I guess. It didn't mean so much to me. Like
scratching an itch."

The two women are having lunch at an outdoor cafe on the Intracoastal Waterway. Sitting at an umbrella table. Picking at fruit salads. Sipping iced tea. Watching pleasure boats plow up and down.

Overcast day. Hot and humid. Weak breeze from the south barely moves the umbrella fringe. At a nearby table, a fat woman wields a palmetto fan. But she looks ready to faint.

"Then I met the man I'm going with now," Sally continues. "His name's Harry. I never told you that, did I? Being with him has been a revelation to me. What sex with love can be. It's like an added ingredient. Salt in the stew. It's made me realize how second-rate recreational sex really is. I mean it just doesn't *work*."

"Does he love you, Sally?"

"Not the way I love him. I know he feels an affection for me, but that's about it. We had a long talk about all the different kinds of love there are. We agreed we'd each do our own thing. I settled for that. It's a hundred times better than what I had."

"But not what you need?"

"You're very perceptive, Angela. No, it's not totally what I need. Whatever that is. But it's all I'm going to get from him. Do you want some ice cream?"

"I don't think so, but you go ahead."

"No, I better skip. I just feel so restless today. It's probably the humidity. Very oppressive."

"Let's finish up, and get back to air conditioning."

On the drive back to their motel, Sally says, "I

have some little bottles of wine cooler in my
fridge. It's like a very mild sangria. Would you
like to try it?''

"Sure. Anything cold. Do you want me to come
to your place?''

"No," Sally says. "I'll bring it to yours."

She totes a four-pack of California Cooler into
Angela's room. They open two. Swig from the
bottles.

"This is better," Angela says. "I don't know
why we went out in that heat. Are you calming
down?''

"I hate to dump my problems on you, honey,"
Sally says. "I know you've got your own. But
talking to you is a real help.''

The other woman leans forward. "Don't ever
think you're bothering me. You're not. I only
wish I could help you more.''

"Just listening is the greatest thing you can do
for me. I've never had a girlfriend I could talk to.
Just men. They're okay, sometimes, but it's not
the same.''

They kick off their shoes. Stretch out. Sally
unbuttons her shirt down to the waistband of her
jeans.

"You never wear a bra, do you?" Angela says.

"Not if I can help it.''

"I do. All the time. And I don't know why. It's
like putting a saddle on a Pekinese.''

They both laugh. Comfortable with their intimacy.

"If I had your body," Angela says, "I'd rule
the world.''

"I used to think that. But it doesn't work out
that way. It did for a while, but not anymore.

Having a good body is just genes and luck. It's not something *I* did. I try to keep the carcass in shape, but I didn't create it; I just inherited it. Sometimes I think it's a curse. Every man I meet wants to jump on my bones.''

"Harry, too?"

"No, he's different. Maybe that's why I love him. He never comes on. I notice I always have to make the first move. Then he's willing enough. But he's also willing to spend a quiet evening just talking or walking the beach. A strange man. Very intelligent and very deep. I still haven't figured him out completely."

"Is he married, Sally?"

"He was. But his wife passed away a few months ago, and I don't think he's gotten over it yet. Sometimes I believe that's why he acts the way he does. He's very moody."

"Maybe he feels going to bed with you is cheating on his wife. His dead wife."

Sally looks at her. "That's exactly what I think. I said you were perceptive. So my competition is his memory of a woman who's six feet under. That's probably why he can't love me the way I'd like him to."

"You think he'll ever ask you to marry him?"

"Oh no," Sally says. "Out of the question."

"Why is that?"

Sally looks away. "Various reasons. It's just not possible."

"Why don't you leave him?" Angela asks. "If the relationship is making you miserable."

"Not miserable. Exactly. Just not what I'd like it to be."

"Maybe you could find another man who'd

love you the way you need."

"I don't want another man," Sally says. "That's not the answer."

Angela Bliss now has no doubts whatsoever that Sally Abaddon will never succeed in converting Harry Dancer. She is breaking the Department's first rule for field agents: Never get personally involved. Every agent is to be a salesperson for the Department's creed. There is no reason for personal relationships that exist for themselves and don't yield results.

If Angela is to be faithful to her vows, she must report Sally's dereliction to Ted Charon, and let him take it from there. It is possible that Sally's punishment will merely be removal from the Harry Dancer case and an official reprimand. Possible—but not likely. The Department has many degrees of retribution. Most of them severe.

Angela Bliss looks at the creamy body of the other woman. She decides. But has enough wit left to reflect that if she is rejected, then Sally must surely suffer. It is bitter to realize how she is putting this beautiful woman at risk. But she cannot help herself.

She pulls her armchair alongside Sally's. Puts an arm across her shoulders.

"It hurts me to see you unhappy, dear," she says. Her own voice sounding strangled to her. "You deserve the love you want."

Sally tries to smile. "I'll survive," she says.

Angela isn't so sure of that. She brushes Sally's hair aside. Moves her lips close to Sally's ear.

"Let me love you," she whispers. "Please, darling. Let me. I know what you're looking for. I can give you that. Please let me."

Sally looks at her strangely. "Not just physical love," she says. "That's not the answer. I want—"

"I know, I know," Angela says. Words tumbling out. "Devotion. Strong and absolute. A religion of two. Isn't that it? Something steady and forever. Lasting, lasting . . . That's what I want, too. We could do it, sweetheart."

Slides a hand into Sally's open shirtfront. Cups a warm, heavy breast. Feels the flutter.

"Could we?" Sally breathes. "Do you think we could?"

"Oh yes! Yes. That's what love should be. A paired world. Sharing. Belonging to each other completely."

Leans forward. Kisses the other woman on the lips. Mouths open. Tongue tips touch.

"Can we try?" Angela Bliss pleads. Almost weeping with fervor. "Please, lover, let's try."

Then, fumbling, awkward, rushing, they are naked in bed together. Seducing each other with words. Love. Devotion. Belonging. Sharing. Belief. Faith. Forever and ever.

While they discover each other's body. Explore and learn. With searching fingers. Mouths hot and sliding. Frantic cries. Shrills of delight. Everything new and promising. Maddened by tenderness. Then whirling away into their fresh universe. Convinced they are creating.

Angela thrusts away. Curls into the fetal position. Eyes squinched with tears. Thin arms pressed tightly across thin breasts. Keening comes from her.

Sally bends over her. "Honey, what *is* it?"

The other woman whirls to face her. Reaches to

touch Sally's lips. "We can't begin with a lie. Can't! We must be absolutely honest with each other. Absolutely open. Isn't that right? Isn't it?"

Sally stares. Face slowly congealing. "Honey," she repeats, "what *is* it?"

Angela's confession spills out. She tells everything. She's with the Department. Internal Security. Brought down from Chicago to check Sally's loyalty.

"Briscoe thought you were turning," she says.

The story of her bedridden husband is a lie. She is unmarried. She is at the motel to make contact. Become friends. Win Sally's trust.

"I report to Ted Charon," she says.

"I'm dead," Sally says. Dully.

"No, no! I swear, lover, I haven't told him a thing. About how you feel or—or anything. As far as they know, you're clean. I've covered for you since day one."

"Why did you do that?"

"Don't you know, sweetheart? Because I've loved you from day one."

Sally sits up in bed. Puts her back against the headboard. Broods. Angela slips away. Brings them two more opened bottles of wine cooler. Sally takes hers absently. Sips.

"Angela," she says, "why didn't you tell me all this before today?"

"Because I was afraid if I did, you might have said you love me just to protect yourself. You'd have thought it was a kind of blackmail. Wouldn't you?"

"Probably. But what if I had rejected you an hour ago? Would you have turned me in?"

"I don't know," Angela says. Convincing herself that was the truth. "I honestly don't know what I would have done. But I love you so much, I had to take the chance. Do you believe me?"

Sally turns her head to stare at the other woman. Suddenly she smiles. All sunshine. "Yes, honey, I believe you. I've *got* to believe you. You're the only chance I have."

"The only chance *we* have," Angela says. "I meant everything I said to you. With all my heart. This day has opened a whole new life for me. For us. I'm a tough cookie, lover. I may not look like it or act like it, but I'm steel. I really am. And I'm not going to let you go without one hell of a fight. I love you, Sally, and I want you. Do you want me?"

Low voice: "I need you."

"We need each other. Alone, we're just half-women. You realize that, don't you?"

"Yes."

"Then we've got to put our heads together and figure out how we can get what we want. Listen, I've worked for the Department a long time—and I know you have, too—and when you come right down to it, the Department isn't some great, mysterious, all-powerful organization. It's *people*. Isn't that right? People make the rules. It's managed by people. And most of them are no smarter than we are. Believe me, darling, I *know*. So don't think we haven't got a chance. We have!"

"You're sure?" Sally says. "You think we can get out?"

"Of course we can. But we just can't take off; you know that. They'd catch up with us, sooner or later."

"Then what are our options?"

"Let's think about it," Angela says. Taking the bottle of cooler from Sally's hands. Placing it on the floor. "Let's talk about it. Later. Right now, let me show you how much you mean to me."

"Yes," Sally says. "I'd like that. Lover."

The Chairman of the Department, with the assistance of the floor supervisor, rises slowly from his reinforced throne in the War Room. Leaning on a blackthorn cane as thick as a cudgel, he makes his way laboriously to his private office. Carrying with him the latest intelligence on the Harry Dancer case.

Alone, he collapses into a club chair upholstered in bloodred leather. Reviews the most recent reports and computer printouts. Pulls fretfully at his thick lower lip.

The Dancer thing started out so simply. Now it is a can of worms. Human passions are distasteful to the Chairman. He is at home dealing with black sins and white virtues. But this grayish swamp of steamy emotions dismays him. Good or bad he can handle. Vagaries are troubling. And sometimes defeat his most precise planning.

Take this matter of case officer Shelby Yama, running the field agent in the Dancer campaign. According to Internal Security, Yama has had repeated unauthorized contacts with an individual identified as a Corporation agent. In addition, he has been observed passing material to that agent. Query from Southeast Region: Will you approve termination of Shelby Yama?

The Chairman ponders that decision. Yama has a good record. Not brilliant, but good. However, there is some evidence of erraticism. Perhaps due to his theatrical background. Or maybe the mercurial nature of the man himself. He seems to be drama-oriented. Not the strongest, most dependable employee on the Department's roster.

The Chairman, reasoning, reflects on the possibilities open to him. One: Remove Shelby Yama from the Dancer case. Replace him with another case officer. Who would require a period of orientation. Resulting in a further slippage of the schedule, and an added drain on the budget.

Two: Bring Yama in for stiff interrogation. Using state-of-the-art truth drugs. But how could he possibly justify his recent activities vis-à-vis a Corporation agent? In any event, the questioning, regardless of its outcome, would damage his confidence and erode the morale of his staff.

Three: Terminate Yama. Forthwith.

The Chairman sighs heavily. Buzzes for his male secretary. Dictates a message to the Director of the Southeast Region. Authorizing the immediate elimination of case officer Shelby Yama. By means to be determined by the Director.

The Chairman then considers the problem of a replacement. He decides on Briscoe.

"The right man at the right place at the right time," he tells his secretary.

Harry Dancer is confused. And aware of it.

He is confused by the wild libertinism of Evelyn Heimdall. In a period of weeks, she has shed her image of a cool, steady, disciplined woman. Become profligate. Tropical climate and Florida's physicality cannot account for the change. She is new. To him and, he suspects, to herself.

"Why not?" has become her constant refrain. After he rebuffs outlandish proposals. She wants more of everything. Insatiable and demanding. He can't keep up with her. Admits he finds her abandon daunting. And frightening.

"Calm down," he tells her. Trying to smile. "Tomorrow's another day."

"How do you know?" she challenges. "Tomorrow may never come."

He has no answer to that.

He is confused by the metamorphosis of Sally Abaddon. That butterfly seems to be folding her wings. Withdrawing into herself. Reentering a cocoon.

"Is anything wrong?" he asks her. "What's troubling you?"

"Nothing," she answers. "Everything is fine. What would you like to do tonight? I'll do anything you say."

But he senses an unfamiliar reserve. He recalls the old folk saying: "You can't really know anyone until you go to bed with them." In bed, Sally goes through the motions and pleases. But a vital part of her is detached and gone. He is left with a professional actress playing a role. Too long, too often.

But most of all, Harry Dancer is confused about himself. Memories of Sylvia . . . He tries very hard to keep reality and fancy distinct. But boundaries blur. He finds it increasingly difficult to separate actuality and dreams.

Frantically he digs out old letters, postcards, menus, programs, photographs, birthday cards—all the memorabilia of their life together. Seeking clues to what they did. When. Where. He needs evidence to reassure him. Anchors to the real.

He sits on the bedroom floor. Surrounded by the detritus of a shared life. Trying to re-create a vanished time. Thoughts go whirling away . . .

One of Harry's wealthier clients sends him an invitation to a posh dinner. Really a command. A thousand dollars a couple. For a worthy charity.

"Did you ever hear of an *un*worthy charity?" he grumbles to Sylvia.

It is a black-tie affair. Held in an enormous tent erected on the grounds of a Palm Beach mansion. Harry digs out his conservative dinner jacket. White shirt. Black tie and cummerbund.

"You look like a daddy penguin," Sylvia says. "A *splendid* daddy penguin."

She wears a slinky sequined sheath. All glittering green and gold. Diamond stars pinned into her hair. Bare, tanned shoulders and arms. Face alight with eager anticipation.

"You look good enough to eat," he tells her.

"Well?" she says.

It is a stunningly opulent home. Mizner-designed. Formal gardens. Two swimming pools. Stable and six-car garage. Forecourt paved with Italian tiles. Ballroom in the main house. Fourteen bedrooms.

"Let's buy it," Sylvia says.

"What on earth would we do with fourteen bedrooms?"

"You know."

"Sex fiend," he says.

"I plead guilty, your honor."

There are two bands for dancing. An enormous buffet table that almost justifies the thousand-dollar "contribution." Three bars are busy. Catering personnel circulate with trays of champagne. There are gold compacts for the ladies; cigarette lighters for the gentlemen.

Sylvia and Harry saunter about. Carrying champagne glasses. Stop to chat with the few people they know. Visit the ballroom to dance a few sets to old Irving Berlin melodies. Come out again to fill plates at the buffet. Take them up to the terrace of the main house where cast iron tables and chairs in Victorian filigree have been set out.

Resplendent night. Calm and creamy. Modest crescent moon and scented breeze. They dig into crystal pots of caviar, sip champagne, listen to muted strains of "They Say It's Wonderful" coming from the ballroom.

"Happy?" Dancer asks his wife.

"Not yet," she says. "When I finish this filet, I will be. What are these things?"

"Japanese mushrooms. Delicious."

"And this?"

He samples. "Slices of black truffle."

"Gee, professor, you know everything."

"I know you're the most beautiful woman here tonight."

"And you're the handsomest man. But let's not tell anyone; it'll be our secret."

They finish their dinner in record time.

"Super," Sylvia says. Sitting back. "Another

five pounds—but I don't care. Do we have to
wash our own dishes?"

"That I doubt. Would you like dessert? Coffee?"

"Not yet."

"I noticed cognac at the bar. How about a
balloon of that?"

He brings the brandies.

"Let's go exploring," she suggests. "I'd like to
see the gardens. They're lighted."

Carrying the oversized snifters, they stroll down
flag walks to inspect precise beds of flowers.
Copses of ornate palms. Topiary in bizarre animal
shapes. They come to a wall of box hedge at least
seven feet high, with a narrow opening. Posted
sign reads: THE DEVIL'S MAZE. ENTER AT YOUR
OWN RISK.

"Let's try it," Sylvia says. "Maybe we'll get
lost and have to spend all night."

Harry is dubious. "Are you sure, Syl? It's getting late."

"Come on, grumps," she says. "Take a chance.
Live a little."

They stroll into the maze. Trying to remember
directions, false turnings, blank walls of hedge.
They pass other couples meandering about. Giggling. Calling to each other.

"This way," Sylvia says. Taking his hand.
"We're getting close to the center. Trust me."

"Haven't I always?"

They find the middle of the maze. A little
pergola with a stone bench. They rest gratefully.
Sip cognac. Listen to shouts and cries of other ex-
plorers, still straying about.

"I hope they stay lost," Sylvia says. "This place

is ours." Leans forward to kiss her husband. "Let's make love. Right here."

"On a stone bench? Thanks, but no, thanks."

"We should, you know," she says. Looking down at the little puddle of brandy in her glass.

He has a pang of something awry. "Syl, is anything wrong?"

She turns a bright, smiling face. "What could be wrong? It's a heavenly night. I'm glad we came—aren't you?"

"Absolutely."

"I'll remember it," she says. "Always."

He catches melancholy. So foreign to her. "Let's get back," he says. "I'd like another dance before the band starts playing 'Auld Lang Syne.' "

She seems suddenly listless. This time he takes her hand, leading. But they wander hopelessly. Lost. Continually coming up against blank walls of hedge. It is funny. At first. But frustration grows. Wee touch of panic. They hear other voices. Meet other wayless strangers. They are caught. Doomed to wander forever.

No longer joking. Desperation. Imprisoned and erring. It is almost twenty minutes before they stumble upon the exit. Their brandy long gone. Both trembling. Sylvia clutches his arm tightly.

"Let's go home," she says.

"Yes," he says, "I think so."

They are silent on the drive back. Finally . . .

"As soon as we get in," he says, "I'm going to mix us the biggest shaker of plasma we've ever had. We deserve it."

"And then we'll go to bed," Sylvia says, "and make love, and you'll hold me."

"You better believe it."

In their own home, with drinks, naked in bed, they wait for dread to ebb. But it does not. They cannot shake the memory of their fear in the maze. Helplessness.

Later, when he is drowsing, almost off, she tells him softly about her illness. He rushes to the bathroom and vomits. Champagne, caviar, mignon, brandy. All. Future. Life.

He kneels before the toilet bowl. Head bowed. Sylvia comes in to sponge his face with a damp cloth. Strokes his hair.

"It's not so bad," she croons. "Really, darling, it isn't."

Was that the way it happened? Exactly? It's the way he remembers it. Splendor turned to pain. Triumph to defeat in a few short hours. Started with jazz. Ended with a dirge.

He sits on the littered bedroom floor. Staring at the engraved invitation to the charity dinner. Trying desperately to recall details. Did so much occur in one evening? Or is his jumbled brain combining events of several nights? Making a mishmash of history. A fantasy.

"Sylvia?" he says. Aloud. "Help me, honey."

There is no answer.

The three men meet in the Director's office. Door closed and locked. Norma Gravesend has not been called in to take notes.

The Director waves a flimsy. "An authorization from the Chairman to delete Shelby Yama. As soon as possible. In a manner of our choosing."

"All right, sir," Ted Charon says. "I'll take care of it."

Briscoe can't let that happen. Shelby Yama may talk before he is eliminated. Reveal that Briscoe is aware of the reason for his contacts with Willoughby. That the material he passed to the Corporation agent was merely the Department's recruiting brochure.

"Director," Briscoe says, "I feel a personal responsibility for what's happened. Yama was case officer, true, but you ordered me to ride herd on him. I failed to prevent his defection."

"You're not to blame," the Director says. "The man was obviously flawed."

"I know that, sir, but if I had been more alert, I might have been able to prevent it. I'd like the assignment of terminating him. I feel it's my duty."

The Director looks at Charon. "Ted, do you have any objections?"

"None, sir. I can understand how Briscoe feels."

"All right then," the Director says, "we'll do it that way. Briscoe, after Shelby Yama is, ah, out of the picture, the Chairman suggests you take over as case officer on the Harry Dancer action. I concur."

"Thank you, sir."

"And I urge you to bring this Dancer campaign to a successful conclusion as soon as possible."

"I can promise you that, Director."

"Good. One final detail . . . This Corporation agent who was trying to turn Yama—what's his name? Willoughby?"

"Yes, sir," Charon says. "Willoughby."

"Perhaps he should be punished as well," the

Director says. "I don't like the idea of the Corporation attempting to convert our personnel."

"I'll handle it," Briscoe says.

Evelyn Heimdall concedes her life is becoming disheveled. She loses all sense of order. For the first time, she knows the pleasure of whim. She explores a ruleless world. Marveling that she could have wasted dear existence on discipline and dedication.

She is conscious of her dissolution in so many ways. Renouncing vows. Ignoring rituals. Mocking sacred myths. All these sins wither when she grapples the satiny body of Martin Frey. Presses close. As good and evil suffer meaning, sensation becomes a faith.

She is converted, with the excessive passion of the new believer. She, in her turn, wants to proselytize the world. So that all may share her discovered joy. Martin Frey is her first recruit. His betrayal of the Corporation is as complete as hers.

Their shared treachery is an added spice. Guilt spurs them to wilder intemperance. Remembering what they are betraying, kisses are sweeter. They couple with the franticness of the condemned.

Lying naked, cooling, on the tiles of Evelyn's balcony. Staring blearily at a wavering sky with tilting stars. Their world tipped. They feel themselves sliding off.

"Can you stop time?" she asks.

"No," Frey says. "Never."

"We do," she insists. "Not so long ago. The

now went on and on. Lasted forever. Didn't you feel it?''

"I wasn't conscious of time."

"That's just the point. It was obliterated."

He turns. Stares down at her mellow breasts. Puts tongue to her. Laughs at her turgid reaction.

"You're always ready," he says.

"Oh yes," she agrees. "Always and all ways."

She rolls to face him. But keeps apart. They have learned the tang of teasing. Offering, promising, denying. Love game that never palls. He touches her. She touches him. Concupiscence stirring.

"I saw Harry Dancer last night," she tells him.

"I know," Frey says. "All night. I kept calling."

"It was no good. For him or for me. I've lost interest in bringing him over to the Corporation. We never talk about it. And I think he's lost interest in me. He's still a sweet man. But he's gone somewhere. Distant. I couldn't get through to him if I tried."

"You think the Department is winning him?"

"No, I don't think so. He's so far inside himself. No one is getting to him."

Trace each other's bodies. Pinch. Pluck. Soft pain and stirrings.

"Here?" he says. "Like this?"

"Yes," she says. "Just like that."

"Have you thought any more of what we must do?" he asks.

"I've tried, darling, but I can't concentrate. On anything but you. On us. When I'm away from you, I think of what we've done and what we're going to do. I almost faint with longing. I get all wet."

"I know. I'm the same way. I almost get sick to my stomach. Literally. Wanting you so much. Dreaming of new things we haven't done yet."

"But will. You know that."

"Oh yes. Everything."

Close now. Faster rhythm to their deliberate fondlings. Banked fires beginning to blaze. Excited flesh hardening. Above, stars spin their ascending courses.

"Should I ask Glitner to replace me?" she says. "I'll tell him I'm getting nowhere with Dancer. Tony already knows it. He'll bring in someone else."

"What good would that do?" Frey says. "You'd be reassigned, and so would I. We'd be apart. Is that what you want?"

"Never!"

"Then do nothing. Ev, we've been over this a dozen times."

"Let's not think about it. Right now. Tell me some of the new things you dreamed for us to do."

He tells her.

"Oh yes," she says. Eyes widening. "I want to do that. Let me."

There is no talk of "Do you love me? Yes, I love you; do you love me? Yes, I love you." Their love is rut. So powerful and overwhelming that emotion becomes skimmed stuff. Whispers cannot be heard in their howls.

They seek the limit. But there is no limit this side of death. They push at the boundary. Physical craving replaces hunger and thirst. They believe no one else has ever done these things. In all history. Like youths, they think they are the first and the only.

Their passion has the sour taint of desperation. Louder cries. Sharper bites. Surrender to frenzy. Until they become insentient. Nothing to them but raw response. Mindless and tingling. Return to the ooze.

World forgotten. Faith lost. God forsaken.

The Chairman, in his private Cleveland office, is suffering. The Department's resident physician has diagnosed his complaint as "a bad cold with low-grade upper respiratory infection." Which, considering the Special Powers granted to key Department personnel, is laughable and humbling.

A box of tissues is on the Chairman's desk. Wadded tissues engulf his wastebasket, litter the rug around it. He reviews progress reports of current actions. Pausing frequently to ram a tissue onto his bulbous nose and trumpet. He is disgusted with upper respiratory infections. With himself. With life in general.

He is intelligent enough to recognize how even minor physical ailments can affect one's spirit and mental attitude. But convinced his depression is not totally due to a runny nose. Even if he was enjoying his usual robust good health, he would acknowledge that things are not going well.

Take this Harry Dancer campaign, for instance. Authorization granted to terminate case officer Shelby Yama on suspicion of treachery. To be replaced by Briscoe. So far so good. But it is Briscoe's suspicions of field agent Sally Abaddon's loyalty that led to the assignment of Internal Security agent Angela Bliss. That investigation has yielded no results. And Dancer is still not won.

The Chairman sits brooding. Dabbing gently at his cherry-red proboscis. Now swollen and sensitive. Not for the first time he ponders the difficulties of the Department in making converts. From what the Chairman considers a logical point of view, there should be no problems at all.

The Department promises wealth. Power. Physical delights. Or a combination of all three. It even, in special cases, promises revenge. Sweetest gift of all. Would not any reasonable man or woman avidly seek such rewards?

But, the Chairman reflects, so quirky and inexplicable is the nature of human beings that a distressing number do not.

In contrast, the Corporation offers such returns as suffering, sacrifice, and duty. Duty! Not happiness, but *duty*! The Chairman will never comprehend how the Corporation can continue to exist with such a program. And not only exist, but occasionally flourish. It is beyond understanding.

And, as if all that wasn't enough to confute good sense, the only hope the Corporation offers is an eternal, halcyon Life Beyond. The Department offers today. The Corporation promises tomorrow. Ridiculous! And yet the soft-minded continue to opt for an unknown, unproved future.

The Chairman is certain that Harry Dancer has been lulled with these same vague assurances. Lulled and defrauded. The subject is apparently an educated and thoughtful man. Has he never heard that a bird in the hand is worth two in the bush? Or, considering his occupation: Take the cash and let the credit go?

Why *is* it, the Chairman wonders, that some people deliberately choose the pain of duty in preference to unlimited pleasure? They must recognize the ephemerality of life. Ah-ha! Perhaps therein lies the success of the Corporation.

For with their offer of Life Everlasting, are they not playing on their converts' dread of death? Promise a dying man even another day of existence, and would he not pay any price to ensure it? The more the Chairman explores this thought, the more convinced he becomes that the Corporation's essential appeal is based on fear of mortality.

If that be true, then perhaps the Department's recruiting program should be reassessed. As of now, it makes no mention of the price that must eventually be paid for favors granted. But perhaps a description should be furnished of a fictitious eternal paradise as well as earthly pleasures.

Many people, the Chairman knows, have a disturbing tendency to surrender present joys for future happiness. By offering both, the Department might well surpass the Corporation in winning men and women who recognize the wisdom of eating their cake and having it, too.

The whole subject, the Chairman decides, will serve as an excellent memo, a lengthy memo, to his superiors. Outlining suggested changes in the Department's appeal to potential converts.

He blows his nose with a triumphant blast.

"Do you think Briscoe is out there?" Angela Bliss asks. Gesturing toward the parking lot. "Watching us?"

"Probably," Sally Abaddon says. "Him or Shelby Yama. Or maybe one of Ted Charon's thugs. Does it worry you?"

"Your safety worries me. I don't care about myself."

"I care about you," Sally says. "I care about *us*."

Sizzling day. Smoky. Sky hidden behind a scrim of haze. Blurry sun. Westerly wind from the Everglades brings flights of giant dragonflies. Swooping and soaring. Wings glittering. One perches on the rim of Angela's iced tea glass. She waves it away.

"All those people," she says. "Briscoe, Yama, Charon. The Department. It's amazing how little I think about them anymore. A part of my life that's gone. I can't believe I ever belonged."

"I know," Sally says. "Sometimes it seems to me like a dream. And now I'm awake."

"It's over, dear. Finished and done with."

Both slack. Infected with the torpor of that steamy day. At an umbrella table alongside the pool. Trying not to move. Gnats, beetles, love-bugs skitter about. A golden boy, stripped to the waist, guides a power mower over the lawn at the far end of the pool. They can smell the mown grass. Perfumed.

Lazy talk about their girlhoods. Parents. Places they lived. People they knew. How they were recruited into the Department. What they did. Thought. Felt.

No hurry to learn each other. They think they

have forever. It is sweet to spin it all out. Come
closer slowly. Asking questions. Every detail.
Opening completely. First for both. Freedom!
This is who I am. Warts and all. Ecstasy of confession.

"I can be naked with you," Sally says.
"Totally. Tell you things I've never told anyone
else."

"I want you to know my secrets," Angela says.
"Everything."

Lock stares. A look so intimate it frightens. It is
all so foreign. They are learning a new language.
Searching with wonder an unknown land. Breathless with fear and hope. Love grows, buds,
flowers. Are there no limits?

"Are you seeing Harry tonight?" Angela says.
Looking away.

"Yes. For dinner. I think I'll be home early.
I've lost him. I knew that even before I met you.
He's off somewhere. Drifting. He responds, but
mechanically. With a kind of glassy smile. His
mind's a million miles away."

"With his wife?"

"Possibly. Probably. He's acting strangely. The
oddest expression when he looks at me. I don't
understand him at all."

"You could tell your case officer you're getting
nowhere and want to be replaced."

"And be reassigned? Shipped somewhere else?
You know I can't do that. Be parted from you."

"Ah, sweetheart, I was hoping you'd say that.
Go along for a while. Until we figure out what
we're going to do."

Into the pool. Surface dotted with blown blades
of cut grass. Drowned dragonflies. They paddle

slowly together. Arms touching. Legs. Sleek skin burning.

"Tonight," Angela says, "when you get back—will you come to me?"

"Of course."

"Darling, I can't sleep anymore unless I know you're there. Next to me."

"I'll be there, lover," Sally says.

That night Harry Dancer is in what he calls a "blue funk." He apologizes. Insists on taking Sally to the Boca club. They dine on red snapper that's been overcooked.

"Just the way I feel," Dancer says. "Dry and juiceless."

"You'll come out of it," Sally comforts. "We'll go back to your place, and I'll have you dancing the fandango."

He gives her a wan smile. "Thanks, but not tonight. I'm just not up to it. Literally and figuratively. We'll make it another time."

She reaches to cover one of his hands with hers. "Harry, what *is* it? Have I done something?"

"Oh my God," he says, "of course not. It's not you, it's *me*. I'm just trying to glue my life together again. It's slow going."

"Do you want to cut out the salary checks? We agreed—no questions asked. If you want to take me off the payroll, that's okay."

"And have you go back to the Tipple Inn? Or another place like it? I don't want that, Sally, and I don't think you do either. Let's keep going the way we have. I'll come out of it, eventually, and get back to normal. Whatever the hell that is."

She looks around the ornate room. "Did you and your wife come here?"

"Oh yes. Frequently."

"You haven't told me much about her. What was she like?"

She opens the floodgates. He starts talking and can't stop. Sylvia, Sylvia, Sylvia. How she looked. What she said. Did. Tennis. Dancing. The way she dressed. Her jokes. Taste. Fey spirit. Crazy things. No fear. Her wildness. Just what he needed. To lift him. Give his life joy and lightness.

Listening to him, Sally knows again she will never succeed with him. Nor will anyone else. Department or Corporation. The man is locked into the memory of a lost love. Someday he may be converted. But not soon.

He runs down. Rueful. "Sorry about that. I didn't mean to get so mouthy."

"She was a very lucky woman," Sally Abaddon says.

"Lucky?"

"To have you."

"She deserved more," Harry Dancer says.

He drives her home. She goes running into Angela's motel room. Face streaky with tears. Angela embraces. Soothes.

"Sweetheart, what *is* it? What happened to you?"

Sally tells her about Harry Dancer. What he said.

"He loved her so much. And he lost her. It's crushed him. I know exactly how he feels. What if I lost you? It would crush me."

"You're not going to lose me," Angela says. "Ever."

They agree, solemnly, like all lovers, that bed is very, very important—but not *the* most important. Physical love is marvelous, wonderful, exciting, intoxicating. But it is icing. The cake is total emotional commitment. Surrender and conquest. Complete sharing. Absolute belonging.

"It's the only meaning I know," Sally says.

"A reason for breathing," Angela says.

Lying naked together is not so much sexual sport as a path to closer intimacy. Assure each other they could sleep clasped and never become aroused. It is the *nearness*. If they could inhabit each other's body, they would. Their love is one.

But they are betrayed by their fervor. If physical contact feeds emotional involvement, that fidelity in turn impels the lover to pleasure the loved. If they seek oneness, then their caresses become a kind of self-gratification.

More correctly, they each worship a third. Their union and harmony. It is that glowing entity they kiss, nibble, and gently bite. They lose their identities in the unity of their love. Paying homage. Bringing vows and sacrifices. Submitting to their faith.

Reasoned so, sexual passion becomes an offering. Burning incense or lighting candles. They are not too far from flagellants. Scourging themselves and each other to prove the intensity of their belief. In their love.

They cannot get enough. Prove enough. Greedily woo delirium with grasping mouths. Frantic tongues. Sliding over each other with sweat-slick skins. Courting death, if necessary. It would be the final obeisance to their new god.

Then, faint with exhaustion, they roll apart. Shaken by the magnitude of their worship. Lie silently. Cooling. Excitement of flesh yielding to hearts' resolve.

"I love you."

"I love you."

Spoken in scarcely heard voices. Whispers and murmurs. Adding intimacy. Soft privacy.

"Are you all right, dear?"

"Drained," Sally says. "You?"

"Wrung out. And frightened."

"Why?"

"It's so—so strong. It sweeps me away. I must learn to cherish that. Complete loss of control. I've always been so disciplined. And now this. I'm not used to it. Don't know how to handle it."

"You don't have to handle it. Just accept."

"Yes, I know that. I'm learning. But it's shattering."

They lie awake. Whispering. Murmuring. Outside light comes dimly through slats of the venetian blinds. Air conditioner hums. Airliner drones over. Someone laughs raucously. They hear a siren wail and fade. Motel plumbing chugs. But they are alone in all the world.

"I've been thinking," Angela says. "There is a way out for us."

"What?"

"Defect. Go to the Corporation. Ask for religious asylum."

Silence. Then . . .

"Will they take us?" Sally asks.

"I think so. We can deliver intelligence they want. Names. Methods. Chains of command. Codes. Things like that."

"Can they protect us?"

"They have offices all over the world. They could assign us anywhere. We'd have to cut a deal with them. That we'd never be separated. That would be our Number One demand."

"And no more active field work," Sally says.

Beginning to dream. "We'll type, learn computers, be secretaries—whatever. As long as we're together."

"Right! Let's talk about it, darling. Plan how we're going to do it. Who we go to and what we say. I can't think of any other chance for us. Can you?"

"No," Sally says. "No chance at all."

They huddle. More murmurs. More whispers. How they may protect their own creed in a bigoted world.

Top Secret manuals of the Corporation devoted to proselyting have evolved over centuries. Are constantly being updated. The current Chief of Operations himself has contributed a modern section dealing with the converting of computer specialists and high-technology workers.

The Department's fat Chairman is not far off the mark when he reasons that the Corporation succeeds by appealing to the human fear of mortality. But that is only one of many missionary techniques taught during the training of case officers and field agents.

Another is the Life Beyond gambit: Paradise promised to the afflicted and downtrodden. A third strategy, called the Placebo Effect, woos potential recruits by convincing them that worldly cares and anxieties can be overcome by the single demand of faith. Duty eclipses and eliminates all earthly concerns.

But probably the most successful operational

technique used in the field is based on the human
need to love and be loved in return. The Corporation views love as a most powerful motivating
force. A separate training manual is concerned
with the varieties and complexities of affection for
another.

The manual begins by terming love an "instinct" which, though it exists in every human
newborn, nevertheless needs nurturing if it is to
survive and thrive. The Corporation refuses to admit there may be individuals, young or old, who
lack the hunger and capacity to love.

Based on this premise, field agents are in-
structed to lead potential recruits "up the ladder
of love." At first the subject may evince no more
than a gentle kindness to a pet—dog, cat, horse,
etc. Or ardor may be felt for a home, a city, a
nation. Even the arts—painting, music, literature
—are considered fit objects of emotional attachment.

It is the agent's task to nourish this craving. To
increase it by leading the target to a loving human
relationship. This step is frequently accomplished
by a process of transference in which the agent
becomes the object of the subject's fervor.

The final step, in an ideally conducted conversion, brings the pilgrim to the glory of sacred love.
God becomes the love object. And in return for
devotion, reveals benevolent concern for His
lovers.

This "ladder of love" technique is far from in-
fallible. But it has achieved a higher conversion
rate than any other Corporation strategy. Computer studies show the most difficult step in the
process is that final rung from human to sacred
love. Many potential recruits cannot make an

emotional commitment to a Supreme Being with
no corporeal existence.

The Love Ladder plan was selected for use in
the Harry Dancer campaign. The Chief of Operations reasoned that the subject had already, in his
marriage, displayed a well-developed capacity to
love. With the death of Dancer's wife, the Chief
supposed the subject would be eager to find
another outlet for emotional attachment. Bringing
him up that final degree should not have been difficult.

But the Chief has been in the business too long
to assume success in any action. Like the Department's Chairman, he is aware of the quirky and
inexplicable nature of human beings. About
whom nothing is predictable. Except that nothing
is predictable.

Reason tells him their life could not have been
that airy and free of strife. But memory insists. It
was an existence unplagued by rancor. Aggravations were laughed away. Arguments defused with
groans and kisses.

Harry Dancer remembers it as a sunny time.
Did it never rain? All he can recall are shimmering tennis courts, shining beach, a light-drenched
racetrack with sharp shouts and the flash of
colors.

"God, are we lucky," Sylvia kept saying.

And they'd both cross their fingers or knock on
wood.

Is it true that everyone, eventually, must pay for

happiness in this world? What a dour view! And yet . . . And yet . . . Give to charities. Attend church on Easter and Christmas. Try to avoid unkindness to others. Slide quietly through life, sideways, and hope the powers that be don't take note of your bliss and mark you for doom.

It didn't work.

Once again he is thrown back to awe of chance and accident. Events unforeseen. Then life becomes a crapshoot—does it not? Roll of a die or flick of a card. Leaving you with no control over your own destiny. We are all born in Las Vegas.

Feeling that way, immured by doubt, raddled by desperation, he snorts memory like a drug. Hungry for the rush and the high. No longer caring if he is dreaming or recalling actual events. Does it matter?

They are at an amusement park. Somewhere. Whirring rides. Cries of barkers at take-a-chance stands. Screams of children. Cotton candy. Smells of frying foods. Clicking of wheels of fortune. Surging crowd seeking the painted promise: Fun! Fun! Fun!

Sylvia is wearing a picture hat. Summery frock of yards and yards of chiffon. Sashays through the throng. Wants to try everything. Do everything.

They throw baseballs at wooden milk bottles. Crash Dodgems. Look over the entire carnival from the top of a Ferris wheel. Eat taffy. Frozen custard. Pork sausages. Drink warm beer. They giggle their way through a House of Mirrors. Gawk at the Fat Lady, Siamese Twins, Skeleton Man, a dead lamb with two heads, a strange object called Moby's Dick.

Finally, surfeited, ready to leave, Sylvia begs for a final ride on the carousel. Harry can't resist; the calliope is playing "Meet Me in St. Louis, Louis." They buy tickets. Merry-go-round stops. Hop aboard. Sylvia swings onto a rampant lion. Harry mounts a haughty llama.

They begin to whirl. Now the music is "June is Bustin' Out all Over." Round and round they go. Grabbing for the brass ring on every turn. And missing. Sylvia has taken off her wide-brimmed hat. Beating the flanks of her lion. Like a rodeo cowboy on a bronco. Whooping and hollering. Filmy skirts billowing in the breeze.

Harry Dancer, upright on his llama, holding the leather reins tightly, feet in steel stirrups, cannot take his eyes from the image of his flying wife. She races ahead of him. Laughing. He might reach, but could never catch her.

On she speeds in mad circles. Head thrown back. Kicking her heels into the wooden beast she rides. Delighted with the swift movement. Elated with the moment. Yelping with enjoyment. Dancer finds himself leaning forward. Yearning toward her. He wants to capture that free spirit. Hold it for his own. And knows he cannot.

They drive home singing bits of carousel tunes. At one of the games of chance—tossing rings onto spikes—Harry has won, at great expense, a little teddy bear. Unaccountably, the button eyes are crossed. Sylvia cuddles the stuffed toy in her arms. Insists on calling it "Irving."

They arrive home late. Harry mixes their first decent drink of the day: gin gimlets with wedges of lime. Kick off their shoes, slump, talk about the sensations and adventures of the day.

"It was fun, wasn't it?" Sylvia says.

"Yes, it was. I'm learning."

"Learning what?"

"How to have fun."

Looks at him. "You have to learn *that?*"

"Oh yes. A lot of people—me included—don't know how to have fun. We've got to be taught."

"You're putting me on, professor."

"I swear I'm not. You were born with the art or skill or ability—whatever you want to call it. I was not. You're teaching me how to do it."

"You like it?"

"Love it. But it depresses me when I think of all the time I've wasted."

"That's part of having fun—wasting time."

"You're very clever," he tells her.

"I've got a brain, buster. I know you married me for my 44-C cup boobs and glorious tresses so long I can sit on them—but I do think occasionally."

"Have I ever denied it?"

"No," she says. Smiling fondly. "You never treat me like a simp."

"Because you're not a simp," he says. "A nut maybe, but not a simp."

"Hungry?"

"You kidding? After all that junk food we had today?"

"I'm worn out. I'll take a refill, go upstairs, shower, and turn in. Join me?"

"In a while. You go ahead. I'll lock up."

"See you later, pappy," she says. Flipping a hand. Winking at him.

"I hope so."

But after she's gone, he doesn't move. Sits thinking about the day's events. It *was* fun. And he hadn't lied to her about his inability to feel joy. Until he met her. But she is teaching him, and he is learning. Whole new scary world. He wouldn't dare venture without her. Like a blood transfusion. Hot. Steamy. Same type.

He has one more gimlet. Crunching ice between his teeth. Then rises, wanders about, locking up and turning off downstairs lights. But the upstairs is bright. He hears Sylvia singing. He is not alone.

She is already in bed. Sheet pulled to her chin. Wearing half-moon reading glasses. Flipping through a paperback romance at her usual speed. Devours a dozen a week. Hands them on to their Cuban cleaning lady who comes in on Tuesdays and Fridays.

Harry goes into the bathroom to shower. Washes his hair. Brushes his teeth. Pulls on a tissue-thin seersucker robe. Comes back to sit on the edge of the bed. Takes the book gently from his wife's hands. Puts it aside.

"One of these days," he vows, "I'm going to get you to read Trollope."

"Trollope?" she says. "Is that a kind of fish?"

"Sure it is. Caught off the Keys. Great eating."

"Broiled or fried?"

They both laugh. He leans forward to kiss her cheek.

"You smell nice," he says. "Soap and cologne and *you.*"

"No pork sausage, taffy, or cotton candy?"

"Not a whiff. Where's Irving?"

She gestures. The stuffed teddy bear is propped up in an armchair. Watching them with crossed eyes.

"I was going to bring him to bed," Sylvia says.

"Put his head on your pillow. But I thought you might be jealous."

"I would have been. I want to be the only man in your life."

"You are," she assures him. "That's the trut', the whole trut', and nothing but the trut'."

"I believe you. Feel like another drink?"

"No, I've had enough. You?"

"I don't think so. I'll sleep without it."

He takes up her hand. Kisses fingertips. Palm.

She takes off her glasses. "And what, pray, is the reason for this unbridled passion?"

"You're beginning to talk like those schlocky novels you read. No reason. I just feel very affectionate tonight."

"Did you take a cold shower or a hot shower?"

"Lukewarm."

"That," she says, "I can handle. Come under the sheet with me."

"Lights on or off?"

"On."

He goes over to the armchair. Turns Irving so the bear's face is pressed into the upholstery. "I don't want anyone watching."

"Very wise. What he'd see might stunt his growth."

Harry takes off his robe. Slides into bed alongside her. She comes into his arms. Feeling cool. Satiny. "It was a good day, Harry," she says. "Wasn't it?"

"A grand day. We must do it again."

"Not the same thing," she says. "You can never repeat. If you want to have fun."

"I'll remember," he says. "I told you I was learning."

In no hurry. Languid lovemaking. Slow and

thoughtful. All the sweeter.

"Husband," she says.

"Wife," he says. "Did you ever believe anything legal could be so marvelous?"

"That marriage license was the best investment you ever made."

"Don't think I don't know it. Saved me a lot of money."

"Swine!" she says. Punching his arm.

Her skin is cream. Warm, eager parts of her. Tiny folds. Corners. Secret places. All scented. Tingling.

"I'll never get to the end of you," he tells her. "Never in a million years."

"If you did," she says, "you'd lose interest."

She senses his need to love her. Usually she is the lover. So bouncy he can scarcely keep her on the bed. But tonight she looks at him with widened eyes. Stroking his hair. And lets him.

She is the only woman in his life who is able to get him out. Not by anything she does, but just by being *her*. Gets him out of himself. Makes him forget his doubts and torments. He is transfigured and transformed by love. New being. Born again. By her.

So supple. Softly hard. Hotly responsive. He tells her she is a musician. Playing him. She laughs, but it is true. She draws music from him. Before there had just been tunes. But she knows his chords and sonorities.

He surrenders to her. As simple as that. Casting off all reason and restraint. Her power terrifies, but he cannot resist. Love so intense. He weeps with happiness and fear. It is no small thing to give yourself over to another. Death of will. Voluntarily.

Sees the world in her throat's hollow. Glimpses eternity in swoop of back. Her body solves cosmic mysteries. Kissing a silken thigh becomes an affirmation of faith.

He is aware of all this. But is she? It doesn't matter. It cannot be explained to her. To anyone. And a sneaking part of him holds back. Not wanting to try. To reveal his weakness. Dependence. On a shoulder's sheen or ear's velvet. On an elfin woman who spurs a flying lion.

Their coupling is a minuet. Eyes open in a lighted room. All the more zesty for its deliberateness. Time expands. Love can do that: magnify a minute to an hour. Live a lifetime in a single day.

"It's possible," he says. Aloud.

But she is beyond hearing. Eyes swollen with wonder. Clutching him. Mouth opened in a silent shout. They both grin ferociously. Sharing their triumph. Their pas de deux circles down. Nothing left but the music's end. The bows.

Much later, she says, "Sweet dreams."

The Director of the Southeast Region, a compleat bureaucrat, specializes in survival. Knows all the management tricks of claiming credit and shifting blame. Tempers boldness with caution. Smiles at superiors, frowns at inferiors. Never says Yes, never says No.

"Let me think about that," he says. Thoughtfully.

Not so much intelligent as shrewd. Dresses like a bank president and thinks like a rug dealer. In another age he might have brewed potions for the Borgias.

Sits grandly at the polished desk in his private office. Scans the latest flimsies from Cleveland. Including an ill-tempered diatribe from the Chairman demanding to know when he can expect results on the Harry Dancer action. The Director puts it aside. Initials a few memos, signs a few letters. Thinks suddenly of a new computer operator on the floor below. She is young. Very young.

The Director is a womanizer. Hopelessly addicted. He believes he conceals it from his staff and the Department hierarchy. But beneath his bishop's robes is a randy stud. The Department allows excess, of course. But not at the expense of efficiency. The Director thinks himself efficient. And discreet.

Norma Gravesend knocks, enters to gather up signed memos and letters. He looks upon her benignly. What a loyal employee! Eager to give her all. Which she does—when ordered. Strange woman. As unobtrusive as wallpaper. But not without a certain attraction. Different. Perverse.

"Is Shelby Yama still around, Director?" she says.

"Of course. Why do you ask?"

"It's just that I haven't seen him lately. I wondered if he had been transferred. Would you like to do the budget estimates now?"

"Later," he says. Watches her leave the office.

Her casual question about Yama disturbs him. Why did she ask? She has never before exhibited any special interest in the case officer. Yet now she inquires about him. Curious. The Director is an old hand at this business; he doesn't believe in happenstance or coincidence.

Shelby Yama is slated for sanction. But how could Norma Gravesend possibly be aware of that? She was not shown the authorization from Cleveland. She was excluded from his meeting with Ted Charon and Briscoe during which Yama's fate was discussed. So why should Norma suddenly be interested in the man?

The Director considers the possibilities. Believing, as he does, that everyone, including himself, is capable of treachery—if the price is right. He subscribes wholeheartedly to the Department's creed. Which is simply to disevangelize the entire world. But that belief requires the total elimination of faith. Trust no one. Person or god.

Norma Gravesend could have obtained the Chairman's sanction to cancel Shelby Yama if she wished. She knows the regional office. How records are shuffled. The route and storage of top secret documents. It would be easy for her to read and copy the decoded message from Cleveland.

The Director's glance falls on his desk intercom. He runs his fingers lightly over the buttons. What if, during his locked-door conference with Charon and Briscoe, the switch connecting him to Norma's desk had been depressed? Could he swear it had not been? No. Was it possible she had heard what was said? Yes.

It is, he assures himself, very thin stuff. Paranoiac suspicions. But the bureaucrat's instinct for survival cannot be denied. He saunters out of his office. Smiles at Norma.

"I'll be downstairs, dear," he says. "Watching the wheels go 'round."

She nods brightly. Turns back to her typewriter.

The Director goes immediately to the Internal

Security Section. Enters Ted Charon's office without knocking.

"I want you to put your people on Norma Gravesend," he tells a startled Charon. "At once. Twenty-four hours a day."

"If you say so, Director."

"I do say so. When you have anything to report, call me, and I'll come here. Is that clear?"

"Yes, sir."

The Director then strolls down the staircase to the lower floor. Exchanges nods with supervisors and station chiefs. He looks about. Finally locates the new computer operator seated before her console.

Comes up behind her. Puts a stroking hand lightly on her warm shoulder.

"How are you getting along, my dear?" he says. In the kindliest way imaginable.

The easy way, Briscoe knows, is to use Special Powers. Zap both Shelby Yama and Willoughby. But that would be stupid. After the inexplicable deaths of Jeremy Blaine and Herman K. Tischman, the cops might start wondering. Asking questions. Investigating links between the victims.

Briscoe likes problems like this. Solved by action. He gives it a lot of heavy thought.

Southern Florida is a network of canals. Designed for flood control. Also useful for dumping bodies. Briscoe reads the local newspapers; he knows. Figures a canal would be an ideal place to get rid of Yama and Willoughby. They might never be found. And if they were—so what?

He checks local canals. Finds none that will suit his purpose. Too close to traveled roads. Or too shallow. Or too well illuminated. And there's the problem of a car. If he's to give the cops a plot they can live with, he has to leave a car at the scene. Also, death in a ditch lacks the high drama he enjoys.

He forgets about the canal scenario. Scouts the Deerfield church where the two men have been meeting. Sees the possibilities immediately. It has a bell tower six or seven stories high. With a railed observation deck on top. Interesting.

Checks it out carefully. Winding steel staircase goes up to the platform. Church isn't locked until midnight. Briscoe spends several evenings wandering in and out. Exploring. No one stops him. No one questions. Services go on in the nave while he tramps up the stairway. Timing his climb.

It begins to come together. He likes it. Goes to Ted Charon's equipment section. Signs for a "cold" handgun that can't be traced. A .38 Colt Detective Special revolver. In prime condition. Loaded. Briscoe also requisitions a kilo of cocaine in a plastic bag.

Now he's got the props. Goes back to the bell tower of the Deerfield church. Carrying a small wrench. He's alone up there. On all his visits, he's never met anyone admiring the view from that lofty perch.

Loosens the bolts holding a section of the railing to the concrete deck. He is so clever at this work that he pads the jaws of the wrench with a rag so no nicks will be left on the bolt heads. He tries the railing. It wobbles satisfactorily.

Shadows Yama's meetings with Willoughby for a week. Decides Wednesday night will be best. A late prayer meeting sparsely attended. By ten o'clock the church has emptied out. Maybe one or two believers in the pews, heads bowed. Minister back in his rectory.

Briscoe goes over his plan again and again. Writing out the time sequence. Studying it, then destroying it. An outlandish scheme. Depending on boldness. That he has—and the victims don't. He's depending on their shock, inability to react swiftly. The two of them could take him. Easily. But they are not doers.

Parks two blocks away on Wednesday night. Walks back to the church. Waits patiently in the shadows of thick bottle palms. Eventually the church doors open. People stream out. Shelby Yama and Willoughby together. Talking and laughing. Tall Corporation agent stooping to listen to the case officer.

Briscoe comes up behind them in the parking lot. They hear his footfalls. Turn. Yama is startled.

"What are—" he begins. Then sees the revolver in Briscoe's hand.

Willoughby sees it, too. He looks at the gun, at Briscoe's face, at Shelby Yama. The agent's lips begin to move. Silently. Praying?

"The two of you," Briscoe orders. "Back into the church. Through the front door. Make a hard left. Up the staircase. Let's go."

"Hey," Yama says, "what *is* this? What's going on?"

"Move!" Briscoe says. Raising the revolver.

Marches them back to the church entrance. Gun in his jacket pocket now. But no one around to see. Up the stairs. Slow climb. No talking. They come out onto the deserted observation deck. Sweet night. Clear sky. Stars. Balmy breeze. Everything nice.

Briscoe glances over the railing at the parking lot below. Two cars out of the way. Turns back to his pigeons. Gun out now. Covering both of them.

Shelby Yama starts talking rapidly. What's going on? He can't understand this. It isn't in the script. He told Briscoe he was turning the Corporation agent. Let him talk to the Director. He'll explain everything. Somebody's making a big mistake.

Briscoe doesn't listen. Doesn't reply. His original plot calls for him to shoot Yama dead. Leave his body on the platform. Push Willoughby through the loosened railing. With one bullet in him. Leave the sack of cocaine near Yama's body. Wipe off the revolver and drop it down onto Willoughby's corpse.

Drug deal turned sour. That's what the police will figure. Two pushers fighting for the dust and the gun. Both shot. One dies on the platform. One goes over and dies in the parking lot. No fingerprints found on the gun. That'll puzzle the cops, but they won't have the time or manpower to dig deeper. Just another dope killing. Good riddance.

But now, high in the sky, Briscoe finds that plan flat and unfulfilling. It is a lordly scene. Black vault of heaven above. Pricked with glittering stars. And below, sparkling lights of earth. He feels the power of the night. Is filled with its majesty.

King of it all. He wants to throw down those who oppose his will. His faith. They cannot inhabit high places, but must be tumbled to destruction. Cast out and cast down. Removed from the kingdom of darkness.

"Listen," Yama says, "can't we—"

Briscoe leaps suddenly at Willoughby. Puts a hard shoulder into the man. Railing gives way with a screech. The Corporation agent offers no resistance. Topples backwards. Arms and legs outstretched. Flying.

Unexpectedly, the Department's case officer tries to fight back. Struggling. Clawing. Biting. No match. Briscoe wrestles Yama to the edge. Tosses him over. Leans to watch the dark form float and hit. Atop Willoughby. Dead embrace.

Briscoe drops the bag of cocaine. Sees it split open in a white cloud. Forces himself to turn away and start down the stairs. Walking slowly, calmly. Gun back in his pocket. If his life ended at that instant, he would be happy. Fulfilled.

Strolls back to his car. Drives home. Remembering, savoring the moment. Casting out. Descent from heaven. In the finest traditions of the Department. There is poetry there. Something moving. Exciting. Religious experience.

For the Others are religious, too. In their way.

The Chief of Operations kneels at his prie-dieu. Too distraught to think clearly. And so turns to prayer. For poor Willoughby. Other agents have died in the line of duty. But the pain never lessens. The Chief wishes he had a power akin to canonization. He does not. There is a bronze Honor Roll to which Willoughby's name will be added. His only reward. On earth.

The Chief drags himself back to his office. Forces himself to make a list of victims in the Harry Dancer affair. Jeremy Blaine. Herman K. Tischman. Shelby Yama. Willoughby. All lost in the struggle for one man. Is it worth it? Four lives for one? The arithmetic baffles him. He cannot define the moral choice.

Depression corrodes his will. How can he possibly justify such sacrifice? Four for one? A blasphemy. Unless . . . Unless the one is gold, and the four are dross. But that presupposes quality. Antidogma. Are we not all equal in God's eyes? Perhaps. But not in the Chief's eyes.

He calls Anthony Glitner in Florida. Speaking over an unscrambled line.

"Tony," he says, "I wish to express my condolences on the passing of our dear friend."

"Yes," Glitner says. "Thank you, sir."

"I know how you must feel. Believe me, I do. But we cannot let this unfortunate accident keep us from our duty. If anything, it should strengthen our resolve."

Silence.

"Do you agree?"

"Yes, sir."

The Chief doesn't like Glitner's tone.

"Tony, do you want to be replaced? It won't count against you."

"No, Chief. I'll see it through."

"You feel up to it?"

"Yes. I'm a little numb at the moment. I'll come out of it."

The Chief tries to be hearty. "Of course you

will! Temporary setback. You'll recover. We'll all recover. Is there anything you need? Personnel? Equipment?''

"Not at the moment, no, sir."

"How is the field agent taking it?"

"No problems."

"None? That's odd."

"Yes," the case officer says, "isn't it?"

When he hangs up, Glitner reflects that it *is* odd. News of Willoughby's murder has little effect on Evelyn Heimdall. She murmurs conventional expressions of sorrow. Then regains her bubbly manner. Spinning a breezy tale of her growing intimacy with Harry Dancer. How the man is responding to evangelizing.

The case officer, a diffident, self-effacing man, conceded he may not be tempermentally suited to honcho the Dancer operation. He cannot compete with Briscoe's brutality. Glitner is cerebral; physical violence is foreign to him. As it was to Willoughby. Dead Willoughby.

The question of Evelyn Heimdall is subtler. But no less frustrating. And frightening. He is aware of her new looseness. "She's coming apart at the seams," he tells himself. Then wonders if he is imagining. Counterintelligence agent Martin Frey reports her straight. But Glitner's doubts persist.

She is on a high. Wildness there. He sees her drifting out of the Corporation's orbit. Doesn't know how to bring her back. He decides to push. Discover how far she's gone.

"I like Florida," he tells her. "Do you?"

"Love it, love it, love it," she says. Snapping her fingers. Doing a dance step. "Sooo relaxing. I feel a hundred years younger. Don't you?"

"At least," he says. Smiling. "I must get out to

the beach one of these days. Get some color.''

"Of course you must. Tell me when. We'll make a day of it. Picnic lunch. Bottle of cold wine. The whole bit.''

"Sounds great.''

"And you'll see my new bikini,'' she says. Laughing at him. "Two postage stamps and a Band-Aid. Dancer loves it.''

"I can imagine,'' Glitner says. Not liking this talk. Against his will, aroused by it.

He is almost convinced she is ready to turn. But that would mean that Martin Frey is either a hopeless incompetent or a partner in her betrayal. Either way, the Harry Dancer action is compromised.

Tony Glitner, glooming over the permutations and combinations of this unsavory situation, decides not to send a panic signal to the Chief of Operations. The case officer is responsible for his field agent. He will not sacrifice her until he has proved her treachery.

He knows how he might do that. It dismays him.

"Ted Charon is on line two, sir,'' Norma Gravesend says.

"Thank you, dear,'' the Director says. Pushes the button.

"Yes, Ted?''

"Director, I wonder if you could stop by my office for a moment? Something's come up on that matter we discussed a week ago. Could you drop by for a moment?"

"Of course. Be there immediately."

In Charon's office, the Internal Security Chief says, "I thought it best if we met here to talk about the Norma Gravesend investigation."

"That was my original suggestion," the Director says testily. "What have you got?"

"We've had close surveillance on her for the past week. She's making contact at the public library with a middle-aged man. Passes a book to him every time they meet. We tailed him to his home. Did a B&E while he was out. His name is Leonard Gabriel. He's got enough radio equipment in his house to reach Mars. We were unable to find any code books."

Two men stare at each other. Gradually the Director's ruddy face drains to chalk. Realizing what this means. Wondering how long he has been harboring a Corporation mole in his private office. Isn't that what the Chairman will ask?

"How did you get on to her, sir?" Ted Charon asks. Sympathetic, but already trying to establish his distance from this breach of security.

"Instinct," the Director says. "I always had my suspicions. What do you suggest we do now?"

Drawing me in to share the blame, Charon thinks. Not what do *I* do now, but what do *we* do now. The bastard wants me to clean up his mess.

"Pick up this Leonard Gabriel," Charon says. "Wring him dry. I've got some experts; Gabriel will talk. Then we go to Norma. Tell her what we've got. Convince her that her only hope of survival is to turn again. Become a triple agent. Help us feed disinformation to the Corporation."

The Director feels a thrill of hope. Perhaps his neck is safe after all. If they can persuade Norma to switch sides again, surely the Chairman will be more lenient in the punishment he decrees. He might even be willing to let the Director continue in his present position. With nothing worse than an official reprimand.

Two days later they call Norma Gravesend into the Director's office. Lock the door. Show her Polaroid photos of what's been done to Leonard Gabriel. Watch her face closely. Hoping for tears and hysteria. See only stony strength.

"Did you have to do that?" she asks. "To that dear man?"

"Do you deny you were part of the conspiracy?" Charon says.

"Don't waste your time," she advises. "I deny nothing. I admit everything. I've been a Corporation agent ever since I came to work for that monster."

Jerks a contemptuous thumb at the Director. He begins to sweat.

"Norma," he says. Trying to be avuncular. "Before you say anything more, dear, think of the consequences. You don't have to share Gabriel's fate. There is a way you can redeem yourself. And save yourself."

"I'm already saved," she says.

"Work for us," Charon urges. "Just keep doing what you have been doing. We'll tell you what to send to the Corporation."

"No," she says. Lifting her chin. "I expected that someday I might have to face this, and I made up my mind. I don't care what you do to me. I will not go against the Corporation. It's all I have."

"Stupid woman!" the Director shouts at her.

"You may change your mind," Charon says. Turns to the other man. "Do I have your permission to work on her, sir?"

"Yes, yes. Just get her out of here and do what you have to do."

When they were gone, the Director sits slackly. Deflated. Thinks of how much Gravesend knows about the inner workings of the Department and what she must have told the Corporation. Worse is what she knows about his private habits. All that now in his dossier in Corporation files. He squirms with embarrassment.

Her betrayal shocks him, then angers him. After all his kindnesses to her. Repaid with vile treason. The Director's eyes sting as he reflects on the injustice of it all. His personal life made public. Subject of crude jests, no doubt. His career endangered. His very existence at risk.

Sighing, wiping his eyes, he takes out a pad. Begins to compose a message. Wondering how he can possibly inform the Chairman of what has happened without making himself seem an incapable dolt. Worthy candidate for termination with extreme prejudice.

Briscoe's game plan is working wonderfully. Sanction of Shelby Yama gives him the title of Case Officer. As well as the power. Now he can lean on Sally Abaddon for results. Threaten reprisals if she doesn't obey orders.

Even better is the Norma Gravesend defection —the talk of the entire Southeast Region. Briscoe figures it means the end of the Director. If that happens, and his job is open, who would be better suited than Briscoe? Especially if he scores a win in the Harry Dancer campaign.

Problems there. Abaddon swears she's bringing Dancer around. But offers no proof. Angela Bliss, supposedly running a security check on the field agent, reports Sally is clean. But Briscoe is getting bad vibes from the whole operation. And too much is at stake to ignore his instincts.

He assigns himself the task of tailing Abaddon. Discovers that, as she claims, she is seeing Harry Dancer two or three times a week. But, Briscoe notes, their meetings are short, and becoming shorter. Lunch. Dinner. A few hours in Sally's motel or Dancer's home. But they no longer spend a night together.

Sally and Angela spend nights together. Frequently. And poolside days together. Shopping trips. Movies. Strolls on the beach. It may all be part of Angela's job: getting close to the subject. And then again it may be a different kind of intimacy.

That doesn't shock or offend Briscoe. The Department approves amoral personal conduct. What worries is how the relationship of the two women may affect the outcome of the case. If it endangers the winning of Harry Dancer, then Sally Abaddon will have to go. And Angela Bliss.

Briscoe is a sexless man. His needs are power and status. Even money is a secondary consideration. But he can act, if he must. And only by acting, he decides, can he test Sally Abaddon's loyalty to the Department.

It is not a role he relishes. But her future, and his, may depend on his performance.

The dying ask questions that cannot be answered. "Why me?" Resignation comes slowly. But before that is a period of unfocused fury against the living, the happy, healthy living. Finally: acceptance. Smiling-sad remembrance. Revisiting the past.

Harry Dancer, so far down he believes he is never going to come up, recalls Sylvia in that mood. Nostalgia for everything. Old songs, old times, old friends. "Remember when—" obsesses her. She seems intent on re-creating a life. Finding value in her few years. Making them shine with a golden glory.

With loving patience, he joins her in the summing up. Indulging himself as he indulges her. Hoping to dull the pain. Instead, sharpening it to knife-edge. Two misers counting their wealth before it is lost.

"I want to go to the club," she tells him. "By myself."

He looks at her. "All right."

"I want to sit at the bar. A single woman. Then you come in and pick me up."

A ghastly idea. He feels like weeping. But knows what she seeks. Reassurance. To be wanted again. Reclaim her youth. Playacting an adventure. All pretend and make-believe. But precious to her. Vital. He is determined to see it through.

"Let's do it," he says. "When?"

"Tomorrow night. I'll take a cab. Get there about eight. You drive up around eight-thirty."

"Fine. What are you going to wear?"

"You can't know. I'll be a stranger to you."

Following evening. He dresses swiftly. Leaves the bedroom to her. Takes a small gin out onto the patio. Sits there until he hears a cab arrive. House door slams. Cab takes off.

Harry comes back into the kitchen. Has another gin. Larger. Finds he is clenching his fists. Praying he can get through this evening without breaking. Takes a deep breath. Stalks about the empty house. Wondering what kind of role she wants him to play.

When he walks into the club, he sees her at the far end of the bar. Finishing a vodka gimlet. He stops suddenly. She is wearing the same dress she wore on their first date. Short-hemmed sheath of silver lamé. He didn't know she still had it. Marvels that it fits so beautifully.

Takes a chair two seats away from her. The bartender comes over. He knows them. Looks quizzically from husband to wife. Separated. Makes no comment.

"Good evening, James," Harry says. "Beefeater on the rocks, please."

When the drink is served, he glances at Sylvia, then says to the bartender, "Would you ask the lady if I might buy her a drink."

James, figuring he's in the middle of a family squabble, moves over to speak to Sylvia. Comes back to Dancer.

"Sorry, sir. The lady says to thank you for the offer, but she'll buy her own."

Harry nods. Watches while James mixes a fresh gimlet for Sylvia. The two sit there without speaking. Occasionally glancing at each other in the bar mirror. Then quickly looking away.

He sees her take out a pack of long Benson and Hedges menthols. Searched through her tapestried bag for matches. Looks about helplessly. Harry is at her elbow in an instant. Flourishing his lighter.

"Allow me," he says.

"Thank you, sir," Sylvia says. Very cool.

He holds the flame for her. Hand trembling slightly.

"Are you a member?" he asks. "I don't believe I've seen you here before."

"A new member."

"I'm sure you're going to like it. My name is Harry Dancer. May I join you?"

"If you wish."

He brings his drink. Takes the chair next to her. The bartender looks on approvingly.

"That's a lovely dress you're wearing," Harry says. "Did you get it in Florida?"

"No. Manhattan."

"Oh? Are you from New York? I used to live there."

"I've never lived there, but I go up two or three times a year on shopping sprees."

"Do you play tennis?"

"Oh yes. That's why I joined the club."

It is a pickup. Questions and answers. Learning about each other. They talk weather, tennis, Florida beaches, restaurants. She tells him her name. Sylvia Lloyd.

"May I buy you a drink, Sylvia?" he asks.

"Thank you, Harry," she says. "That would be nice."

They have dinner at the club. Young strangers meeting for the first time. And after a while it becomes real. The tension. Will she or won't she? Will he or won't he? Excitement and fright. Hope and fear of rejection.

Over coffee and brandy, he says, "Do you live nearby, Sylvia?"

"Quite near. I walked over here. I have a small

condo, but I'm looking for something larger. Where do you live, Harry?"

"As they say in Florida, down the road a piece. I have a beachfront home."

"Beachfront? Sounds divine."

"Too big for me, and decorated like a warehouse. But yes, it's nice. Like to see it?"

Lock stares. Then she stubs out her cigarette.

"I'd love to see it," she says. "But only for a few minutes. Then I've got to get home. Tennis date in the morning."

"Of course," he says.

They will not break up into laughter or tears and end the farce they are playing. Suddenly it is essential to both. Their life together born again. First stirrings. First bloomings. They are young. Nervous and eager. Afraid of making a false step. Pushing too hard or surrendering too easily.

He shows her around his home. Kitchen. Patio. Upstairs. Everything. They stroll out to the beach. Listen to the sea. Watch palm fronds whip crazily in a gusty wind. Saunter back to the house.

"It's beautiful," she says. "Really beautiful."

"I know," he says. Laughing. "But there's so much you could do with it."

"Yes, there is."

"Would you like another brandy?"

"I shouldn't, but I will."

They kick off their shoes. Slump down in deep armchairs. Regard each other without smiling.

Now or never, he thinks. "Sylvia," he says, "do you really have to get back to your place?"

"Is that a proposition?" she asks.

"Yes."

"I could cancel the tennis date."

"Well then?"

In the bedroom, they leave the lights off. Undress hurriedly in the darkness.

"I want you to know," she says, "I don't usually do—"

"I know," he interrupts. "I don't usually either."

They are deliberately awkward in bed. Fumbling. Reality is lost, so well are they acting their roles. Once again it is the first time. They want it to be grand. They are alternately crude and tender. Testing. How may I please her? What does he like best?

Eventually she yields. And so does he. Then they are raw pulses. There is nothing they will not do. He has never known such a madly passionate woman. Nor she such a determinedly striving man. Their furies fuse.

"Here."

"Now."

"This."

"Oh!"

"Do me."

"This?"

"God!"

"Don't stop."

"Ah."

"I love you."

"I love you."

Memorable lovemaking. An event. Shattering them. They hug tightly. Holding, hiding their secret. Knowing in that brief coupling their lives are changed. They have entered each other. Become one.

Still playing his part, Harry says, "When do you want to leave?"

"I don't want to," she says. "Ever."

Now, Sylvia dead and gone, Harry Dancer is convinced that evening actually happened. In exactly the way he recalls. They played a trick on time. Doubled a moment, from past to present. And now it is past again.

He is vaguely aware of what he is doing: duplicating his dying wife's nostalgia for a life lost. Now he is the one bridging past to present and ignoring the future. The golden glory was there; he calls it back to memory. No longer worrying if it is yesterday's reality or today's dream.

Anthony Glitner sits hunched on the beach. Cowering from the midday sun. Wide-brimmed hat pulled low over dark sunglasses. Towel across his pale, freckled shoulders. Another towel protecting his drawn-up knees. Still he feels the sun's sear. Draining his juices.

Beside him, Evelyn Heimdall lies prone on cotton blanket. Head nestled on forearm. Bra strap undone. Oiled back glistening. Oiled arms. Oiled legs. Golden girl toasting. She seems part of the sun, sand, sea. Glitner tries not to stare.

They have finished their picnic lunch. Hamper emptied of barbecued chicken, potato salad, tomatoes and cukes. What little wine left is too warm to swallow. They are incapable of moving. Replete and melted down.

"So nice," Evelyn says drowsily. "Perfect day."

"Hot," Tony says. "You like the heat, Ev?"

"It thaws me. Gets rid of all my aches and

pains. My miseries just *ooze* out.''

He looks seaward. Catamarans with gorgeous sails tack against the wind. Rubber floats bob about. Swimmers dash into waves, shrieking. And over all, the pitiless glare. Sky is open. No sky at all. Just blue emptiness and flaming sun.

''More oil,'' Evelyn murmurs. ''Please. On my back and shoulders. I don't want to peel.''

Obediently he leans forward to smooth velvety skin. Feels the heat of her. Firm muscles. She is taut. Tight in her body's envelope.

He begins his pitch.

''I'm getting all excited,'' he says. Massaging that vibrant back.

''That's nice,'' she says. ''So am I. You have good hands, Tony. A sweet touch.''

''Thank God we're in public. If not—who knows? I might throw myself upon you with a hoarse cry.''

She laughs. ''Be my guest. You're not married, are you?''

''No.''

''Girlfriend?''

''Not at the moment.''

''Poor Tony,'' she says. ''What a shame. Regulations got you down?''

''No,'' he says. Hating what he's doing. ''Regulations got me *up*.''

When she giggles, her whole body moves in a sexy paroxysm. Flesh ripples. He spreads oil into the cunning hollow behind her knees. Looking at the way her thin bikini panties cleave to her buttocks. Deep crease.

''Relax, Tony,'' she advises. ''Rules are made to be broken; you know that.''

''I've got no one to break them with.''

She lifts her head to stare at him. "I'm here."

He tries to smile. "It would be an act of Christian charity."

She lowers her head. Closes her eyes. "I'm a charitable woman. My training . . ."

He is torn. What started out as a simple test had become more complex. He fights temptation. The physical scene melts his resolve. So easy to succumb.

"Could we?" he says. Voice choked. "I don't know."

"Don't worry it so," she says. "It's not that important. Don't even think about the Corporation."

"I've got to. Heavy decision."

"All right then, think about it. I'll be around. Ready, willing and able."

She shouldn't have said that. Confirming his fears. His momentary lust dissolves. Now all that matters is how to deal with her hedonism. What would be best for the Corporation? For the Harry Dancer campaign?

"I'll be good for you, Tony," she says.

That night, in Martin Frey's sweaty embrace, she tells him of the afternoon on the beach with Glitner.

"He came on to me," she says. Laughing. "Can you imagine? And I always thought he was such a straight arrow."

Frey moves away from her. Sits up. Stares at her. Shocked.

"What did you say?" he demands. "Your case officer made a pitch?"

"Did he ever. A real hard-on."

"And how did you react?"

"Went along. Teasing. If he wants to, fine. If

he doesn't, fine. It's got nothing to do with us.''

He groans. "Ev, it's got *everything* to do with us. It was his suspicion of you that brought me down here in the first place. But my reports clearing you haven't satisfied him. He still thinks you're turning.''

She begins to bite a knuckle. "Martin, are you *sure?*"

"Of course I'm sure. You told me yourself that he's a perceptive man. Sensitive. Ev, he was *testing* you. Has he ever gone off the code before? To your knowledge?''

"No. Never.''

"Then he *is* a straight arrow. Just trying to find out how far you've strayed.''

"It might have been the sun, the beach. Maybe he's thawed. The way I have.''

Frey shakes his head. "I was trained in counter-intelligence. I know the techniques. Glitner was entrapping you. And you walked right into it.''

"I really thought he meant it.''

"You were wrong. He was putting on an act.''

She turns a dulled face to him. "Oh God, Martin, what do we do now?''

"Do we have a choice? What we talked about before—go over to the Others. Make the best deal we can.''

"Will we be together?''

"Absolutely. Or we don't turn. Listen, there's a lot of top secret stuff we can deliver. The Department would be crazy to turn us down. They may be evil, but they're not crazy. And if they're going to pump us dry, we want something in return. Being together is the first thing. It'll work out, hon; you'll see.''

"How do we do it? Who do we surrender to?''

"Let me handle it. In cases like this, it's best to go to the top man. Someone who can cut a deal."

Shivering with fear, she flings back into his arms. Now the enormity of their treachery inflames them. Denying all. They couple like the plague-stricken. With hysterical intensity. Into a flaming maelstrom. Awaiting a thunderbolt that might destroy them. Or worse, a judgment that might condemn them to an eternity of suffering.

The Chairman, seated on his War Room throne, scans the latest intelligence briefs from the Southeast Region. Groans with anger. That section is providing more aggravation than the nine other regions combined.

Treason of the Director's private secretary is the last straw. Stupidity of the man! To harbor a Corporation mole in his own office. If the Chairman acted on impulse, he'd have the Director terminally demoted immediately.

But the Chairman rarely acts on impulse or whim. Too dangerous. To his own career. So he reviews carefully the actions that must be taken following the Norma Gravesend disaster.

Codes will have to be changed, of course. Key personnel switched. Informants protected. Communication techniques revised. All because a fathead Director employed a spy. The Chairman tries not to let his fury cloud his judgment.

Eliminating the Director is easy. But what is important is the outcome of the campaigns being supervised by that idiot. Like Harry Dancer. With

Briscoe in as case officer, the Chairman hopes the Dancer thing may prove to be a solid win. But removing the Director abruptly could jeopardize the conquest of Dancer and a dozen other potential recruits.

So, sighing, the Chairman decides to temporize. The Director of the Southeast Region can be chopped at any time. The Department's shoguns are not interested in individuals. Only numbers. A steadily increasing congregation.

He will let the Director stay on. For the present. With no reprimands, no communications whatsoever. Let the cretin sweat. Wondering when the blade will fall. Meanwhile, affrighted, he might put spurs to his case officers. Demanding converts.

Like Harry Dancer.

Briscoe walks in on Sally Abaddon early in the morning. Without calling first. Knocks on the door, she answers, and there he is. Wearing polyester slacks in a hellish plaid. Knitted shirt with the Department logo over the heart. Short sleeves reveal hairy, muscled arms. Left forearm is badly scarred.

"Hi, babe," he says. Steely grin. "Let's you and me have a talk."

She lets him in. He asks for a cup of coffee, orange juice, a beer—anything. She brings him coffee. Then he asks for a pastry, Danish, toast —anything. She brings him a powdered doughnut. Having established who's boss, he sits negligently in a deep armchair. Slurping his breakfast. Watching her steadily as she moves about.

"This woman you're spending all your time with," he starts. "The one who lives next door—what's her name?"

"Angela Bliss."

"Yeah. You got a thing going with her?"

"We're friends. I can't spend twenty-four hours a day with Harry Dancer."

"That's right, you can't. Well, this Angela Bliss belongs to the Department. Internal Security. Ted Charon brought her down here from Chicago to do a job on you. Did she tell you that?"

Abaddon turns away to find a cigarette and light it. She answers with her back to him.

"No, she didn't tell me that."

"Well, she's a shoofly cop all right. I had nothing to do with it. Before he got snuffed, Shelby Yama had his suspicions about you. So he got Charon to sic her onto you to see if you're behaving yourself."

"And?" Sally asks. Voice tight.

"You're clean. Bliss swears you're true-blue. So she's being pulled off the case. Sent back to Chicago for reassignment. She'll be out of your hair by tomorrow."

Abaddon finally sits. Facing him. Crosses her legs. Robe falls open. He looks at her knee, smooth calf. Watches her bare foot jerk up and down.

"Nervous?" he says.

"Of course not. Why should I be nervous? She cleared me, didn't she? I don't know what Yama was suspicious about."

"Maybe he got worried because you weren't closing the Dancer deal. Maybe he thought you weren't seeing enough of him."

"I'm going to see him this afternoon. For lunch."

"For lunch? And a matinee?"

"If he wants. Look, Briscoe, some guys you can push, and some guys you can't. Dancer is the kind of man who sets his own pace. I've got to go along or risk losing him. I know my job."

"Sure you do, babe. But Cleveland is only interested in results; you know that."

"You'll get results."

"Yeah? When?"

She lights another cigarette. "I can't say."

"A week? A month? Make a guess."

She snaps at him. "Get off my back, will you? This is a difficult case. The man is still dreaming about his dead wife. It's going to take time."

"Not good enough," Briscoe says. Shaking his head. "Your annual Fitness Report is coming up. I'd like to say something nice about you. Catch my drift?"

"Oh, I catch it all right."

"You're still balling Dancer?"

"Of course."

"Well, that's your hook, isn't it? Lean on him. Threaten to cut him off if he doesn't come across."

"I'm not sure that'll work."

"Then what in hell *will* work?" he yells. Stops. Tries to control his anger. "Want to play the recordings for him? Show him the tapes? He's got a responsible position. People depend on him. Tell him if he doesn't see things our way, he's down the tube."

She stares at him. Trying to keep her face expressionless. "Give me another week, Briscoe."

"You're stalling," he accuses.

"No, no. Give me a week to bring him around. If I can't do it, then we'll try the recordings and tapes."

"A week?" he says. "You've got it. See how easy I am to get along with? Just a pussycat—that's me."

"Oh sure," she says.

She hopes that's the end of it. He has finished his coffee and doughnut. She wants him to leave. But he sits there. Staring at her bared legs. She pulls the robe closed. His gaze slowly rises to her face. She never before noticed the color of his eyes. Muddy ice.

"You're seeing Dancer this afternoon?" he asks. Voice suddenly flat. And tense. Flat and tense at once.

"That's right."

"So you're not doing anything tonight," he says. "All by your lonesome."

"I have things to do."

"With Angela Bliss? Forget it. She's on her way out. There's nothing there for you, babe."

She doesn't reply.

"I'll come by around eight," he says. Rising. "You and I should get to know each other better. Now that I'm your case officer."

Still she is silent.

"Eight o'clock," he repeats. "Okay? Remember the Fitness Report."

"Sure," she says.

She peeks through the venetian blind until she sees him drive away in the black Mercedes. Then she starts weeping. It is five minutes before she can control herself enough to phone Angela Bliss.

"Can you come over?" she pleads. "Right away."

"Darling, what *is* it?"

"Please . . ."

"I'll be right there."

They sit huddled. Holding hands. Sally relates what Briscoe said. What he implied. Nuances. And the way he looked at her.

"He knows," she tells Angela. "About you and me. Everything. He's coming by tonight. To test me. And he says you'll be gone by tomorrow."

"He may be lying."

"Even if he is, it's just a question of time, isn't it? Before we're separated. And he wants me to blackmail Harry with the recordings and TV tapes we've got. Angela, I can't do that."

"Of course you can't. Sweetheart, we've been talking about it a long time, but now we've got to *do* it. Go over. To the Corporation. It's our only hope."

"But Briscoe is coming here *tonight,*" Sally wails. "We need more time to find out who we defect to. Figure out what we're going to say."

Angela puts a palm to the other woman's cheek. Smiling. "Not to worry. Leave it to me. I know how these things are handled. You go have your lunch with Harry. By the time you get back, I'll have a plan."

"And I won't have to make love to that creep?"

"Absolutely not. Don't even think about it. Darling, do you trust me?"

"You know I do. Till death do us part."

"Will you do whatever I tell you? It may be rough. Really bad."

"Does it mean we'll be together?"

"That's exactly what it means."

"Then I'll do anything," Sally Abaddon says.

Afternoon of the same day. The Director cringes in his office. Hair disheveled. Suit unpressed. Two days' growth of beard. "Let the cretin sweat," the Chairman had vowed. And so the cretin is. Awaiting the judgment that never comes.

Meanwhile he tries to get through the routine of his business day. Has even installed the new computer operator as his personal secretary. Hopelessly inefficient, but so young. Tender. Too bad he has no desire to test her loyalty. Defection and termination of Norma Gravesend have neutered him. He wallows in despair.

When his phone rings, he almost faints. Certain the summons has arrived. Picks up the receiver with a palsied hand. Answers in a cracked voice:

"The Director speaking."

"Sir, this is Martha at the switchboard. I have a man on the line who insists on speaking to you personally. He won't state his business nor give his name. How do you want me to handle it?"

"Tell him to talk to Internal Security."

"I've already suggested that, sir. He says he'll hang up if I switch him to anyone but you. He claims it will be to your benefit to talk to him."

That hooks the Director. He considers. If the call turns out to be from a crazy, he can always hang up. But if the caller really has something to offer . . .

"All right, Martha," he says. "Put him on."

Man's voice: "Is this the Director of the Southeast Region?"

"That is correct. To whom am I speaking?"

Caller ignores his question. Asks a question of his own. "Are you supervising the Harry Dancer action?"

The Director catches his breath. What crazy would know that?

"I'm not sure what you're talking about," he answers.

"Stop playing games," is the impatient response. "The Harry Dancer campaign. Your case officer is Briscoe, ever since Shelby Yama got chilled. Your field agent is Sally Abaddon. Now do you realize I know what I'm talking about?"

Shock. Has there been another security breach?

"What do you want?" the Director asks.

"Sanctuary," the man says. "I am a Corporation counterintelligence agent. I have with me the field agent on the Dancer case. We'd like to discuss the possibility of coming over."

The Director holds the phone away. Stares at it with amazement. Tiny flame of hope begins to flicker.

"Hello? Are you there?"

"I'm here," the Director says. Hastily. "You're talking about defection?"

"That's right."

"Well," the Director says. Expanding. "I think that can be arranged. We have a program that—"

"Cut the shit," the caller interrupts. "I said we want to discuss the possibility. You know the Atlantic Avenue bridge over the Intracoastal Waterway?"

"Yes."

"They raise it every thirty minutes. On the hour and half-hour. The moment it closes after two o'clock this afternoon, we'll meet you in the middle, on the span. Then we'll talk. You come alone."

"The two of you will be there?"

"That's right."

"Then I must insist on bringing an associate."

Silence. Then: "Who? Ted Charon, your Chief of Internal Security?"

Again the Director is startled. Man seems remarkably well informed. Which supports the genuineness of his proposition. "Yes, Charon," he replies. "Two on two. It's only fair."

Silence again. Finally . . .

"All right. On the Atlantic Avenue bridge. Right after two o'clock. Be there."

Click.

The Director sits back. Pulls a deep breath. If the call is legitimate, what a coup! Turning two important Corporation agents. Weakening—maybe fatally weakening—their Harry Dancer operation.

More important, maybe saving the Director's ass.

He and Ted Charon arrive at the bridge a half-hour early.

"I've got two cars," Charon says. "One at each end. Three men in each car. If we can't cut a deal, we can still grab them. If you say so, sir," he adds.

"Let's play it by ear," the Director suggests. "Keep your men back until we find out what they want."

Charon looks around. "I don't see any other occupied cars parked at the bridge ends. Or anyone who looks like heavies. Maybe they are coming alone.''

They wait patiently. Bridge parts and rises at two o'clock. Two cruisers and a sailboat pass up the Waterway. Bridge closes. Barricades rise.

"All right," Charon says. "Let's go."

Walk slowly to the middle of the span. Stop, backs to the railing. Look in both directions. Nothing.

"Maybe they're not coming," the Director says. Beginning to sweat again. "Maybe they spotted your cars and took off."

Charon refuses to take the blame for failure. "They'll come," he says. "It was their idea, wasn't it?"

Finally, they see a couple sauntering toward them from the western end of the bridge. Man and woman. Holding hands tightly.

"That could be them," Charon says. Takes off his cap. Wipes his brow with a handkerchief. Alerting his men.

The four meet. Stand staring at each other.

"Director?" the man asks. He is young. Handsome. Olive skin. Woman is almost as dark. Solid body. Short, sun-bleached hair. She looks frightened.

"That's correct," the Director says. "And this gentleman is Ted Charon, our local Chief of Internal Security."

"Could we see some ID, please," Charon says.

The two strangers look at each other. Man nods, takes out his wallet. Woman fumbles in her purse. They hand plastic cards to Charon. He examines them. Looks up to compare faces and photos. Returns the ID cards.

"Martin Frey and Evelyn Heimdall," he reports to the Director. "That checks out with our intelligence. The lady is Corporation field agent on the Dancer case. Frey works out of Counterintelligence in Washington."

"You want to come over?" the Director asks them.

"If we get what we want," Frey says.

"Which is?"

"The usual protection. Plus a promise that the two of us can stay together. Work together. We're a team. That has to be understood."

"And what do we get in return?" Charon asks. "Besides a team."

Frey shrugs. "Whatever we've got. Codes. Personnel rosters. Recruiting techniques. Names, dates, and places. We won't hold back. We know we're gambling on your good faith, but we're willing to take the chance. We can be very valuable to the Department."

"More than just the intelligence we can deliver," Heimdall says. Speaking for the first time. "Valuable to the Department as active agents. We know our jobs. And we're enthusiastic."

"You realize what it entails?" the Director says. "No one resigns from the Department. You're aware of that?"

They both nod. The four talk another fifteen minutes. Details of the actual surrender. When, where, and how. Professionals dispassionately discussing terms of treason. Documents to be signed. Safe houses. Reassignment. New roles for the converts.

Finally, the Director looks at Ted Charon.

"What do you think?" he asks.

"Let's take them," Charon says. "They've got no place else to go."

Evening of the same day. Sally Abaddon and Angela Bliss go over their plan a half-dozen times. Looking for things that might go wrong. Figuring how they will react. Trying to anticipate Briscoe's countermoves. They are frightened by the man's strength and brutality.

"Where did you get the gun?" Sally asks.

"It's mine," Angela says. "Department issue. Everyone in Internal Security gets one."

"Have you ever used it?"

"Not off the range, no. But I'm a good shot. Sweetheart, are you sure you can see this through?"

"I'm sure," Sally says. "We don't really have any choice, do we?"

"No choice at all."

They discuss renting a car. Decide that will complicate things unnecessarily. Wonder about the need for rope or handcuffs. Injection of drugs. Anything to immobilize him.

"No," Angela says. "We've got to keep it as simple as possible. The fewer things that can go wrong, the better. Oh God, I'm nervous. Are you?"

Sally holds out a trembling hand. "Look."

"I know, darling. I feel the same way."

"What we're doing—going to do—it's not the best way to start our new life, is it?"

"We'll be forgiven. It's justified. He's an evil, evil man. He takes pleasure in hurting people. I know his record."

They are in Sally's motel room. Surrounded by all the tawdry props used to lure Harry Dancer. Now it has the dead and dusty look of an unused stage set. They cannot bear to look at the fleshy nudes on the walls. Orange-tinted mirrors. Sad, kitschy furnishings.

"Can we make love?" Sally asks. Suddenly. "Please. It's important to me."

"Yes," Angela says. "Oh yes."

Naked in each other's arms. Shivering with fear and delight. Their plot an added spur. Brought closer by danger. Risking all for each other. Their embrace is desperate—and all the sweeter.

They have learned each other's bodies. Confessed wants and hidden pleasures. Their lovemaking is assured and giving. It has the tang of newness, leavened by love. Their fresh world expands; they see no limits.

"Let me," Sally says. "My turn."

Angela's thin, hard body has become dear to her. Something to cherish. Bone and muscle, skin and vein. All warm and eager. Mouths seek. A conspiracy of two. Secret agreement. Love is theirs alone. They surround, protect, and nourish it.

In their ardor, doubts vanish. There is nothing they might not do. Kisses banish fear. Probing tongues confirm their resolve. Coupling, they become stronger. Decision reinforced. Two are one body, one will.

Drawing apart, they stare into each other's eyes. Stroking, stroking. Murmuring things. Feeling sheen and satin. Pressing. Tugging. Smiling at their puppy play. Flooded by happiness. Swollen with bliss. Both throbbing with a single pulse.

"No matter what happens . . ." Angela says.

"Yes," Sally says, "no matter what . . ."

They loll. Groaning with content. Then rise, dress, make final preparations. Both wear black jeans, black T-shirts, black sneakers. Midnight assassins.

"The important thing," Sally says, "is not to let him use the Special Powers."

"He won't get a chance," Angela says. "Trust me."

They share a drink—a single vodka loving cup.

"Dutch courage," Angela says.

"We don't need it," Sally says. "We have each other."

"Always," Angela vows.

Briscoe is late. It is almost eight-twenty before Sally, peering through the blinds, sees the black Mercedes roll up to a stop across the parking lot.

"He's here," she announces.

Two women embrace. Clutching tightly. Pressing.

"I love you."

"I love you."

Angela takes up position behind the door. Sally turns off the overhead light. Leaves only the dim bedside lamp burning.

His knock is like the man himself: sharp, loud, authoritative.

Sally opens the door wide.

"Hi!" she says.

He steps in. Almost smiling. Angela pushes the door closed. Moves up behind him. Puts the muzzle of her revolver behind his left ear.

"A gun," she says. "Loaded. Don't move."

He stands motionless. Sally pats him down. No weapons. She takes his keys. Angela prods again with the revolver. He says nothing. His silence scares them. They see his glinty eyes roving. Calculating.

"Go, Sally," Angela says.

Abaddon slips out the door. Closes it softly behind her. Bliss moves back a few paces. So she can't be taken if Briscoe whirls suddenly. Revolver steady in her fist.

"No Special Powers," she tells him. "Unless you want to die."

"You haven't the balls for it," he says. Speaking for the first time. Arid voice.

"Try me," she says.

Then they stand with no more talk. Angela waits for Sally to bring the Mercedes up close to the motel. So they won't have to march Briscoe across the parking lot at gunpoint. Finally she hears a light horn tap. The signal.

"All right," she says, "we're going out now. You first. I'll be right behind you. Get in the back of the car. Press yourself into the far corner. Keep your hands in plain view. If you think you can take me, be my guest. I'd love to pop you right here."

But he attempts nothing. Almost docilely he follows orders. Goes out the door. Gets into the back seat. Far over. Angela follows him in. Holds the gun with both hands. Aimed at his chest.

"He's behaving, Sally," she says. "Let's go."

Abaddon drives out onto A1A. Turns south.

"You're defecting," Briscoe says. Licking his lips. "Going over to the Corporation. The two of you."

"That's right," Angela says. "We're getting out."

"So?" he says. Shrugging. "What's that got to do with me? You want to go? Go. I can't stop you. But why involve me? We'll just assign another field agent to the Harry Dancer action. It's not as important as you think it is."

"If you were any other man," Angela says, "I'd believe you. But I know your record, Briscoe. I know the kind of devil you are. You might let us walk away, but you'd never let us live. You couldn't take that defeat. All your plans, your ambitions, down the drain. Wherever we went, you'd come after us. And eventually you'd find us. We'd have to keep looking back for the rest of our lives. The Department might cross us off the roster and let us go. But not you. You'd never forget or forgive. Because we made you look like an incompetent fool. And you'd come gunning. Isn't that right?"

He doesn't reply. Looks straight ahead through the windshield. Watches as Sally makes a right onto Atlantic Boulevard. Heading west. They cross the bridge where, several hours ago, Evelyn Heimdall and Martin Frey surrendered to the Department. But none of them know that.

"Let's make a deal," Briscoe says.

"No deal," Sally says. Voice sharp.

"Just listen a minute," Briscoe says. "It makes sense. Take me to the airport. I promise to behave. Put me on the first flight out. Anywhere you say. That'll give you time to contact the Corporation. They'll give you protection. I'll be in the air, out of the picture for hours."

"Forget it," Angela says. "You'll come back

and start looking for us.''

"I give you my word of honor I won't.''

The women laugh.

They drive in silence awhile.

"You know,'' Briscoe says, "every now and then I think about switching. Tell me why you're doing it; I'm really interested.''

They don't bother answering.

"Getting close,'' Angela says to Sally. "Another street or two. No U-turn. You'll have to go around the block.''

Traffic is light in a fine drizzle. Sally starts the wipers. Drives slowly. Leans forward to peer ahead. Makes the turns. Comes out onto Atlantic Boulevard again. Heading east. Briscoe glances out the window. Sees the shimmer of streetlamps on the dark surface of a canal.

"Not here?'' he cries. Offended by their amateurism. "With lights? Traffic? At this hour? You're out of your minds!''

"We'll take the chance,'' Angela says.

"We have nothing to lose,'' Sally says.

"Two women with one man,'' Angela adds. "Who's going to think anything's wrong? We're going to do it, Briscoe. Believe me.''

For the first time they hear desperation in his voice.

"Look,'' he says, "let's talk about this. You think the Corporation will be happy to take in a couple of killers?''

"They won't know,'' Angela says. "Will they?''

"The car!'' he shouts. Brain befuddled. Grabbing at foolish details. "How are you going to get rid of my car?''

"Easy,'' Angela says. "Wipe it clean and park

it somewhere. Next block, Sally. Pull over. Leave the motor running."

"I know," Sally says.

She slows and stops. Hops out. Jerks open Briscoe's door. He almost falls onto the ground. Angela scrambles after him. Presses the gun against his neck.

"Down to the canal," she says. "Fast!"

He opens his mouth to scream. She slams the revolver against the side of his head. Stunned, he stumbles forward. They half-support, half-carry him to the canal. He is mumbling, shaking his head. They haul him to the edge of the scummy ditch.

Angela turns. Looks back at the boulevard. Waits until a heavy truck speeds by. Then motions Sally clear. Whirls Briscoe around. Shoots him twice in the face. Gouts of blood. He topples back. Head and shoulders splash into black water.

"Give me the gun," Sally says.

"What?"

"Give it to me!"

Angela hands it over. Sally aims, closes her eyes, shoots Briscoe two more times in the chest and stomach. Opens her eyes. Stares at the other woman.

"Both of us," she says. "We both did it. Together."

They prod and kick Briscoe's body deeper into the canal. Corpse slowly sinks. They watch white bubbles subside. Then they turn and run for the car.

Anthony Glitner, at 2:30 A.M., feels everything
is falling apart. Evelyn Heimdall has not made her
routine check-in calls for the past twenty-four
hours. The case officer has staff searching for her.
But she has vanished.

He informs Washington. In turn, Corporation
headquarters tells him they are unable to locate
Martin Frey. Messages fly back and forth. A
Grade-A flap.

Glitner might have been able to cope, but he is
still depressed by the murder of Willoughby. That
sweet, eager man. So strong in his faith. Gone. To
a better life, Tony devoutly believes. Still, it is
hard to lose a dear comrade.

Even harder to endure the treason of a believer.
And that, the case officer is convinced, is what has
happened to Evelyn Heimdall. And Martin Frey.
The Corporation has suffered a shattering loss.
Glitner accepts responsibility for the twin defection. He should have been more perceptive, more
alert. Asked for a replacement for his field agent
when he first suspected her weakening.

He wonders, again, if he may be burned-out.
Exhausted by continual conflict with the Department. Unending. Victories and defeats. But never
with a firm sign of eventual triumph. Which leaves
only faith. Thin reed at two-thirty in the morning.

Even the strongest believer must, occasionally,
doubt. The Corporation may be certain. But the
Corporation is a creed. A body of laws. Adherents
are human individuals. Subject to all the frailties
of living in an irrational world. Pain? Undeserved
suffering? How to account for those anomalies in
a universe parsed by the Word?

Riven, shredded by uncertainty, Anthony Glitner paces the floor. Praying for *proof*. Incontrovertible proof that life has meaning. That *his* life is valuable, his work significant. He wants assurance. A pat on the head, he ruefully admits.

When the phone rings, he leaps for it. Hoping Evelyn Heimdall is finally calling. That problem solved. His fears groundless. But it is an unfamiliar voice. Female.

"Anthony Glitner?"

"Yes. Who is this?"

"It's not important at the moment. What is important is that I am an agent of the Department, division of Internal Security. My friend is the field agent in the Harry Dancer action. We both wish to defect. To come over to the Corporation. Can we meet and discuss it?"

Glitner is stunned. Silenced.

"Hello? Mr. Glitner? Are you there?"

"Yes, I'm here. When do you wish to meet?"

"As soon as possible. Right now if you can make it."

"All right. Where?"

"Can you come to us?"

"Is that wise? You may be under observation."

Pause.

"Yes," the woman says, "you may be right. Very well, we'll come to you. We have the address. We'll be there in twenty minutes."

Tony hangs up softly. It may be a trap—but he doesn't think so. She sounded definite, assured, professional. Two Department agents wanting to defect. Victory!

But he feels no sense of triumph. Just sadness. And weariness. Reflecting on the faults and weaknesses of people in his profession. Burn-out comes, sooner or later. They work in such a highly charged atmosphere. At fever pitch. Eventually they are scorched.

Because of the rawness of their decisions. Life or death—and nothing in between. Every choice vital, every act essential. They are spiritual surgeons. Is it any wonder that their hands might falter?

He wrenches his mind from these dismal thoughts. Begins to straighten up his disordered motel suite to keep busy. Plans how to handle these two would-be converts. What they will ask, and what he will offer.

It is not total compensation for the death of Willoughby and the dereliction of Evelyn Heimdall. Still it is a—

Stops suddenly. Recalls his brooding of an hour ago when he yearned for a sign. Assurance that his faith is justified, his life of value. Is this the portent he seeks?

Door bell rings. He moves to answer. Smiling.

The day is a glory. Early morning sun brave in a pellucid sky. Palm fronds rustling; gentle northeast breeze dries and cools. Ocean calm with small pages turning an endless volume onto the beach.

"This is why we came to Florida," a neighbor calls, and Harry Dancer nods and smiles.

Sitting close to the water. Wearing his faded khaki swimming trunks. Knees drawn up and clasped. Sees kids frolicking on the strand. Joggers. Shellers. A few bright floats bobbing out there. Catamarans getting nowhere. A young creamer falling off her windsurf board. White foam over the nearest reef. Everything familiar and cherished.

Stares out and beyond at the gently curving earth. Water and sky color one enormous globe. No sharp corners. Just lulling arcs. Wooing the eye, soothing the spirit.

"Take a swim, Syl?" he asks. "Way out?"

"Maybe," she murmurs. "Later."

She is lying prone beside him. On a big beach towel printed with a portrait of Mickey Mouse rampant. Her bronze body dazzles. He looks at her with love and longing. Never to know completely this total woman.

"The best loves are incomplete," he says.

"If you say so, professor."

He reaches out to touch a glowing shoulder. One fingertip. Brief contact.

"What was that for?" she asks.

"Just to make sure you're there."

She chugs a single laugh. "Oh, I'm here, darling. Always will be."

"Promise?"

"Absitively, posilutely. I wouldn't leave you alone."

"No," he says, "don't do that. Bring you a drink? Sandwich?"

"Nothing, thanks."

"Caviar? Champagne? Diamonds? Rubies? Emeralds?"

"Now you're talking." Then she lifts, props up on an elbow, stares at him. "You're awfully generous this morning. And romantic.''

"A mood. It'll pass.''

She grunts, puts her cheek down on her forearm again.

"No,'' he says, "it won't pass. I love you so much, Syl. It scares me. Losing you would be an amputation. The best part of me.''

"You're not going to lose me.''

"Keep telling me that,'' he begs. "It's the only thing that keeps me going.''

"Don't you think I feel the same way? What would I be without you? Couldn't endure it.''

"Sometimes . . .'' he says. Feeling foolish but wanting to say it. "Sometimes I think of us as more than married. Blood-related.''

"Sister and brother?''

"Yes,'' he says, "but twins. You know?''

"The closeness,'' she says. "Yes, I do know. A beautiful thought.''

"It's the way I feel.''

She reaches behind her back. Hooks her bra strap. Sits up. Leans on his clasped knees. Grins at him.

"Incest,'' she says. "That's what we've got going here.''

"Something like that,'' he agrees. "Something wonderful.''

They smile, turn toward the invisible horizon. Squinting against the sun's glow. They look at forever. World without limit. Everything stretching. Sylvia takes his hand. Holds it tightly.

"It's all ours, Harry,'' she says. "Isn't it?''

"Has been,'' he says. "Since I met you.''

"And it will never end,'' she vows. "I swear to God.''

They sit there. So near, so near. Seeing the bright, living beach scene. Part of it, but apart from it. World of their own. The two sufficient.

"That swim," he says. "I'm going to take it now."

"Are you sure you want to, love?"

"Have to," he says. "Need to. No choice."

She squeezes his hand tighter. "All right, Harry. I'll be with you."

He rises slowly. Stretches. Flexes his shoulders. Walks easily down to the water's edge. Stands a moment, ankle-deep. Looking out at the gentle depths. His gaze becomes unfocused. Seems to see a tide rolling backward. Spilling froth far out. Ready to bear him. Beckoning.

Wades into a winy sea. Doesn't dive, but waits until he floats away. Then strikes out with calm deliberation. Steadily swimming. Pulling toward forever. Lifting arms, moving legs. Toward his goal.

On he goes. Breathing smoothly. Smiling with happiness as he feels his muscles' strength. No limit. Past the waders, the shouters. Past the floats and boats. Into the quiet where all he can hear is the susurrus of his own tender waves: Sssylvia, Sssylvia, Sssylvia.

How long? He doesn't know, doesn't care. He lifts his head occasionally. Peers. Makes certain he is heading toward forever. Feeling the start of weariness. Comforting warmth. Arms and legs beginning to flail. Churning now. Body rolling.

Happy with his weakness. Sensing the end. Hearing "Sssylvia, Sssylvia, Sssylvia." He does not have to call her name. She is with him. Her love draws him on. Reaches for her with leaden arms. Seeking. Aching to reclaim.

Wallowing. Drained body slowing. Until, gasping, he lets the sea enter his open mouth. And gives himself over with joy. Sinking slowly. Bubbles jagging up.

And he is home.

The Chairman, in his office at Cleveland headquarters, is enduring questioning by the Department's Inspector General. Snide man with the smarmy smile of a mortician.

"We lost Sally Abaddon and Angela Bliss," he says. Accusing.

"And we gained Evelyn Heimdall and Martin Frey," the Chairman reminds him.

"Briscoe was eliminated."

"So was Norma Gravesend."

"What about Shelby Yama?"

"What about Willoughby?"

They glare at each other. Then simultaneously sigh.

"The operation was a disaster," the Inspector says.

"There I agree with you," the Chairman says.

"The bottom line is that we lost Harry Dancer."

"The bottom line is that no one lost or won Harry Dancer. Everyone concerned, Department and Corporation alike, underestimated the man. There was more to him than we realized."

"You should have known."

The Chairman shrugs his fat shoulders. "As I have observed several times, Inspector, we are not dealing with packages of breakfast cereal. Our targets are living, breathing human beings—with all the hopes, fears, prejudices, and foolish dreams that implies. This is not a science, you know; it is an art."

"Apparently our artists are not exceptionally talented."

The Chairman slams a meaty hand down on his desk top. "I will not have my ability questioned," he says wrathfully. "The statistics are available to you. They clearly show that my record is excellent. I win many more than I lose."

"More, perhaps," the Inspector sniffs, "but not many more. Chairman, our disappointment in the outcome of the Harry Dancer affair is not solely based on the loss of a single potential recruit. There are also budgetary considerations involved."

"Money," the Chairman growls. "It always comes down to dollars and cents."

"We are running a world-wide operation," the Inspector General says. "We would be derelict in our duty if we were not constantly aware of income, expenses, personnel costs, and cash flow. Now let's go over your projected budget for the coming year. I believe that revisions are required in some of your more, ah, optimistic estimates."

"Yes, Inspector," the Chairman says. Surrendering.

At almost the same time, a somewhat similar postmortem is taking place at Corporation headquarters in Washington. The Chief of Operations and case officer Anthony Glitner are toting up the balance sheet on the Harry Dancer action.

"About even, sir," Glitner concludes. Voice dulled, dispirited. "Lost some, won some."

"And no one won Harry Dancer," the Chief adds. Searching through his pockets for antacid tablets. "It was not one of our more glorious campaigns."

"My fault," Tony says. "I let it get out of hand."

"Nonsense," the Chief says. "You're not to blame. The whole thing hinged on the personality and character of Harry Dancer. Our failure was insufficient intelligence. I have already composed a memo on the subject. From now on, our analyses of possible converts must be much more detailed. In-depth probing. So we know exactly whom we're dealing with."

"Do you think that would have helped in this case, sir?"

The Chief stares at him. "What do you mean by that?"

"Perhaps the man was unknowable."

The Chief finds a single, dusty Tums. Pops it into his mouth. "Tony, I prefer not to dwell on the mysteries of the human spirit. The important thing is to concentrate on conversions. That is our only reason for being."

They sit in silence a few moments. Heads lowered. Brooding.

"Sir," Anthony Glitner says, "where do you think the soul of Harry Dancer is now?"

"Oh . . ." the Chief says. Wearily waving a hand. "Out there somewhere. Floating . . ."